WIFEY

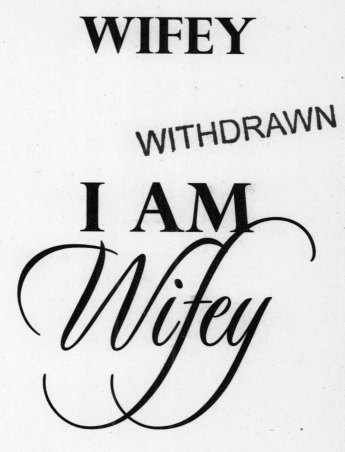

I AM *Wifey*

BUY

FOR MELODRAMA

WIFEY

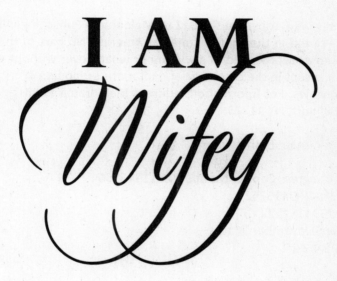

I AM *Wifey*

ERICA HILTON

This is a work of fiction. All of the characters, organizations, and events portrayed in this novel are either products of the author's imagination or are used fictitiously.

www.melodramapublishing.com

Library of Congress Control Number: 2011946166
ISBN-13: 978-1934157527
ISBN-10: 193415752X
First Edition: November 2012
10 9 8 7 6 5 4 3 2 1

Interior Design: Candace K. Cottrell
Cover Design: Marion Designs
Editors: Brian Sandy, Candace K. Cottrell
Model: Jaz

ALSO BY
ERICA HILTON

ONE

Jasmine sat silent, stone-faced, and confused.

"Did we answer all of your questions?" Agent Dowd asked her.

She closed her eyes. All she could do was wonder if Nico was fucking Mia at that very moment as she sat in a room full of FBI agents trying to convince her to become a snitch.

"Jasmine, if something is on your mind, now is the time to speak," Agent Battle said to her.

"You wanna know what's on my mind? I ain't no snitch!—That's what's on my mind. What's on my mind is, why the fuck am I sitting here? Why the fuck I ain't see a judge yet? Why the—"

"Jasmine, you're right. You're not a snitch," Agent Dowd said, quickly interrupting her rant. "What did we tell you twenty minutes ago? We told you that we want you to be a *source*. There is a huge difference between a source and a snitch."

The room went quiet. Jasmine looked at the agent and rolled her eyes.

"So, yeah, like I said, I wanna see a fuckin' judge. Y'all trying to isolate me, like I'm some dumb bitch or something. I don't wanna be your *source*. Lock my black ass up. Do whatever the fuck you feel you gotta do. But I tell you one thing—Y'all better come correct, because I'm gonna make sure my lawyers go so fuckin' hard on y'all asses for embarrassing me at the restaurant and having me in custody for more than twenty-four hours without seeing a judge. Hello! This is New York City. I know my rights. I'm suppose to see a judge within twenty-four hours!"

Agent Battle, the only black agent in the room as well as the only female agent, motioned to the other two agents to keep quiet. She pulled up a chair, placed it right in front of Jasmine, and sat so her torso was facing the back of the chair.

"So you a ride-or-die chick? You gonna ride for your man because he loves you, right?"

Jasmine looked at Agent Battle and didn't say anything.

"Your pussy is just so tight and juicy that you know that nigga loves you, right?"

"Whateva."

"Jasmine, I been where you at—Fuck this badge!" Agent Battle unclipped her gold shield from her belt and threw it on the table behind her. "I'm talking to you straight up as a black woman. You sitting there now with an attitude and think you can handle anything that's thrown at you, but I'm telling you that your life ain't worth no nigga that's fuckin' the next bitch as we speak. You would have to be crazy."

"I would have to be crazy? But how do I know them photos are real and it ain't no Photoshop tricks?"

"The photos of Nico with Mia?" Agent Battle asked, just to be clear.

"Yeah. I mean, those pictures could be old."

"You right. They could be old, they could be fake, but ask yourself this—If your pussy is so good, and Nico is so in love with you, how come you ain't lawyered up right now?"

"Y'all muthafuckas got me in here handcuffed and isolated from everybody, just like I just finished saying. Can't nobody help me if they don't even know where I'm at. What the fuck?"

Deep inside Jasmine wondered if Agent Battle was right.

Agent Battle picked up her badge from off the table and clipped it back onto her belt. She knew she had to be careful, because the FBI desperately needed Jasmine to cooperate with them, and they didn't want her to call their bluff and continue to insist on being formally arraigned in court.

Agent Battle motioned to Agent Dowd to undo the handcuffs on Jasmine's wrists, and she walked out of the room without saying anything.

"Oh, my God! What the fuck? I'm tired! I'm hungry! I wanna either go home, or I want to see a judge. I got civil fuckin' rights that y'all are violating."

Agent Battle came back into the room and handed Jasmine a cell phone. "Call your man," she said.

"Thank fuckin' God!" Jasmine immediately dialed Nico's number, but it rang out to voice mail.

◆◆◆

Mia loved riding Nico's dick in the reverse cowgirl position. As she ground her pussy so that every inch of his dick was inside of her, she couldn't hold back the tears that streamed down her face. She was glad her back was to Nico because she didn't want him to see her crying.

Mia cupped both of her breasts and pinched her nipples. Nico's dick inside of her had never felt as good as it did at that moment. Just as she was about to explode, she could hear his phone vibrating in his pants on his bedroom's hardwood floor.

"Don't answer it, baby," she softly pleaded in a moan mixed with a teary voice.

Nico clearly wasn't as into the fuck session as she was. He lightly tapped her twice on her ass cheeks and told her to get up for a second. After she slid her pussy off his dick, he sat up on the bed and quickly reached over and picked up his pants from off the floor. He grabbed his cell phone and looked at it without answering it.

Mia ran her hand down her face while she sat on the edge of the bed. She was trying to wipe away the tears. "Everything okay?" she asked him, her eyes red.

"You was crying?"

Mia stood up and walked over to Nico. She buried her head into his chest, and her tears instantly began flowing again. She held on to Nico as she sobbed.

"The fuck you crying for?"

"Because I'm so happy right now. You make me feel so good," she replied, Nico's rock-hard dick pressing up against her thigh as he scrolled through his phone, looking at his text messages.

Mia looked up at Nico as she held on to him. "Baby, I am so sorry for what I did. It really was nothing, really nothing at all. I was just tore-up drunk, high, and confused, and things just happened," she explained. "I love you." She kissed Nico's chest.

Nico didn't immediately respond, and before long, his cell phone was ringing again. Mia asked him again not to answer it, and she bent down to her knees and began sucking on his dick and massaging his balls to keep his mind off anything but her.

Jasmine ended the call without leaving a message for Nico.

"I need *my* phone. He ain't answering because he don't pick up numbers he don't recognize."

None of the agents replied, and Jasmine decided to try Nico a second time, with no luck.

Jasmine didn't want to show it, but she was annoyed. She didn't know what to make of it, but she didn't want to assume anything.

"Jasmine, he's not answering because he's concerned with one thing, and that's looking out for himself. You really need—"

"I really need *my* phone," Jasmine said, cutting off Agent Battle.

"No. You really need to look out for yourself and seriously consider what we're asking you to do."

At that moment one of the agents who had left the room came back with Jasmine's cell phone and her oversized Gucci bag, which he placed in her hands.

"You're free to leave," Agent Battle nonchalantly said, surprising Jasmine. She handed Jasmine her card. "Think about the evidence we have stacked against you. Think about your future and give me a call. But, either way, we'll be in touch."

Jasmine took hold of it, looked at it, and placed it inside her bag. She stood up and prepared to leave.

"Where's the bathroom?" Jasmine asked.

Agent Battle told Jasmine to follow her, and she escorted her down the hall. Jasmine's high heels echoed throughout the halls as she walked.

"When you're done, you can take that elevator down to the lobby," Agent Battle said, and she returned to her office.

Jasmine went inside the bathroom, washed her hands, and threw water on her face. She shook her head when she looked in the mirror and saw how ragged she looked with bags under her eyes from lack of sleep. She was thankful she had a pair of sunglasses in her bag. She reached for them and put them on before fixing her hair.

After she used the bathroom, she called Nico again. This time, after the third ring he picked up. A relieved half-smile appeared on her face before she sighed into the phone and spoke.

"Oh, my God, baby, where are you?" she asked, tears beginning to form in her eyes.

"Where the fuck you at?" Nico barked into the phone.

"What you mean, where am I at? I'm in the precinct."

Nico hesitated before speaking. Jasmine's words were echoing because she was still inside the bathroom, but he had no way of knowing that. He pushed Mia's head away from his dick and motioned for her to stop pleasuring him.

"Why your phone echoin' like that?"

"Nico, I don't know. I just want to go home. Come get me."

"Come get you? You with the lawyer?"

"Why are you asking me a million and one fuckin' questions? Shit! Just come pick me up, so I can get the hell outta here. We'll talk when I see you."

"A'ight, I'll hit you right back."

Nico called his lawyer, and the lawyer explained to him that he was still trying to find out where Jasmine was. He told him that Jasmine wasn't at the Midtown South Precinct when he got there and that the cops wouldn't give him any information on her. Then he went to Central Booking and she wasn't being held there. The Manhattan District Attorney's office also wouldn't give him any information.

After Nico ended the call with his attorney, he called Jasmine back. "Where they holding you at, baby?"

"Downtown, on Reade Street."

"What happened to the murder charge? What they saying?"

Jasmine sighed with annoyance. "They didn't charge me with nothing. NYPD held me for eighteen hours, and then they transferred me down to the feds, and I been down here for eighteen more hours. And I'm tired, I'm aggravated, I'm dirty, I'm hungry, and I want to get the fuck outta here."

"So all they did was question you?"

Jasmine kept her mouth shut, her blood beyond boiling.

Nico was quiet, his brain working, trying to figure out what was up. The NYPD couldn't hold her for twenty-four hours unless she saw a judge, so he was real suspicious and feeling paranoid. "A'ight, Reade Street, right?"

Jasmine sucked her teeth and sighed.

"Give me forty-five minutes, and I'll be there."

"Thank you."

TWO

"Finish fucking me, baby," Mia said.

Nico wanted to leave and head to his lawyer's office, but at the same time Mia's body was looking right, and he wanted to reclaim the pussy she had given to some other nigga in a moment of weakness.

"Turn around," he instructed her.

Mia turned around so that her bare ass was facing him, and she braced herself by placing both of her hands on the bed. Her pussy was soaked and throbbing in anticipation of Nico's dick reentering her.

"You feel so good," she turned her head and said to Nico as soon as he slid his dick back inside of her.

In a matter of seconds, Nico was fucking Mia hard, and she was enjoying every bit of it. Before long she was coming all over his dick, and once again, tears of joy began to flow out of her eyes.

◆◆◆

Exactly forty-five minutes had passed, and Jasmine was standing on Reade Street in the sweltering sun waiting for Nico to arrive. The fact that she still had on yesterday's clothes was beyond irritating to her. She called Nico to see what street he was on. The phone rang twice then stopped ringing.

She looked at her phone and realized that her battery had died. "I can't believe this shit!" she screamed.

The people on the street looked at her, trying to figure out what was up with her.

Jasmine looked inside her bag and realized that she didn't have her wallet with her, nor a single coin of loose change.

She walked back inside the FBI building, and a black-uniformed officer manning the metal detectors and the building's entrance asked her if everything was okay. She nodded to him, and after going through the metal detector, she stood still for a moment and thought about what she should do.

Out the corner of her eye she could see out of the lobby and onto Reade Street, where she had just been standing, and she was certain that she saw Nico's Maybach. A huge smile appeared across her face, and she instantly felt relief. She quickly bolted from the building and returned to the blistering sun.

Jasmine removed her shades so she could see better, and when she did, she realized that the car she thought was a Maybach wasn't even close to being a Maybach. The red light changed to green, and the car drove off.

Not wanting to seem like a crazy chick, she decided to just stand in the sun and wait for her man. It seemed like a thousand cars passed her by as she stood on the street corner looking like a helpless panhandler. A half hour had gone by, and to her it felt like two hours.

She walked back into the federal building, and the uniformed officer smiled at her and waved her through the metal detector.

"You sure you all right? You need help with anything?"

Jasmine knew her options were limited, but she didn't want to resort to Agent Battle for help. So she asked the uniformed officer if she could use a phone and explained to him that her cell phone was dead. The officer pointed in the direction of the dinosaur-looking pay phones in the rear corner of the lobby, sparing her the embarrassment of asking for change by giving her three quarters.

"Thank you so much," Jasmine said, way too exasperated to even smile.

When she dialed Nico and his phone rang out to voice mail, her exasperation was turning into desperation.

"Nico, my cell phone is dead, so if you call me, you aren't going to get me. But I'm on Reade Street right near Duane Street. Where the hell are you?" Jasmine ended the call. She had no choice but to hang up the phone and go back outside and wait.

"Come inside me, baby," Mia pleaded to Nico. She always knew when he was about to come because his strokes became much more rhythmic.

She was laying on her back with her legs wide open while Nico fucked her, and just as he was ready to come, she wrapped her legs around his body and interlocked her feet and pulled him into her and made sure that he didn't pull out.

"You wild. You know that, right?" Nico smiled and said to Mia after he came inside her pussy.

Mia unclasped her feet, and Nico pulled his dick out of her and stepped back and looked at her. Mia propped both of her feet on the bed. She looked as if she was preparing for a gynecologist to examine her pussy. She told Nico to look at her, and she contracted her pussy muscles until his come began to ooze out of her. Then she scooped up some of it with her middle finger and put it in her mouth and sucked her finger clean, like she was finishing off the last bits of a Popsicle.

She smiled after swallowing Nico's come, and she didn't say anything else to him. She was right where she wanted to be, and she had Nico right where she wanted him.

It had been a full two hours since Nico was supposed to pick Jasmine up. As much as she hated to, she went and sat down on a nearby park bench. Jasmine was a germaphobe and hated things like public toilet bowls, train cars, and public seating, but her feet were aching, she was feeling dehydrated, and she knew that if she didn't sit down she was going to pass out.

Five minutes passed, and before she knew what was up, she'd dozed off on the park bench. She wasn't in a deep sleep, so when she felt something tap her hand, she instantly woke up. She looked around and didn't see anyone standing near her, but she couldn't believe what she did see. She looked at the back of her right hand and saw what looked like bird shit.

"No, this is not happening to me! This is not happening to me!"

With her left hand, she took off her shades and looked at her hand, and she confirmed that it was warm, purplish bird shit that had just landed on her. She jumped to her feet in a panic, shaking and trembling in disgust. She used her left hand and rummaged through her bag and found some tissue to wipe the pigeon shit off, but there was no way she could wipe away the disgust she was feeling.

Jasmine marched back into the federal building, and after going through the metal detectors, she found a bathroom. She washed her hands for five minutes straight, but was unable to wash away the icky feeling.

After exiting the bathroom she went back to the pay phone and tried calling Nico again, but this time his phone didn't even ring; it went straight to voice mail. She knew he'd turned his phone off, but a part of her wanted to believe that he was driving through the Midtown Tunnel and didn't have any reception.

She put the phone on the receiver and stood with a blank look on her face.

"Miss, what's your name?" the officer who'd given her the change said after he had walked over to her. There were other officers manning his post while he went on his lunch break.

"What?"

"Your name."

"For what? What difference does it make?"

"Let me help you." The officer was definitely attracted to her, but at the same time he was genuinely concerned.

"If you wanna help me, call my man and find out where he's at."

"Oh, you waiting on a ride?"

Jasmine wasn't in a talkative mood, so she didn't reply.

"My shift ends in a couple of hours, so if you still need a ride, I could look out for you."

Jasmine didn't even look him in his face. She nodded, and he walked off. She walked toward the exit of the building. She thought about taking him up on his offer because she was clearly out of options, but she knew it would look way too crazy if Nico caught wind of a cop dropping her off at the crib.

Like a true soldier, she walked back to the corner of Reade Street and waited loyally for her man to come scoop her.

Unfortunately for Jasmine, another hour passed by, and still there was no Nico. It seemed like ages had passed since the feds had shown her those photos of him with Mia, and she was wondering if, in fact, those photos were real. She did her best to shake the thoughts from her head. As soon as she was able to convince herself that those photos were a result of Photoshop tricks, she heard Agent Battle's words playing in her head when the agent had mockingly asked her if she was a ride-or-die chick.

Jasmine walked back into the federal building one last time and stood in front of the pay phone, wondering what she should do. She was down to her last quarter when she saw an advertisement sticker for a cab service plastered on the pay phone. She knew her best bet would be to use that quarter to call herself a cab, and that was exactly what she did.

When the cab arrived, Jasmine instructed the cab driver to take her to her mother's house in Queens. She was hoping that either her mother or father would be there so that she would be able to pay for her cab, take a shower, and change her clothes.

As the cab made its way from Manhattan into Queens, all kinds of thoughts ran through Jasmine's head. Something had told her not to go to Nico's sprawling Long Island estate that she shared with him, so she decided to follow her gut.

THREE

After a good night of sleep at her parents' house, Jasmine was in no mood to go to school. She ate breakfast and then headed out to Long Island, where she let herself inside Nico's mansion with her spare key. Nico wasn't home, and Jasmine still hadn't spoken to him. She dialed his number from his home phone, but he didn't answer.

"So you good?" Nico asked Mia.

Mia nodded, and Nico reminded her that he would be sitting in the rental parked right across from the only entrance to the Marriott Hotel in Hartford, Connecticut.

"Baby, I'm good." She gave him a kiss on the cheek and exited the Holiday Inn hotel the two of them had checked into an hour earlier.

Mia left the room with 32 ounces of "China white" heroin in her Louis Vuitton shoulder bag, her heart pounding as she made it to the hotel parking lot. She placed the bag in the trunk of the rented Volvo and got behind the steering wheel, pushed the ignition, and headed downtown to the Marriott, while Nico followed her in another rental.

After the ten-minute ride to the Marriott, Mia parked the car and called and reported the rental car stolen. She left three hundred and fifty thousand dollars worth of pure heroin inside the trunk of the car, got out, and headed to Room 605 on the sixth floor with another Louis Vuitton bag that held inside only her makeup, wallet, and other personal items.

A buff African dude named Twist opened the door to the hotel room.

"Twist?" Mia asked.

Twist nodded and invited Mia into the room. There were two other African dudes in the room seated at a table, smoking cigarettes and drinking Jack Daniel's.

"You drink?" one of the dudes asked her.

"I'm not here to drink and socialize," Mia said in a no-nonsense tone. If any of these dudes were federal agents, she would be looking at football numbers behind bars, but she did her best to not let her nervousness show.

Twist started speaking in his language, and soon the other two dudes started to laugh.

"Have a seat," Twist said to her.

Mia remembered Nico's instructions. She told Twist she wanted them to meet at the bar downstairs, near the lobby.

Twist smiled and said something else in his language, and the other two dudes again started laughing.

"Have a drink. Just sit and relax," Twist said to her, while his boy poured a drink for her, and his other boy got up and went to another room.

"Listen. No disrespect, but can you do me a favor and speak English? I don't wanna hear all that African jungle voodoo language shit that I can't understand."

Twist looked at Mia and smiled. "African jungle voodoo shit?" Twist said with a thick Kunta Kinte-sounding accent. "You're funny."

Mia didn't smile because this wasn't a game to her.

"So where's Nico?" Twist asked.

"Why the fuck you asking all these questions? I told you I'm not drinking, and I told you we gotta go downstairs."

Twist's man came back into the room with a black knapsack and tossed it to him. He unzipped it and showed it to Mia.

Without saying anything, Mia immediately turned and walked out of the hotel room. She knew there was always the possibility that the room could be wired with cameras, so she said as little as possible. She only wanted to talk business at the bar.

Twist followed her.

"Sweetie, I only talk in bars and lobbies."

Twist nodded, and they made their way down to the bar, where Mia ordered a soda for herself and a Jack Daniel's on the rocks for Twist. After about five minutes, one of the dudes from in the room came downstairs and placed the black knapsack near Twist's feet and walked off. Twist sipped on his drink, and then he looked around the bar and asked Mia who she thought was five-0.

"You tell me," she replied.

Twist motioned his head at someone seated not too far from them. "That's one right there, and see homie that just walked in . . . that's a cop; he's wearing a vest."

Mia looked at Twist and shook her head. She sipped on her Sprite and placed it back down on the counter. "That's my shooter with the vest."

Twist looked at her and smiled.

"It's three-fifty inside the bag, right?"

Twist nodded, and then Mia instructed him to take the car key that was sitting on the counter.

"Walk out front, and in the second row you'll see a gray Volvo. Check the trunk."

Twist was expecting to handle everything inside the hotel room, but he knew that if he wanted the deal to go through, he had to play by Mia's rules or he'd run the risk of having her think that he was a cop.

"I ain't going nowhere," Mia told him.

Twist took the key and made his way to the Volvo. He checked the trunk and saw what was inside the Louis Vuitton bag. A smile flashed across his face, his white teeth contrasting with his blue-black skin.

"You think your girl will like the bag?" Mia asked after he'd returned to the bar.

Twist smiled. "She'll love it."

"That's what's up."

Mia placed a twenty-dollar bill on the counter, knelt down and scooped up the black knapsack, and headed out of the bar. She tried to walk as normal as possible, but she felt like she was going to shit on herself. It seemed as if every step took the equivalent of two minutes. She was praying that federal agents didn't swarm her and slam her to the ground and arrest her.

When she made it to Nico's rental car, Nico moved to the passenger's seat, and she got in the driver's seat. Mia put the car in drive, and she and Nico drove off. She reached over and kissed him on the cheek.

"I told you I got you, baby," she said.

Nico looked inside the black knapsack and smiled.

FOUR

Nico had a lot on his mind. He had an uneasy feeling that Bebo was planning to take him out, and he constantly looked over his shoulder. Not only did he feel that his life was in danger, he could also sense that he was close to being indicted. He just didn't know how close. His lawyer had warned him to be careful over the next couple of weeks and to avoid talking on the phone.

Despite the warning, Nico reached out to Jasmine on his way back from Connecticut.

Jasmine picked up on the first ring.

"Jasmine."

Jasmine broke the silence when that anger she felt when she was left stranded at the federal building instantly returned.

"Nico, how the fuck could you just leave me stranded in Manhattan like that with no money or nothing, after you told me you was on your way to come get me?"

"Where are you right now?"

"I'm in the house!"

Nico was quiet.

"So are you going to tell me what happened or what?"

"I might pass through later on tonight, but I'm not sure. I got some moves I gotta make." Just as Nico said that, the prepaid phone he had recently purchased began vibrating. He saw it was his right-hand man BJ.

"Yo, let me hit you back," he said to Jasmine.

"Nico, don't hang up this phone!"

Nico abruptly ended the call.

Jasmine's blood was boiling, and she really couldn't take any more of Nico's bullshit.

"Ugggghhhh!" She slammed her phone down on the bed.

"BJ, what's good?" Nico asked.

"Bebo want us to come through for a meeting tonight."

BJ was also speaking on a prepaid cell, since he too knew that the feds had stepped up their surveillance.

"Call that muthafucka and tell him to suck my muthafuckin' dick!" Nico barked into the phone. "Shit is hot as hell right now, and this muthafucka setting up play-date meetings and shit, like we're fuckin' two-year-old kids."

"A'ight," BJ said, not wanting to question Nico's bravado. After a moment of silence, he asked, "How that thing go?"

"Everything's good. 'Bout to cross back into New York right now."

Both of them were silent for a moment.

"You want me to go through just to see what Bebo is saying, or what?"

"If you go to that meeting, you ain't coming outta there alive. Trust me on that."

Nico's main cell phone began ringing. It was Jasmine. He picked up. "I'll hit you right back." He ended the call without giving her a chance to say anything.

Jasmine was beyond enraged. For the first time she truly contemplated her options, wondering just what was up with Nico. Now it seemed like he was purposely avoiding her, like she had the monster or something.

BJ was about to hang up, thinking that Nico was talking to him.

"Nah, nah, not you. I was talking to Jasmine. She just hit me up on my other phone," Nico explained.

"But, BJ, trust me, if you go to that meeting, I'll be going to your funeral next week. Fuck Bebo! This is my muthafuckin' shit! This is my muthafuckin' crew and my muthafuckin' city!"

BJ and Nico ended their call. Nico didn't have to spell things out for BJ. He knew it was just a matter of time before Nico called on him to murder Bebo.

But what Nico didn't know was that Twist was working for Bebo. The two had met while in prison. Bebo was furious that Nico had crossed him and cut him out of a deal that he thought Bebo knew nothing about. More importantly, he had no clue who was supplying Nico with that 95% pure heroin.

Bebo knew that he had to maintain his rep at any cost, even if it cost him the life of his top lieutenant. Most of his anger stemmed from his envy of Nico. He took it as Nico was trying to outshine him. Nobody outshined the master.

FIVE

Nico wanted to stay off the radar until he could figure out for sure what was going on after he came back from Hartford with Mia. He had Mia open up a safe deposit box at a Chase Bank branch in White Plains, where he stashed the three hundred and fifty thousand.

Mia was more than willing to do whatever Nico asked of her, and she was right by his side when the two of them checked into the W Hotel in midtown Manhattan, where they decided to stay for a couple of days before heading out to Las Vegas.

◆◆◆

Jasmine still hadn't spoken at length with Nico to find out where his head was at, but she decided to just chill and give him space and not press him. She was trying her best to go about things as normally as possible, but it was hard because she was insecure about what the future held for her.

She had started to get real close with a Puerto Rican girl from her school named Narjara. Narjara was a little younger than Jasmine at eighteen. She was from Washington Heights and lived with her man. Jasmine liked Narjara because she was real cool, she was pretty, and she had swagger that Jasmine liked. Plus, Narjara sort of looked up to Jasmine like she was the big sister that she never had. Narjara was always complimenting her on how beautiful she was and was always asking her for advice. Narjara's man was a mid-level drug dealer from Newark, New Jersey, and he was real abusive to her.

When Narjara called Jasmine, crying and hysterical after getting her ass beat by her man, Jasmine didn't hesitate to tell her to take a cab to Long Island and come chill with her. Jasmine wasn't really in the mood to entertain company, since she had so much on her mind, but she figured it would be a much-needed distraction for her.

When Narjara arrived at Jasmine and Nico's estate, she called Jasmine on her cell phone, and Jasmine ran out to greet her and to pay for her cab.

"Oh, my God!" Jasmine covered her mouth with her right hand, looking at Narjara's face in disbelief as she escorted her into her house. "You gotta go to the emergency room and get that eye checked out."

Narjara's right eye was closed and swollen shut, and her bottom lip was split and swollen. She looked as if she had been on the receiving end of head shots from Floyd Mayweather.

"I can't, Jasmine."

"What you mean, you can't? You don't have a choice; I'm taking you myself. You could lose your eye. That shit don't look good at all. What the hell happened? That muthafucka can't be putting his hands on you like that!"

Narjara, on the verge of tears, shook her head. "It's always the same bullshit. It's like no matter what I do, I can never make him happy. He always finds something to scream on me about. I get so tired of him reminding me how, if it wasn't for him, I would still be working a stripper's pole somewhere."

"For real, for real, you ain't fuckin' with his ass no more, and I mean that shit. You can just chill here until we figure something out."

Narjara went to the mirror and looked at her face. "It wasn't even this bad when I got in the cab." Right after she said that, she fell to the floor.

Jasmine screamed, and then she ran to her aid. "Narjara! You okay?"

Narjara had fainted, but she quickly came to. "Yeah, I'm okay. Just real dizzy," she said from the floor, trying to sit up.

"See, this is what I mean—Your ass is going to the hospital right now. I was going to drive you, but I'm calling an ambulance."

"Jasmine, no. I'm all right!"

"No, you aren't all right. You fuckin' just fainted. You getting checked out by a doctor."

"And what am I gonna tell them happened to me? That my boyfriend beat my ass? Then they'll call the cops. And I just don't feel like dealing with that drama."

Jasmine shook her head. She blew out air out from her lungs. At that very moment, her front doorbell rang. She wasn't expecting anyone to come by at such a late hour. She was hoping it was Nico; that he had forgotten his key or something.

The bell rang again, and Jasmine told Narjara she would be right back.

She looked on the security camera and saw Bebo. A smile came to her face. She knew if Bebo was there that Nico was more than likely right behind him.

"Hey, Bebo," Jasmine said, after opening the door. She leaned over to give Bebo a kiss on the cheek.

Bebo brushed past her without accepting the kiss, not even bothering to say hello. Two dudes she hadn't seen before followed him.

"Where your man at?" Bebo asked.

Jasmine opened her hands and shrugged.

"Jasmine, I asked you—Where was your man at?"

"And I said I don't know!" she replied, sensing something was wrong.

"You shrugged your fuckin' shoulders. Open your mouth and address me with words."

Narjara walked into the living room to see what was going on. She had put on a pair of Jasmine's shades, but her swelling was still visible.

"Are you high or something?" Jasmine asked. "Where the fuck is Nico?"

"I don't know. I thought he would be with you."

Bebo tried to detect if she was being straight up with him. "Nah, he ain't with me. Get him on the phone."

"Okay, hold up. First, tell me what the hell is going on."

"Get the muthafucka on the phone!" Bebo reached into his waistband and pulled out a snub-nosed revolver and pointed it at Jasmine.

Jasmine's heart started racing. Narjara tried to turn and walk out of the living room.

"Don't move, *chica*!" Bebo ordered.

Narjara stopped dead in her tracks. At that moment she would have given anything to be at home with her man, getting her ass kicked.

"Bebo, seriously, I don't know what's going on. I don't. I mean, I was just about to take my girl to the hospital and—"

"Get the muthafucka on the phone! What the fuck?" Bebo yelled, his booming voice startling Jasmine. "I'm not playin' no games!"

Jasmine didn't know what was going on, but she knew in her gut not to test Bebo at that moment. She reached for her phone and dialed Nico. She didn't know if she wanted him to pick up, or ignore her calls as he had been doing.

"It's going to voice mail," she stated, her heart thumping out of her chest.

"Dial that shit again!"

Jasmine complied, and again it went to voice mail.

Bebo, his gun still aimed at Jasmine, walked closer to her and pressed the gun to her temple. "Where-the-fuck-is-Nico?" he asked in a cadence.

Jasmine had never been as scared as she was at that moment. "Bebo, I swear to you, I don't know. I haven't spoken to him in a few days."

Bebo pressed the gun into her temple with more force, and then he cocked it.

"Bebo, I swear I don't know! I swear on everything!"

Bebo could see Jasmine tremble just slightly. His instincts told him that she was telling the truth, but he still kept the gun to her temple. "Call him again!"

Jasmine held her phone out so that Bebo could see she was really calling Nico, and then she decided to put the phone on speaker to prove that she was really calling him.

"See, he's not picking up. I swear to you he's been ignoring my calls. I don't know where he's at. I don't know why he's not taking my calls."

"Who the fuck is that?" Bebo asked, referring to Narjara. He took the gun away from Jasmine's temple.

"That's just my homegirl from nursing school."

"Where the fuck Nico keep his shit?" Bebo again raised his gun to Jasmine.

"He don't tell me nothing about what he do," she replied, a combination of desperation and exasperation in her voice.

"Jasmine, this ain't a fuckin' game! Where the fuck is the safe at?"

"I don't know. I swear to you." Jasmine felt she had no choice but to lie because she had no idea what was up.

WHACK!

Bebo slapped Jasmine across the face with the butt of his gun, and she instantly saw stars and felt woozy, but she didn't fall to the ground.

"Where the fuck is the safe?"

Narjara yelled, "Jasmine!" and rushed to her aid.

One of Bebo's goons stepped up and grabbed Narjara by her hair.

"It's cool. I got this," Bebo said as he held his gun on both Jasmine and Narjara, now standing right next to each other. "Go find the stash. I got these bitches."

In a matter of seconds, Bebo's henchmen were rummaging through Nico's mansion and ransacking every room, looking for Nico's stash. Jasmine was praying that Nico would call her back and help her get out of the immediate hell she was facing, with Bebo starring as the devil.

While Bebo's boys turned the house upside down, Jasmine quietly pressed the record feature on her BlackBerry.

"Get off of me!" Narjara screamed, trying to fight Bebo off.

Bebo had grabbed her by the throat and pulled her toward him before putting her in the headlock. Her back was to his chest, and now he was pressing his gun against her temple.

"Bebo, she ain't got nothing to do with anything. Let her go!" Jasmine pleaded as Narjara scratched and clawed at Bebo's muscular arms, trying to free herself from his grip.

Bebo's arms were cutting off Narjara's air supply, and she felt like she was going to pass out at any moment.

Two minutes later Bebo's boys were back in the living room.

"We can't find the stash, but look at this shit we found, yo." One of Bebo's henchmen handed him FBI Agent Battle's card.

"What the fuck!" Bebo screamed at Jasmine and Narjara. "You snitchin'? This bitch is a fed?"

Bebo began to apply so much pressure to Narjara's neck, he was almost on the verge of snapping the bones in it. Narjara's face was blood red, and her eyes looked as if they were bulging out of their sockets.

"No. No, she's—"

BLAOW!

Narjara's limp body fell to the living room floor like a bag of bricks from the gun blast that had entered the right side of her temple and exited the left. Her blood and brains splattered all across the walls and floor of the living room.

"AHHHHH! Oh, my God! Oh, my God!" Jasmine screamed, trembling with fear. She couldn't believe what she had just witnessed.

"Bitch, I'm asking you one more time—Where the fuck is the stash at?" Bebo asked like a coldblooded hitman. Bebo was furious with Nico, but at the same time he wanted to get his hands on that pure heroin that he had sold to Twist, and he was desperate to find out where he had stashed it.

Jasmine, frozen in fear, wanted to tell Bebo where Nico's two safes were, but she was so afraid for her life, the words simply would not form in her mouth.

She started to backpedal. She was seconds from turning and bolting up the stairs, where she was going to attempt to jump out of a window to safety. She knew she was looking at death, but the only thing she could think of was surviving.

Bebo was like a man possessed. As soon as Jasmine took two steps backwards, without warning, he raised his gun and pointed it at her and fired twice.

BLAOW! BLAOW!

Jasmine had raised her hands in the hair in a defensive motion, but it didn't stop the first bullet from ripping through her right hand and causing blood to splatter everywhere. The second bullet pierced her neck and spun her around, and her body went crashing to the floor. She lay face down, motionless, and bleeding about fifteen feet away from her friend.

Bebo surveyed the room one last time, making sure that Narjara and Jasmine were both dead. "Let's get the fuck up outta here and find that bitch-ass nigga."

He used his baggy shirt to wipe his fingerprints off the gun he had just used. He then walked over to Narjara and knelt down beside her, still holding the gun with his shirt. He then took hold of Narjara's limp right hand and positioned it so that she was gripping the gun.

He chuckled. "It's fucked up how that bitch shot Jasmine and then killed herself," he said to his two partners in crime.

After he'd said that, he and his two hitmen hustled out of the house, got into an all-black Lexus, and sped away.

SIX

Mia and Nico landed safely in Las Vegas, and they took a car service to the Wynn Resort hotel. They checked into a deluxe top-floor corner suite with a panoramic view.

As soon as the couple stepped foot in the room, Mia said, "Oh, my God! Baby, I love this!"

The suite had floor-to-ceiling windows and a fantastic view of the Las Vegas strip. They were up so high, Mia felt like she was on top of the world.

"Nothing but the best," Nico said.

Mia kissed him on the lips, and she went to explore the other parts of the suite.

Nico was exhausted. He sat down on the couch and put his feet up on the ottoman. He smiled when he heard an excited scream come from the bathroom.

"Oversized Turkish towels! I loves it!" she said as she looked at all of the bathroom amenities.

Nico was ready to doze off and get like an hour of sleep before heading out shopping with Mia, but first he wanted to charge his prepaid cell phone so he could check in with BJ. He plugged it in and set it on the dining table.

Mia came back into the room and started massaging his neck and shoulders. "You tired, baby?"

Nico ran his hands down his face. "I'm good. Get me a drink?" He then explained that he was going to lie down for about an hour before they headed out to shop and gamble.

Mia liked the plan. After she poured Nico his drink, she went back to massaging his shoulders.

Nico loved the way Mia made him feel whenever she gave him a massage, and her hands never felt so good.

Nico's phone charged to the point where it was able to turn itself on, and it began vibrating to indicate that he had messages. Nico gulped down his drink and put the glass down. He asked Mia to pass him the phone. Immediately he dialed his voice mail and heard three messages from BJ.

"Yo, call me as soon as you get this," was the first message from BJ.

An hour later, BJ had called back and left another message. "My nigga, I don't know if you touched down yet or what, but get at me ASAP."

Nico knew something was up because BJ never left messages like that. BJ hated the phone and only used it when necessary.

BJ left a third message a little over an hour after he had left the second. "Nico, where are you? Hit me back. This shit can't wait."

Nico unplugged the phone, took the charger, and walked into the bathroom and plugged the phone back in. He called BJ back.

Mia could sense something was up, but she didn't ask any questions. She poured herself a drink, sat down on the ottoman, and turned on the flat-screen TV.

BJ picked up on the second ring.

"What's good?"

"Where you at?"

"In Vegas. Why? What's up?"

"You need to get back to New York. Muthafuckas ran up in your crib and shot shit up," BJ explained.

"What the fuck you talkin' about?"

"My dude, shit is on the news and everything. Something went down at your crib, and people got killed. I don't know what the fuck is going

34

on. Five-0 got shit roped off, and you know they won't tell a nigga shit."

"What?" Nico's mind started racing. He knew Jasmine was probably the only person in the house. "You spoke to Jasmine?"

"Her shit been ringing out to voice mail."

Nico immediately thought the worst. He could sense that Jasmine had been murdered.

After Mia had moved out of the crib, Nico had gotten rid of the security firm he had hired, after dudes had run up in his crib looking for him and Mia was home alone. He was kicking himself at that moment for not keeping the security guards on the premises.

"I'm heading back to New York tonight, and we gonna handle this shit. Find out what the streets is saying. Get Lorenzo and everybody else and tell them niggas to strap up and get ready to go to war," Nico ordered.

"We ready right now, my nigga! We just waiting on word from you before we make a move."

"A'ight, that's what's up." Nico ended the call.

Nico stood in shock and disbelief. He thought about all of the mistakes he had made recently. Without a doubt, he knew his biggest mistake was not staying in touch with Jasmine. Maybe she had been trying to tell him about some new drama, but he didn't give her the opportunity.

Nico emerged from the bathroom and walked back into the living room. Mia took hold of the remote control and turned down the volume to 106 & Park. She asked if everything was okay.

"I gotta get back to New York tonight."

"Why? What happened?" Mia stood to her feet.

"That was BJ on the phone. He told me niggas ran up in my crib, shot the shit up, and people got killed. He said the shit was on the news and everything."

Mia placed her hand over her mouth in disbelief. She didn't want to ask the obvious, but she knew Jasmine was still living at Nico's Long Island estate. Mia couldn't help but think about how lucky she was because she would have been dead at that very moment had Jasmine never stepped into the picture.

"Listen, just chill here. I gotta get to New York and find out what's up. I'll get back out here as soon as I can, and if I can't, I'll fly you back to New York."

"No, baby. I want to go back to New York with you. I can't let you just go back to New York alone by yourself like that." Mia pressed up close to Nico and held his hand.

"Nah, I need you to stay out here. Just hold me down from out here. Trust me on this. I don't want you in New York until I take care of this and sort everything out."

Mia knew not to press the issue. She was perfect at playing her position, so she got on her iPad and started looking for flights for Nico. She found a flight heading out in two hours, and she booked it.

◆◆◆

Nico kissed Mia and then made his way down to the lobby, so he could head to the airport.

As soon as he left the suite, Mia went on Google to see what she could find out about the shooting, and without reading the entire article from New York's Eyewitness News Web site, she stopped and focused on where the article said that the names of the female victims at the location of the suspected drug kingpin's residence were being withheld.

Mia wouldn't have wished that kind of death on her worst enemy. But she couldn't help but plaster a smile across her face. Her biggest competition had managed to eliminate herself, and that brought her joy.

She poured herself a drink of Bailey's Irish Cream on the rocks. She sat down on the couch and smiled at the thought of her and Nico's unimpeded future together.

Mia decided to celebrate Jasmine's demise by treating herself to a luxurious spa treatment, so as soon as she finished her drink, she dialed the front desk and had them book an appointment for her.

With a smile that just would not leave her face, she walked over to the floor-to-ceiling windows and looked out at the breathtaking view. She said out loud to herself in a sinister tone, "She should have just listened to me. I told that bitch that—'I am wifey.'"

SEVEN

Nico's red-eye flight landed at New York's LaGuardia Airport at five thirty in the morning. He had already spoken to BJ, and he would be at the airport when the plane arrived, waiting to drive them to Nico's Manhattan apartment.

BJ had managed to gather what the streets were saying, and one thing was crystal clear—Bebo's name kept ringing out. He was convinced that Bebo was behind the shootings. His theory: Nico had played Bebo by not coming to the meeting Bebo had called.

Nico unbuckled his first-class seat and waited for the plane to taxi its way to the gate. What normally took no more than ten minutes was taking much longer, and he was getting extremely restless.

The pilot spoke through the intercom and apologized to the passengers, telling them they had arrived safely at the gate but, due to a mechanical issue with the plane's door, they would be delayed in getting off the plane for another fifteen minutes or so.

Everyone on the plane was tired and groggy, and they voiced their anger and disgust before returning to their seats, where they had no choice but to sit and wait for the doors to open.

Nico called BJ and told him what was going on with the plane.

"It's all good. I'm here," he said to Nico.

"What's the word?"

"That muthafucka Bebo."

Nico gritted his teeth. "That's what you hearing?"

"From everybody. And everybody can't be wrong on this shit."

Nico was quiet for a moment. "We handlin' this shit today!"

"No doubt."

At that point Nico could see one of the flight attendants opening up the front door to the plane. "I'll be out in like five minutes," he told BJ. He looked down at his seat and on the floor to make sure he wasn't leaving anything behind. Then he stepped into the aisle to exit the plane.

As soon as he looked up, he saw five white uniformed Port Authority police officers. Before Nico could blink, they had him surrounded.

One of the officers said, "Mr. Carter, can you turn around and place your hands behind your back?"

A smirk came across Nico's face. "Y'all niggas serious, man?"

"Mr. Carter, turn around and put your hands behind your back!" the young, rookie-looking officer commanded much more forcefully, his face blood red.

"Get the fuck outta here! Put my hands behind my back for what?" Nico tried to brush past one of the officers.

Two of the cops instantly drew their Taser guns and aimed them at him, while two other cops ordered everyone to go to the back of the plane. The rookie officer tried to grab hold of Nico's wrist to cuffs him as he told him he was placing him under arrest.

"You arrestin' me for what?" Nico demanded to know. "What the fuck is the charge?"

The people on the plane looked on in shock, wondering if Nico was a wanted shoe-bomber or something.

The next thing Nico knew, the rookie cop punched him square in the face and spun him around and had him laying facedown across two seats in row two.

Nico had the rookie cop by at least thirty pounds and knew it wouldn't have taken much to beat his ass, but he didn't want to get tased, or worse, catch a hot one in his back from one of the trigger-happy cops.

The cop applied the handcuffs extremely tightly and yanked Nico up to his feet by his right elbow. In the process he almost pulled Nico's shoulder out of its socket.

Pain shot through Nico's body, but he clenched his teeth. "What the fuck y'all arrestin' me for?"

The cops didn't reply. Two of them flanked Nico and walked him off the plane.

Although it was still early morning, the terminals were busy. It seemed as if every eye in the airport was on Nico as the cops walked him through the terminal and outside to a throng of waiting Port Authority police cars.

◆◆◆

All of the cop cars caught the attention of BJ, who was about ten feet away by the passenger curbside pickup. He watched in disbelief as Nico was stuffed into the back of a squad car in handcuffs. BJ got as close as he could to the police car, trying his best to get Nico's attention, but Nico never looked his way. Bbefore long the squad car pulled off. BJ ran back to his car and immediately dialed the lawyer and told him what happened.

It was still early in the morning, and Nico's lawyer sounded as if he had just woken up. But with as much money as Nico had been paying him, he didn't hesitate to get on things. He told BJ he had to get dressed, but that he would be in touch with the Port Authority police within fifteen minutes.

"Keep your phone on, and I'll get back to you when I know something."

"Ok." He got in his truck and headed to his cousin Lorenzo's house to fill him in on what just went down.

BJ couldn't believe Nico had just gotten arrested, but like a true soldier, he stayed focused. He had to find out where Bebo was. Dominoes were stating to fall left and right, and he was determined to not get caught slipping.

EIGHT

Jasmine lay on the floor motionless, her right hand numb from the gunshot wound, her jaw throbbing from being slapped with the butt of Bebo's gun, and her neck literally on fire. Everything happened so fast, she didn't know if she was dead or alive. She felt like she was in a scene from a horror movie. The room was eerily quiet, and the silence freaked her out. She didn't know if she was about to see that bright light that people talk about seeing when they are on the verge of death, or if she was going to see Jesus or the devil.

Paranoia started to grip her, and with her face down on the ground and her eyes closed, she had to tell herself not to panic and to stay calm. It seemed as if the silence in the room was getting louder and louder, and at the same time her neck seemed as if it was getting hotter and hotter. She knew she had to do something because she was starting to get extremely light-headed.

She began to call Narjara's name. "Narjara," she said in a whisper, sounding like an asthma patient struggling to breathe and talk at the same time. She still hadn't moved her body.

When she didn't get any response, her adrenaline kicked in, and she called out the name a second time. She still got no answer.

She finally had the courage to open her eyes. "Narjara, you all right?" she asked. Again she got no response.

Jasmine still couldn't feel her right hand, but she needed both of her hands to help her sit up. So she placed her palms on the floor, sort of like she was preparing to do a push-up, and tried to push herself up. As soon as she did that, the blood coming from her hand caused her to slide forward, and in the process, she lost her balance and fell forward on the floor. The sight of her own blood scared her.

She struggled to sit up, and when she did, she realized that the sight of her own blood was nothing compared to the huge hole in Narjara's head.

"Oh, my God!" Jasmine screamed in fear as she looked at Narjara lying on the floor dead with one of her eyes wide open, one still swollen shut, and her brains splattered everywhere.

With her heart pounding and her adrenaline flowing, Jasmine saw that the door to the house was wide open. Fear instantly gripped her as she thought Bebo was going to come walking through the open door at any moment and finish her off.

"Where's my phone? Where is my phone?" she said out loud, scrambling around. While looking for the phone, she brought her left hand up to her burning neck, and all she felt was her own hot blood. That freaked her out even more.

Jasmine finally found her phone. Something told her to go lock herself in the bathroom and call the police. She quickly headed up the stairs to the bathroom, staining the walls and the banister with the blood on her hands. As soon as she made it to the bathroom, she locked the door, and with her bloody, trembling left hand, she dialed 9-1-1.

As the phone rang, Jasmine did a little dance like she had to pee, but she was just nervous and couldn't believe that 9-1-1 hadn't picked up on the first ring.

The operator answered the call, "Nine-one-one. What is your emergency?"

Jasmine looked at her reflection in a mirror in the bathroom, and she was a bloody mess.

"Hello. Nine-one-one. What is your emergency?"

"I've been shot. I need an ambulance right away." Seeing herself in the mirror brought the horrors more to life, and it made her feel like she was going to faint.

"Ma'am, did you say you've been shot?"

"Yes."

"Okay, miss, what is your location?"

Jasmine gave the operator her address.

"Who shot you? Was this an accident?"

"Someone broke into my house and shot me."

"Okay, are they still in the house with you now?

"No, but I'm afraid they might come back. Please hurry and get someone here. I'm bleeding, and I'm feeling like I'm gonna die."

"Okay, try to remain calm. We have units on their way to you right now. I just need to get more information from you that will help you and help the people who are coming to assist you. Is that okay?"

"Okay. I'm just so scared, my body is trembling. And my friend is downstairs. They killed her." Jasmine broke down crying into the phone.

"What is your friend's name? Is it a male or a female friend?"

"Narjara; she's a girl."

"Okay. And you said she was killed. Was she also shot?"

"Yes." Jasmine could hear the operator typing away as she spoke. "Miss, please hurry."

"They're on their way right now. They're about three minutes away, okay, sweetie? You're gonna be safe. I'm going to stay on the phone with you until they get there."

"Okay."

"Ma'am, what is your name?"

"Jasmine."

"Jasmine, do you know who shot you?"

Jasmine paused in gripping fear.

"Jasmine?"

"No, I don't, but it was three people, three men."

"Okay. And where did you get shot?"

Jasmine was getting tired of all the questions, but the operator was a comforting voice to her, so she just dealt with it.

"I can hear sirens now," Jasmine said, feeling tremendous relief at that point.

"Okay, but I need you to stay on the line with me until they are in the house, okay?"

"Okay."

A minute later Jasmine heard cops inside the house. "The police are here. Can I go downstairs?" Before the operator could respond, Jasmine disconnected the call and started to scream out to the cops to let them know where she was at in the house.

Two cops ran upstairs to her, while one cop remained in the living room with Narjara, and another checked all of the first floor and the basement.

Jasmine was never so happy to see a police officer in her life.

"Are you alone?" one of the cops asked her.

"Yes, I think so."

One cop escorted Jasmine to the living room and handed her off to two paramedics, who had just entered the house, and he ran back upstairs to assist his partner in checking the second floor.

The paramedics had Jasmine sit down to evaluate her, and they did their best to stop the bleeding to her hand and neck. Within minutes they had an oxygen mask on her face and had her lying on a stretcher, which they wheeled to the waiting ambulance in front of Nico's house. They whisked her away, sirens blaring.

"Am I gonna die?" Jasmine asked the paramedic who stayed with her in the back of the ambulance, her words somewhat inaudible due to the oxygen mask.

"Are you gonna live?"

Jasmine nodded her head to indicate to the paramedic that he had heard her correctly, and at that moment a tear rolled out of the corner of her eye and stopped near her ear.

The overweight white male paramedic wiped away Jasmine's teardrop. "Just relax." He grabbed hold of her left hand to comfort her.

Jasmine squeezed his hand firmly, and at that moment another tear rolled out of the corner of her eye just before both of her eyes calmly closed.

NINE

The Port Authority police ushered Nico into a holding cell, took his handcuffs off, and slammed the steel cell doors shut.

"I need to make a call," Nico said to the cop who pushed him into the cell.

"Shut the fuck up and sit your nigger ass down!" The cop then walked off upset that he had to do lengthy paperwork and even more pissed off that his shift wouldn't end until the Nassau County Police Department detectives arrived and took custody of Nico, so they could question him about the shooting at his Long Island estate.

Nico smiled at the racist remark, but he didn't respond.

"Jimmy, can you fingerprint that black nigger for me? I don't want to have to whip his nigger ass," the cop said to one of his fellow officers. He was purposely talking loud so that Nico could hear him.

"Jimmy, your boy don't got no swag. Tell him it's nigga, not nigger." Nico smirked. He wanted the racist cop to know that nothing fazed him.

The cops looked at Nico and shook their heads. Nico couldn't believe how mentally weak they were.

Officer Jimmy came over to the damp cell that smelled like a wet cat and unlocked it, and then held Nico by the arm and walked him over to a computer cart and began to fingerprint Nico.

"So how much they pay y'all to do this job?" Nico asked.

The cop didn't answer.

"At least six figures, right?" Nico asked. "I mean, with overtime and all that, you making at least a hundred grand, right?"

The cop methodically continued to fingerprint Nico and also took his mug shot. When he was done, he walked Nico back to the holding cell, slammed the door shut, and made sure it was locked.

"We make an honorable living. We work for everything we get, and we don't sell poison to our communities," Office Jimmy said to Nico.

Nico nodded his head with a smirk, but he didn't reply. He knew that he had won the mind game with the weak-minded officers. He sat down on the benches and wondered what he was being held for, and he also wondered how long it would be before they let him make a phone call.

An hour and a half later, two Nassau County cops came to his cell accompanied by the racist cop.

"There's your black nigger right there," the Port Authority cop said to the Nassau County detectives.

The detectives introduced themselves, and then they placed Nico in handcuffs and escorted him to an empty room.

"Yo, what the fuck is up? Port Authority arrests me, but Nassau DTs are questioning me?" Nico asked as he took a seat at the table.

"Do you want anything to eat or drink?" one of the detectives asked.

"I wanna know what the fuck I'm being held for," Nico shot back.

At that moment, a Port Authority sergeant knocked on the door and whispered something into one of the detectives' ears. The detective got visibly upset, his face turning bright red. And he told his partner to step out into the hallway with him.

"His lawyer is here," the detective told his partner.

"What the fuck?" He looked at the sergeant for answers. "We told you guys not to let him lawyer up until we had a chance to question him."

"We never let him use the phone," the sergeant replied.

"That's bullshit! How the fuck is his lawyer here if he didn't make any phone calls?" The lead detective shook his head in disgust.

The larger police departments like the NYPD and Nassau County all looked on smaller police departments like they were inept. And that was definitely what the two detectives were thinking about the Port Authority police at that very moment.

"You mother fuckers are so incompetent," the detective said to the Port Authority sergeant.

The sergeant didn't reply because he wasn't exactly sure if one of his officers had slipped up and allowed Nico to make a phone call.

"Don't just stand there. Get the fuckin' attorney," the detective said with defeated disgust.

Nico's attorney, Ron Thompson was a very well known and very powerful black attorney from Manhattan that most police departments both feared and respected. He was a former prosecutor who had started his own private practice, and he represented many high-profile clients.

The sergeant walked Ron over to the two detectives.

"Gentlemen." Ron held out his hand for a handshake.

The detectives shook Ron's hand, and then they all went into the room where Nico was sitting. The detectives took a seat, but Ron remained standing.

A relieved Nico was shocked to see Ron, but he made sure to keep a poker face after nodding to his attorney.

The lead detective was about to talk, but Ron interrupted him. "First thing, remove the handcuffs from my client's wrists."

The detectives complied, and then Ron asked them for a moment alone with Nico.

"How did you know I was here?" Nico asked.

"BJ called me from the airport after he saw you in handcuffs."

Nico nodded.

Ron sat down across from Nico. "You didn't sign anything or make any statements, did you?"

"I ain't sign nothing, and I didn't say anything."

Then Nico went on to explain how they'd arrested him when he was about to step off the plane but never charged him with anything or told him why he was being arrested.

"Well, you know why?" Ron replied. "The shooting is dominating the news, and they are going to see if they can link you to it."

"I ain't have nothing to do with that shit. I was out of town."

His lawyer nodded. Then he asked him where he went.

"I was in Vegas."

"By yourself?"

"Nah. With my lady."

Ron nodded. "And you don't know nothing about this, right?"

"Only what the streets is saying. But I ain't got nothing to do with that shit. I ain't gonna sanction my own crib to get ran into and shot up."

"All right." Ron stood up and went to the door and motioned for the detectives to come in.

"You're holding my client, and you didn't charge him with anything? What the fuck is this?"

"We didn't arrest him. We just want to question him," the lead white detective replied.

"Don't play games with me. I know who arrested him. They arrested him on your department's request," Ron shot back as he stood in his three-thousand-dollar tailor-made Italian suit, looking like he was about to give closing arguments in a courtroom.

"Ron, look. We got a murder that took place within our jurisdiction at your client's residence. We want to ask him questions pertaining to that."

"No. What you want to do is swoop down on my client while he's getting off the plane and make a dramatic arrest and then question him and get him to confess to a crime that he had nothing to do with, just so you can have him do a perp walk out of this precinct with the news cameras flashing. That's what you really want."

Nico sat back. His lawyer was worth every dime he paid him.

The detective was about to say something, and Ron cut him off.

"Look, are you charging my client with murder or what? If not, then what the fuck are we doing here?"

"We just want to question him."

"You lost that right with the dramatic way you guys decided to handle things. My client isn't talking."

This was what the detectives feared, and that's why they didn't want Nico to lawyer up. The lead detective knew he was stuck. He looked at his partner for help.

"Ron, we're not playing hardball, we just want to question your client. But we can play hardball and lock your client up on a conspiracy charge."

Ron shook his head and smiled. "My client was nowhere in the vicinity of New York when the crimes in question took place, and he can prove that. Now, unless you gentlemen have direct eyewitness testimony and statements that implicate my client in a conspiracy of any kind, then I think he's free to go."

The detectives looked at each other, stumped.

"Nico, you're free. Let's go," Ron said, and the two of them walked out of the interrogation room.

Nico wanted to retrieve his belongings before his lawyer drove him to meet up with BJ. He let the racist Port Authority cop, who was still sitting at his desk doing paperwork, know that he needed his stuff.

Now that an attorney accompanied Nico, the slick racist talk was no longer coming out of the cop's mouth. The cop retrieved Nico's things.

After Nico gathered his stuff and put away his cash and his wallet, he said to the cop, "Remember, it's nigga, not nigger. You gotta add more *ga* into it, you feel me?"

He watched the cop turn red, then patted him on the shoulder. "I'm just fuckin' wit'chu, man. Be easy," he said, a sinister smile on his face.

TEN

While all kinds of drama was going on in New York, Mia was living it up twenty-five hundred miles away in Las Vegas. Although Nico wasn't with her to help her enjoy the good life, that didn't stop her. If she wasn't at the Encore spa getting a massage, she was at the Wynn spa getting a manicure and a pedicure. And when she wasn't pampering herself at the various spas, she was splurging on herself inside Alexander McQueen or buying a dress from the Chanel store. Between spending time at the Hermes, Dior, Graff Diamonds, and Louis Vuitton stores, Mia was in heaven and felt like a walking orgasm.

There was so much to do to keep her busy, she actually thought it was a blessing in disguise that Nico had flown back to New York because she knew all he would have wanted to do was gamble and fuck.

Mia had a slew of fine dining choices to choose from, and she made sure that she ate well for breakfast, lunch, and dinner. She did it all. All except for the nightclubs on the resort. She wasn't in the mood to get hit on by anyone. She also didn't trust herself anymore when she drank in public. The last thing she wanted was to have a repeat of what happened to her when she flew to Miami and ended up getting drunk and fucking a friend of her arch nemesis, Jasmine.

◆◆◆

The doctor acknowledged the police officer who stood guard outside Jasmine's hospital room. He walked up to her bed, where her mom stood on one side and her father on the other.

Jasmine's parents were grateful she was alive, but they were angry with her for putting herself in that position where she'd almost been killed. And they were even angrier with her for resisting their demands that she leave Nico alone for good.

"Jasmine, you heard what the doctor said," her father reminded her. "You were a fraction of a centimeter away from having that bullet pierce your jugular vein, and then what? We wouldn't be standing here talking to you right now."

The doctor patiently waited for an opening to interject.

"But I'm okay!" Jasmine stressed.

As it turned out, Jasmine was extremely lucky. The bullet that had hit her in the neck had actually been more of a deep graze wound. But the bullet had managed to tear off a large piece of flesh from the right side of her neck.

Jasmine's mom and dad were taking turns tag-teaming her while also bashing Nico.

Thankfully for Jasmine, her doctor stepped in. "Excuse me. If I may just interrupt," he respectfully said.

"Sure, sure," Jasmine's father stepped to the side to allow the doctor to get closer to Jasmine.

"I know this is an extremely emotional and traumatic thing that you all have experienced as a family. And although Jasmine's condition had been upgraded to stable, it's important that she gets her rest. The more she can relax without dealing with anything emotional, then the quicker she will return back to normal."

"Thank you for saying that. Now, Mom and Dad, stop stressing me!"

Powerless, Jasmine's mother and father looked at each other. There was an awkward silence in the room.

The doctor tried to put everyone at ease. "So, does anyone have any medical questions for me?"

"Yeah. When can I go home?' Jasmine asked.

The doctor smiled. "We're doing our best to get you home as soon as possible."

Jasmine's mother shook her head. She asked the doctor if the surgery was still planned for the next day, and if he could re-explain what the surgery entailed.

"Yes, the surgery is still on for tomorrow morning. And what we are going to do is repair Jasmine's deep ulnar branch."

Her mom asked, "And what is that again?"

"Well, there are two main arteries that enter the hand—the radial artery and the ulnar artery. You can think about those two arteries as being the trunk of the tree, so to speak. And then think of two big tree branches that grow out of the trunk of the tree. We have to repair that branch that grows out of that main tree trunk."

Jasmine's father nodded his head to tell the doctor that he understood.

Her mother said, "And, if I understand correctly, that branch that you are going to operate on, it also has other smaller branches that stem off of it?"

"You got it." The doctor smiled. "You should have gone to medical school," he joked.

"So is that the only purpose of the surgery?'

"Ugggghh!" Jasmine sighed in disgust. "Ma, what's with all these questions? He's Chinese, so you know he's smart. I'll be fine. Goodness!"

Jasmine's mother was embarrassed, but the doctor smiled. He didn't take offense to what Jasmine had said.

"Yes, that is the only reason for the surgery, and after the surgery, of course, we will have to have a splint for about two to four weeks for the bone fracture in her hand to properly heal."

Jasmine shook her head. "Can I ask you something?"

"Sure."

"I been worried about how everything is going to heal, and I was thinking that what I'll do is just get a tattoo on my hand and on my neck to cover the scars and I—"

"Oh, Lord Jesus, help me!" Jasmine's mother screamed out loud, her right hand held to the sky.

"And I just want to know how soon would I be able to get a tattoo?"

Her father said, "Jasmine, if you get a tattoo on your neck, you better never step foot in my house again! And I mean that."

The doctor didn't know how to respond, but he wanted to remain neutral.

"Well, why don't we take things one step at a time? Let's deal with the surgery first and seeing how quickly we can get you back home and back to normal."

"I feel fine now. I'm ready to leave."

The doctor smiled. "You know, many times people hear about gunshot wounds to the leg or to the arm or to the hand, and they dismiss it as being not that serious. But just as in your case, Jasmine, very often major arteries are impacted, and that is what makes the wounds life-threatening. Never forget just how fortunate you were to be able to get medical attention as soon as you did, because there is always the possibility of losing too much blood to the point where it becomes fatal."

"Lord knows I pray for this child every day," Jasmine's mother said. "Can't nobody tell me the Lord doesn't answer prayers."

Jasmine remained quiet, but she was disgusted that she hadn't yet heard from Nico. She was starting to resent him. She also began to wonder if it was he was the one who sent Bebo to kill her. She desperately wanted to speak to him just to see where his head was at.

The doctor and Jasmine's parents left, leaving her alone with her thoughts. The only conclusion she could come to was, after she had gotten arrested, Nico must have figured she was talking to the police—that she had told them he was a co-conspirator in Shabazz's murder.

That's why he wants me dead, Jasmine thought.

Jasmine was human, and she couldn't help but wonder if Mia was somehow starting to work her way back into Nico's life and reclaim her wifey status.

Oh, my God! I gotta get out of here! she said to herself in a panic.

Her mind was playing all kinds of tricks on her. One moment her mind was telling her that Nico loved her, the next moment Nico had sent Bebo to murder her. Another moment her mind was telling her to just relax, that Nico was just dealing with a lot and that he would explain everything to her as soon as he could. But then again, she kept thinking that Nico was back to fucking Mia.

Jasmine was beyond stressed out. She took a painkiller, which made her feel euphoric, but that soon wore off. She fell asleep wondering if she would wake up and see Nico the next day.

ELEVEN

After a successful surgery on her hand, Jasmine was recovering in the post surgical unit, resting and trying to decide what she would do when she got out of the hospital. She was wondering if it would make sense to go back and live at Nico's estate. She didn't know how safe it would be living there, or if Nico even wanted her there, since she still hadn't spoken to him.

Her options were limited because she hadn't stashed enough money to get her own place, and she definitely wasn't going to move back in with her parents. She thought about asking her friend Simone if she could live with her for a little while, but she quickly decided against that idea. Jasmine knew it would take all of two days for Simone to do something to piss her off, and they would end up in an argument or in some kind of drama she didn't need.

With no viable options coming to mind, she decided not to stress herself out. She reached for the remote control with her good hand and started flipping through the limited channels the hospital had available. As she channel-surfed, she heard a knock on her room door.

Jasmine assumed it was one of the doctors or nurses coming to check on her, but instead she saw Agent Battle walking into her room accompanied by a handsome black man wearing a suit and a tie.

Purposely wanting to be rude, she continued to channel-surf and avoided looking directly at Agent Battle or the man with her.

"Hello, Jasmine," Agent Battle said in a soft, neutral tone.

Jasmine really had no choice at that point other than to acknowledge

Agent Battle, so she returned the hello.

"So how are you feeling? I hope you're recovering well."

"I'm good," Jasmine said, flipping through the channels.

"Jasmine, do you mind if we talk for a few minutes?" Agent Battle asked.

Jasmine turned up the volume on the TV once she found ESPN.

The black guy asked her, "You a Lakers fan?"

Jasmine looked at him and rolled her eyes. She wasn't a huge sports fan, but there was nothing else on TV worth watching. Plus, she didn't know who he was, so she kept her mouth shut and ignored him.

"May I?" Agent Battle said, reaching for the remote control.

Jasmine didn't answer her, nor did she object when Agent Battle took it upon herself to turn off the TV.

"Jasmine, this is Agent Gosling. I asked him to come with me, so I could revisit what we spoke about when we last saw each other."

Jasmine looked at her and didn't say anything.

"Jasmine, let's be straight up with one another. I don't know if you believe in miracles, but I think you would admit that your being alive and able to talk to me right now is pretty much a miracle. Would you agree?"

Jasmine had a nightmare the night before in which she relived the moment when Bebo fired the two gunshots at her. It woke her up in a panic about twelve hours earlier. She slowly nodded in response to Agent Battle's question.

"So tell me—how many more miracles do you want to live through?"

Jasmine wondered why Agent Battle was the one doing all the talking. She asked the black man, "You a cop too?"

Agent Gosling nodded his head. "Yes, I'm a federal agent."

"Cop, federal agent, po-po, fed—it's all the same shit."

"Jasmine, we can talk, right?" Agent Battle asked her in a tone that was trying to get her to lower her guard.

"Yeah. That's what we're doing, right?"

"No. I mean, can we talk black woman to black woman, black man to black woman, no holds barred?"

"Yeah . . . I guess."

"Jasmine, the people who came and shot you, you do know that wasn't just some random shooting, don't you?"

Jasmine wondered if Agent Battle had some specific information about the shooting that she didn't have. She shrugged.

"You can shrug your shoulders, but let me just tell you, when you got shot the other day, please understand that that was a targeted hit on you. There was nothing random about it. There was no other motive behind that shooting other than to take you out. Hits aren't random; hits are planned. You do follow me, right?"

Agent Battle's words confirmed the thoughts Jasmine had been having about if Nico had tried to have her killed for snitching. Still, she made sure not to show her hand to Agent Battle.

Agent Gosling added, "So whoever did this to you will be coming back to finish the job."

"Okay, and? Tell me something I don't know." Jasmine shook her head. "Cops make me laugh. Y'all never around to arrest nobody when shit happens, and y'all never know who did shit after it happens, and then y'all always come around after the fact, talking about the obvious. How about walking in this room and telling me that y'all arrested the muthafucka who shot me?"

Agent Battle looked at Agent Gosling, and in her heart she knew where Jasmine was coming from. "In many ways you're right, Jasmine, and that's why we're here. We can't effectively do our job without sources."

"You mean, snitches," Jasmine interjected.

"No, I mean sources. Snitches do crimes, and then to get their own asses out of a sling, they tell on the people involved with the crime. That's not what our sources do." Agent Battle reached into her jacket pocket and handed Jasmine a photo of Narjara lying naked on a silver coroner's table with a huge hole on either side of her head.

"Why are you showing that to me?" Jasmine hollered. Her blood pressure rose, and her chest began to heave up and down. She dropped the photo on the floor.

"Jasmine, who is that in that photo?"

"You know who it is."

"No. Who was she to you?"

"She was my friend."

"No, she was more than your friend. Yeah, she was your friend who didn't have a felony record, she was your friend who was in college trying to better herself, she was your friend who had all kinds of potential to be whoever she wanted to be. She was your friend who would have been a nurse, and a wife and a mother some day. But you know what?"

Jasmine looked at her and didn't respond.

"Narjara is never going to get the chance to live out her life and chase her dreams. Never. It's over. For Narjara—and you can correct me if I'm wrong—but it was just one random night that ended her life. One night where she was in the wrong place at the wrong time, and just like that"— Agent Battle snapped her fingers—"her beautiful life was snatched away from her through no fault of hers."

Agent Battle took hold of Narjara's picture, and tears came to her eyes. "Jasmine, this could have been my daughter in this picture laying there dead on that table. That could have been you laying on that coroner's table waiting for your parents to come and identify you."

"But it wasn't."

"Exactly. It wasn't. But you know what our sources do? Our sources help us put away the scumbag muthafuckas who have the audacity to do shit like this to beautiful young women who haven't even had a chance to live." Agent Battle handed Agent Gosling the photo, so she could wipe a tear from the corner of her eye.

Jasmine could sense that Agent Battle's tears were real. She couldn't believe that a cop could genuinely care about a victim.

"Jasmine, I'll be honest with you like I was honest with you when you were in the federal building in Manhattan. I could lock you up on a murder charge tomorrow, and a grand jury could indict you with no problem. I am absolutely confident of that. Or you could leave this hospital later today and end up on a coroner's table like your friend. I'm confident of that as well. But whether you leave here and end up dead, or I lock you up and send you to the penitentiary, the end result is just going to be another beautiful life that is wasted. And you know what? Jasmine, I don't want that. I don't want you wasting your life, and when I say that, I mean it."

"Why the fuck do you care so much? I mean, just do what you gotta do and let me do what I gotta do. But I ain't no snitch."

"I care because I have a responsibility to care."

Jasmine held up her hands and looked at Agent Battle with a confused look, as if to say, "What the fuck are you talking about?"

"I have a responsibility to care, just like you have a responsibility to care. And the only difference is, I take my responsibility seriously. Like, if I were you and I had a friend in my life like Narjara, I would look at it as my responsibility to do whatever I had to do to put the people away who did this to her."

"Yeah, but I don't know who shot us," Jasmine lied.

Agent Battle just looked at Jasmine and knew she was lying, so she kept quiet.

"I'm serious, I don't."

Agent Battle got the picture of Narjara from Agent Gosling and attempted to hand it back to Jasmine.

"Don't give me that picture!"

60

"Jasmine, do what's right for your friend, and do what's right for the millions of other Narjaras out there. Do what's right for the millions of parents out there who are trying to avoid their child becoming the next Narjara."

"That's what our sources help us do," Agent Gosling added. "They help us do what's right for everybody. Jasmine, all Agent Battle is asking you is to help us help you, and in doing that, you'll be helping so many other people. Jasmine, you'll be making a difference."

Agent Gosling had done his homework on Narjara and had found out from interviews that he'd conducted with some of her friends that Narjara looked up to Jasmine as a big sister and that she often went to Jasmine during her battering crisis with her boyfriend.

"Help y'all help me?"

"Yes. Just like Narjara would reach out to you for help with her abusive boyfriend."

"How did you know that?" Jasmine asked.

"When you do good like that, word gets around. Good has a much bigger impact on people than evil."

Jasmine had never thought about things from that perspective.

Agent Gosling added, "Jasmine, even in death, Narjara is counting on you to continue to look out for her."

Jasmine did always like feeling like the big sister and protector to Narjara, and when Narjara had gotten shot, she felt like she had failed her big time. Now Jasmine was truly starting to see working with the feds as a way to do right by her dead friend and turn a negative into a positive.

"So if I help you lock up the people who murdered Narjara, you're saying you could help me?"

Agent Battle didn't want to seem too overly excited, but those were the words she was waiting to hear. "Obviously that would be a start. But what we're proposing is that you become a source of ours, a paid source, and the information that you would help us obtain would be information that would hopefully lead to the arrest of the people who murdered Narjara. We would also be looking for you to help us obtain information we could use to help us connect the dots on criminal targets we've already identified."

Jasmine had heard of snitches working with the feds and the police in order to work out plea deals and avoid jail time, but she never knew that snitches got paid by the feds.

"So you said I would be a paid source?"

"Absolutely," Agent Battle said.

"As a paid source, I wouldn't have to worry about any criminal indictments coming my way?"

Agent Battle nodded. "That's correct, but, and I stress the word but, let me be clear. You wouldn't have to worry about any criminal indictments coming your way from any of your involvement in any past criminal activities. But if we agree on things and you become a source, that doesn't give you a license to commit crimes. It's like you help us, and we can wipe your past slate clean, but your future slate is contingent on you doing what's right and abiding by the law."

Agent Battle had to give that spiel, though she and Agent Gosling both knew that the feds and most law enforcement agencies often turned a blind eye to the continued criminal activities of their informants. But there was no way she could just outright say that to Jasmine.

Jasmine slowly nodded, deep in thought as she weighed her options. "Okay, so what kind of money are we talking about?"

"Well, it depends. It's not as if you show up every week and you get a paycheck. It's usually not structured that way. It's more on a per-assignment basis. For example, let's say the information that you source to us leads to us confiscating two kilos of cocaine. Something like that might get you a five-thousand-dollar payment. Or let's say your information leads to us confiscating a million dollars in cash. That might get you a thirty-thousand-dollar payment. Or if we are targeting a specific individual, the payment would depend on the individual. If you got us a high-level drug distributor, that could generate you twenty thousand dollars. And obviously a lower-level drug distributor would get you less."

Jasmine was starting to like the sound of the numbers she was hearing. She could easily see herself making a hundred grand a year for basically maintaining her current lifestyle.

Agent Battle went on to explain, "And, just so we're clear, the payments wouldn't always be so extravagant. We might give you a hundred dollars to make a hundred-dollar marijuana purchase, and for something like that, you would be paid dollar for dollar and would earn a hundred dollars for that purchase."

Jasmine didn't show it, but she was ready to leap out of her bed and do back flips. Jasmine never knew that being a snitch could be so lucrative. She was thinking how she could make a hundred-dollar weed purchase all day every day.

"Question," Jasmine said.

"You got questions, we got answers," Agent Gosling replied with a smile. He and Agent Battle both knew that they had Jasmine where they wanted her.

"This is just hypothetical, so don't read more into it than necessary."

Both agents nodded.

"So let's say I was going to go work for BMW and they were going to pay me fifty thousand a year, but then I found out, for the same job, I could make seventy thousand a year working for Mercedes Benz, wouldn't I be kind of stupid to not go and work for the company that's paying me more money?"

Agent Battle was about to speak, but Jasmine cut her off.

"Okay, okay, what I'm saying is, can other agencies beat the FBI's pay rate for sources. Like, if I could make more with the NYPD or with the

DEA, then why wouldn't I just fuck with them? I mean, no offense or anything, I'm just asking."

"Actually, that's a very good question," Agent Battle responded. "All I can say is, there are no written rules about it. But all the agencies have unwritten rules where we all respect each other's sources, and we don't make it where sources are only going to the highest bidder."

"But would I be wrong or get in trouble if I became a source for other law enforcement agencies? I just want to know up front."

"No, you wouldn't be doing anything wrong per se," Agent Gosling explained. "And there have been times where sources were being handled by different agencies at the same time."

"Just wanted to be clear," Jasmine said with a slight smile that was almost undetectable, since she was trying so hard to suppress it. "Oh, one last thing. I mean, I'm not saying that I will definitely commit and do this whole snitch thing—"

Agent Battle interrupted her. "Jasmine, you would be a *source*, not a snitch. I don't know any other way to convince you of that."

"Source, snitch, confidential informant, yada yada yada—we're talking about the same thing. Okay, but let's say that I did commit to it. Is there any way I could get an apartment or a house out of this? I'm not talking about something that I would own or anything like that. I'm just saying something furnished where I could move into and not have to worry about paying rent or anything. Like, could y'all cover the rent for me?" Jasmine figured she might as well milk it for all it was worth.

Agent Battle and Agent Gosling both knew that the answer to Jasmine's question was yes, but they didn't want to give her the impression that they were desperate. See, the FBI had a lot of leeway with their confidential informants. They knew that the money that they paid them wasn't coming from taxpayer dollars, so they could be flexible. All of the money paid to confidential informants was funded from money that had been confiscated from past drug busts and asset seizures. So Agent Gosling knew she would be able to find a house or an apartment that a government agency owned and let Jasmine use it if she wanted to.

The IRS, for example, had condos in Manhattan that they had seized from someone who had been arrested for tax evasion. It wouldn't be anything other than the FBI filling out paperwork and sending it to the IRS for their approval, and once approved, Jasmine would be able to access the apartment. And, again, that would be at no cost to the taxpaying citizens of the country.

"Well, that's something we could discuss." Agent Battle began to gather her things, preparing to leave.

Jasmine wondered if she had pushed too far.

"I'll leave you with another card and give you some more time to consider everything we spoke about. I don't have more than thirty-six hours for you to think about this, and I would hate to have my agents come visit you with an arrest warrant because, if they do, it would be too late, and the offer we just spoke about would forever be off the table."

Jasmine nodded.

Agent Gosling reached out his hand, and Jasmine shook it with her good hand, and then she reached for the remote control and turned the TV back on to ESPN.

Just as the two agents reached the door to exit Jasmine's room, she said, "You'll hear from me before I hear from you."

Agent Battle paused, looked at Jasmine, and smiled.

When the door closed behind her, Jasmine buzzed the nurses' station and asked them to bring her another painkiller. Within minutes, she popped the painkiller into her mouth, wondering when, if ever, she was going to hear from her man.

But her romantic thoughts about Nico were quickly replaced by thoughts of just how she was going to play both sides of the fence.

TWELVE

N ico and BJ showed up together at the hospital to visit Jasmine, but
when they got there, they were told that she had checked out about
two hours earlier.

"Do you know who she was with when she left?" Nico asked the
petite older white nurse with glasses and gray hair. She looked like she was
definitely eligible for Social Security retirement benefits.

"Oh, sonny, I'm sorry, but I'm not at liberty to give you that kind of
information," she replied.

"No, it's all good. See, I live with the patient. I could give you my
address," Nico said, trying to convince the lady to not be so tight.

The nurse looked at Nico and sighed. "Okay, let me see some ID, and
I'll see what I can do for you."

Nico rarely walked with ID and knew he didn't have any on him at
the time, but he made like he was checking for his driver's license anyway.

"Without any ID, I'm afraid I won't be able to give you any information.
Privacy policies, you know."

BJ went into his pocket. He always carried a wad of hundreds in his
right pocket and smaller bills in his left pocket. He took hold of a crisp
one hundred-dollar bill, folded it up, and discreetly slid it to her.

The nurse looked shocked when she saw that it was a hundred-dollar
bill, but she played it off well. "What did you say your address was again?"

Nico smiled and gave her his address, and the old nurse started spilling
everything, telling him that Jasmine's parents had come to pick her up.

"And you said they left about an hour ago?"

The nurse nodded, and then she motioned for Nico to come closer.

"You two are kind of cute to be cops—Are you married?"

Nico and BJ smiled.

"Nah. We good, ma."

"I have a granddaughter that would be perfect for either one of you. She works in Manhattan. She has a real good corporate job. And I am dying for her to meet somebody nice."

"That's all right, ma, we good, but thanks for the compliment. And good looking out with that info. That's what's up," Nico replied.

And then he and BJ were off to Jasmine's parents' house in Southside Jamaica, Queens. Nico wanted to call Jasmine instead of seeing her, but he'd held back from doing so because he was certain that her phone was tapped.

It took them about thirty minutes to drive from the hospital in Manhasset, Long Island to South Side. BJ did all the driving, while Nico reclined in the front passenger seat of the all-white 760 BMW.

As soon as BJ pulled up to Jasmine's house, they saw Jasmine and her mother and father out front talking to one of their neighbors. Nico could sense that there was going to be some kind of bullshit, so instead of getting out of the car, he had BJ pull to the curb and roll down the driver's side window, since the driver's side was closer to where Jasmine was standing.

◆◆◆

"Who the hell is that?" Jasmine's father walked toward the car.

Jasmine, her hand bandaged and gauze on her neck, instantly recognized who it was, and a smile came to her face. She also walked toward the car.

"Jasmine, go in the house!" her father yelled, trying to restrain her from getting any closer to Nico. "I told you I don't want this nigga coming to my house."

Jasmine broke free of her father's grip and made it to BJ's car, but her father wouldn't let up.

"Listen, I don't want any drug dealers coming to my house. I don't want any drug dealers interacting with my daughter," Jasmine's dad said, bending over and looking into the BMW.

Jasmine said to her mom, "Ma, would you control him please and tell him to stop!"

"We just came to check on you," Nico said to Jasmine after he got out of the car. He chose to ignore Jasmine's father, not wanting to escalate the situation.

Jasmine's mom grabbed her husband by the arm and tried to persuade him to give them a minute by themselves.

"That nigga almost got my daughter killed, and I'm supposed to be okay with him ringing my bell?"

"Sir, with all respect, I didn't ring your bell. And I'm not here to cause no problems. I'm just checking on Jasmine and making sure she's all right, and then I'm leaving. Is that cool?"

Jasmine's father could see the distressed look on Jasmine's face. "Get me from around this nigga before I lose it," he said, retreating to his front door and going inside the house.

"I'm so sorry about all of that," Jasmine said to Nico.

"It's all good." Nico hugged Jasmine and gave her a kiss on the lips.

The hug and the kiss sent shivers down Jasmine's spine, causing an instant smile to appear on her face.

Nico told her, "Get in the car for a minute."

Jasmine got in the backseat, and Nico got in the front seat.

"Hey, BJ."

BJ turned his head to the back seat and acknowledged Jasmine as she leaned forward and gave him a kiss on his cheek.

"You good?" BJ asked.

Jasmine shook her head. "Y'all don't even know.'

Nico asked BJ to pull away from the house. BJ put the car in drive and then headed toward the McDonald's parking lot on the corner of Sutphin and Linden Boulevards, which wasn't far from Jasmine's house.

"Baby, I'm so happy to see you. I didn't know what was going on or what to think," Jasmine said. At that point tears came to her eyes as she relived the night she almost lost her life.

BJ pulled into a parking spot and brought the car to a stop, and Nico got out of the car and asked Jasmine to walk with him.

Nico and Jasmine walked about fifteen yards away from BJ's car and then Nico stopped and hugged Jasmine.

"Why you tearing up?"

Jasmine shook her head. "Baby, I was so scared. I'm still scared. Oh my God, you don't know." More tears came to her eyes and rolled down her cheeks.

Nico pulled her close to him and held her tight. "I gotchu, baby girl. I'm not gonna let anything happen to you."

Jasmine had been longing to see Nico, and he was making her feel safe and protected just the way she knew he would. "I know," she replied, still crying.

"You know that, right?"

She nodded her head up and down.

"So why you still crying?'

Jasmine wiped her tears with the hand that wasn't bandaged.

"You know them alphabet boys is watching me, so I can't move as free as I want to or be on the phone and shit, and that's the only reason I ain't been around."

Jasmine buried her head in Nico's chest. "I just didn't know what to think."

"I know you didn't, and that's why I'm here now."

Jasmine felt so good at that point. She wondered if she could still go through with being a snitch for the federal government.

"Can I ask you something?"

"What's up?" Nico replied.

"Did you want me dead?"

"Jasmine, what the fuck kind of question you asking me?"

"Baby, I been in the hospital, bandaged up, having surgery and nightmares, and all kinds of thoughts just been running through my mind. When I didn't hear from you, I didn't know what to think. And I had never got any answers about why you didn't come pick me up, so I just didn't know." More tears started coming to Jasmine's eyes.

Nico was quiet.

"I'm sorry, but I just couldn't help but wonder if it was you who had sent Bebo to kill me."

All of Nico's muscles instantly got tense when he heard those words come out of Jasmine's mouth. See, the streets had been talking and saying that Bebo was the culprit behind the shootings at Nico's house, but before Nico made a move on Bebo, he wanted to be one hundred percent certain that the streets were right with what they were saying. Jasmine's words had just confirmed it.

"I thought you might have wanted me killed because you thought I might say something about the Shabazz thing."

Nico couldn't help but wonder if Jasmine was wearing a wire. He pulled her close to him and held her. "Shhhhhh," he said into her ear. "You stressing for no reason, baby," he added, massaging her back as he held her close to him.

Jasmine had no idea he was secretly checking to see if he felt any wires or a microphone underneath her clothing.

"Trust me, I'm gonna handle this shit." Nico kissed her on ear and then released her from his embrace.

"I know you will." Jasmine reached for her BlackBerry. "I want you to hear something," she said. "The cops came to visit me, and I been telling them that I didn't know who shot me. I mean, even though I know it was Bebo, at the end of the day, I'm not a snitch."

Jasmine's words made Nico feel like he could put his guard down just a bit.

"Just listen." Jasmine then pressed play.

"Get off of me!"
"Bebo, she ain't got nothing to do with anything. Let her go!"
"We can't find the stash, but look at this shit we found, yo."
"What the fuck! You snitchin'? This bitch is a fed?"
"No. No, she's—"
BLAOW!
"AHHHHH! Oh, my God! Oh, my God!"
"Bitch, I'm asking you one more time—Where the fuck is the stash at?"
BLAOW! BLAOW!
"Let's get the fuck up outta here and find that bitch-ass nigga."
"It's fucked up how that bitch shot Jasmine and then killed herself."

Nico didn't totally understand everything in the recording, but he'd heard enough.

"That was from the night I got shot. Bebo had kept stressing me to call you, and I kept calling you but you wasn't picking up. So after the last time I tried to call you, something just clicked in my head and told me to just hit the record button on my phone."

"Right, right," Nico said, his mind in deep thought. "That's good, that's good. I'm glad you was smart like that. And you said you didn't tell five-o about this, right?"

"No. I wanted you to hear it. I told them I didn't know who it was

71

that ran up in the house."

Nico knew who Narjara was. "That shit is fucked up. What did Bebo mean by what he said at the end of the recording?"

"Bebo put the murder weapon in Narjara's hand to make it look like she had committed murder-suicide."

"That's a grimy muthafucka to do some shit like that to chicks," Nico said with gritted teeth.

The sun was just about ready to set as Nico reached his hand out for Jasmine's. And Jasmine took hold of his, and he pulled her close to him again.

"I hate seeing you like this, all bandaged up."

"I'll be okay. I'm a trooper."

"Yeah, you a trooper, but I should've been there for you."

Jasmine kept quiet.

"Look at me," Nico commanded, and Jasmine looked up at him.

"You trust me, right?"

Jasmine nodded, and then Nico kissed her.

"You not scared anymore, right?"

Jasmine only slightly shook her head, even though she was still scared and knew she would have yet another nightmare later that night.

"I promise you on everything, I'm gonna handle this shit."

Jasmine looked into Nico's eyes and softly said, "Okay."

THIRTEEN

B ebo was a creature of habit. He hung out pretty much every night of the week and usually didn't start his day until one in the afternoon. Unless he had a chick spend the night, by two in the afternoon, after he had showered and gotten dressed, he could always be found at USA Diner in Rosedale, Queens, where he'd order his favorite—fish and grits with a large orange juice.

Bebo owned a barbershop on Merrick Boulevard in the Springfield Gardens section of Queens, not too far from USA Diner. He would leave the diner and head straight to his barbershop and get his head shaved, watch music videos, and just hang out and bullshit with all of the barbers and everybody who came through. Bebo would get his head shaved every day, old-school style, with shaving cream and a straight razor and made sure that his goatee was always trimmed, and he always dressed in brand-new high-end clothes so that his cleanness would match his fly appearance.

"How you doing, baby?" the attractive Jamaican waitress asked him. "I'm surprised you in here alone. Where's your entourage?"

Bebo looked up and smiled and then reached his hand out and grabbed hold of the waitress. Pauline was a bisexual with a short man-style haircut dyed blonde.

He pulled her close to him. "Pauline, where you been hiding at, sexy?"

Bebo always said as little as he needed to. That's why he didn't answer Pauline's question about the whereabouts of his entourage.

"I been around. I was just working the night shift for a few weeks. You want the usual?"

Bebo nodded. Pauline walked to the kitchen to give the order to the cook. Then she came back to talk to Bebo, since her section of the diner wasn't very busy.

"Your boy was in here the other day," Pauline said.

"Who's that?"

"Nico."

"Oh, word?"

Bebo had been looking for Nico, but no one had been able to track him. Nico hadn't been hanging at any of the strip clubs, and he hadn't been seen at any of the spots he frequented. Bebo's interest was piqued, because Nico rarely came to the USA Diner. He knew something was up.

"Yeah, matter of fact, it was two days ago, my last night on the night shift. He was here with BJ and two other dudes I didn't know."

Bebo nodded. "So when you gonna let me get at that again?"

"That's how you talk to me? You think I'm one of these five-dollar, dirty-pussy strippers from the strip club or something?"

Bebo ran his hand down Pauline's thigh and then back up and stopped at her crotch.

"That's not yours anymore." She slapped his hand away. "You don't know how to call nobody, so I gave those privileges away."

Bebo smiled. "Who you gave it away to?"

Bebo's fish and grits were ready, so Pauline went and retrieved his order. She came back, placed his food in front of him along with his glass of orange juice, and then she reached in her apron and put a straw in front of him. Then she took out her cell phone and scrolled through until she found a picture of her girlfriend butt naked on a bed with her face down and her ass up in the air.

"That's who I gave your privileges away to." Pauline smiled as she handed him her phone.

"Waaaowww! That's what the fuck I'm talking about," Bebo replied as he stared at the picture.

"Call me, be nice to me, and stay in touch with me, and I might be able to convince her to let y'all share this." Pauline winked at Bebo before she took her phone back and walked away.

While Bebo flirted with Pauline inside the diner and his driver sat parked and waiting for him in the parking lot, Nico and BJ sat a block away in a black Nissan Altima with dark tinted windows, the engine running. From where they were sitting, they could see Bebo's truck. They had been sitting in the Altima for about a half an hour waiting for him to come out of the diner. Both Nico and BJ had on ski masks, but they weren't planning a stickup.

Finally, after a few more minutes, Nico saw Bebo emerge from the diner. He was standing on the steps of the diner with Pauline.

"Who the fuck is that bitch?" BJ asked.

"I don't give a fuck! Ride on that nigga right now!"

BJ started to drive west on Merrick Boulevard at about five miles an hour.

"BJ, drive this shit. I don't want him to get to his truck."

"But that chick is with him."

"Fuck that bitch! Roll up on that nigga right now!"

BJ hit the gas pedal, and within seconds he was making a right turn onto 243rd Street. Before he could bring the car to a stop, Nico jumped out, ran toward Bebo, and started blasting.

BLAOW! BLAOW! BLAOW! BLAOW!

The first shot hit Bebo in the stomach.

"Ahhh shit! Muthafucka!" Bebo hollered after being hit. He'd left his gun in his truck, so he had no option but to turn and run back inside the diner for cover.

"AHHHHHHHHH!" Pauline screamed. She was so scared and in shock, she froze and didn't run.

Bebo clutched his stomach as he pushed open the double glass doors. *BLAOW! BLAOW! BLAOW!*

Nico fired three more shots. The first shot missed Bebo and shattered the glass door. The sound of gunshots and breaking glass instantly sent the patrons inside the diner screaming and scrambling for cover under their tables.

The second bullet hit Bebo in his ass, and the third hit him in his spine and dropped him to floor, writhing in pain.

Nico had ten more rounds in his 9mm handgun. With Bebo on the ground, he ran up on him and stood over him.

"Yo, chill, man! Don't do that shit! Don't! What the fuck?"

Nico let off five shots, all of which struck Bebo in the chest. He wanted to empty his entire clip into Bebo, but his gun jammed.

Right on cue, BJ ran up the steps of the diner and almost slipped on the shattered glass. As soon as he caught his balance, he pumped four shots into Bebo's chest and two to his head.

BJ tapped Nico, and the two of them ran down the steps of the diner and hopped into the Altima. BJ sped down 243rd Street, made a left turn on 133rd Avenue, and headed north on the Cross Island Parkway.

BJ and Nico were both breathing heavily. Nico told BJ to get off at the Linden Boulevard exit and to pull the car over as soon as he could and just park on any random street. At that point they were less than two miles away from the crime scene and could hear police and ambulance sirens coming from what sounded like every direction.

"You good?" Nico asked BJ as the car came to a stop.

"Yeah, yeah."

BJ then popped the trunk, took out a container of gasoline from in it, and doused the entire car. After Nico and BJ placed their handguns and masks inside the stolen vehicle, BJ lit a match and set the car on fire. In a matter of seconds, the car was engulfed in flames.

Nico and BJ both fled the scene, jogging about five blocks to Linden Boulevard, where they split up. Nico hopped on the first westbound New York City bus he saw, and BJ hopped on the first eastbound Nassau County bus. Prior to parting ways, they agreed to link up later that night via two brand-new prepaid cell phones they had purchased before the hit on Bebo.

The only thing the two of them were concerned with was whether any neighbors or any cameras in the neighborhood had caught a glimpse of them after they'd taken off their masks and torched the car. More importantly, they wondered if Bebo was in fact dead or had somehow managed to miraculously survive so many gunshot wounds.

FOURTEEN

Jasmine was sitting at home on the computer bored as hell and going absolutely stir crazy at her mother's house, where she had been for a full seventy-two hours since leaving the hospital. Other than leaving the house to discreetly meet with Agent Gosling and Agent Battle at a local restaurant to finalize her plans to cooperate, she had been confined to her parents' house. Although she had agreed to help the feds get incriminating information on Nico, she was having second thoughts about her decision. She never told them that she had met with him briefly on the day she was released from the hospital.

Jasmine was supposed to be gathering information on Nico, but she was just genuinely afraid to venture out of her parents' house, worried that Bebo would learn of her whereabouts and come and finish her off. And she definitely didn't want to go back and stay at Nico's house until she heard from him again and knew that he would be staying at the house with her. So, she decided to just stay her ass put.

As soon as Jasmine logged on to Facebook, her cell phone started ringing, and she got a bunch of text messages. Everybody wanted to know if she had heard what happened to Bebo. Initially Jasmine thought that everyone was referring to her and Narjara being shot by Bebo, but that just didn't make sense to her, since that was now old news. She called back her friend Simone, who asked her if she had seen the news.

Jasmine immediately turned on the four o'clock newscast and started watching the story about Bebo being shot multiple times at the USA Diner in Rosedale, Queens.

"It was crazy!" one eyewitness said to a news reporter. "I was just about to get out of my car with my girl and walk into the diner, and the next thing I know, I see a dude running toward the diner firing his gun, so I just took cover. It was multiple shots, like pop, pop, pop, pop, one after the other. I immediately grabbed my girl and pushed her to the ground and laid on top of her. I just couldn't believe it. And then as soon as the shots stopped, they started again. It was almost like the shots wouldn't stop."

"Did you get a look at the gunman?" the reporter asked.

"Nah, things just happened too fast, and we hit the ground. From what I hear, people are saying it was two gunmen. I believe it, because there were just so many shots. I mean, it definitely reminded me of something from the Mafia. Whoever they were after, they were definitely trying to take him out. There's no doubt about that. John Gotti, rest his soul, would have been proud. You feel me?"

The reporter seemed a little surprised by the eyewitness' rhetorical question and his reference to John Gotti, but before she ended her report, she couldn't help but allude to the irony in the eyewitness' comment.

"References to mobsters might not be too far off, as we are learning that the victim of the shooting is allegedly the kingpin of a drug organization known as Ghetto Mafia. In Rosedale, Queens, I'm Sandra Livingston. Now back to you."

Jasmine couldn't believe what she was hearing. She changed the channel and saw another station reporting on the same story. All she could wonder was if Bebo was dead. After watching the story on a different news channel, she was able to confirm that he had in fact died at the scene of the crime.

Jasmine continued to watch and she saw how the police had roped off USA Diner with yellow crime scene tape. She also was able to see Bebo's body lying on the lobby floor of the diner covered with a white sheet and.

Upon seeing that, Jasmine felt instant euphoria. She felt like she could have her life back and walk around in peace without having to look over her shoulder in fear of Bebo. She knew her man had made good on his promise. Jasmine loved a strong man, and she especially loved a man who could protect her. Nothing was a bigger turn-on to her than a man who would kill for her. She couldn't wait to fuck his brains out for doing only what a king would do for his queen. After all, she was wifey.

◆◆◆

The FBI had given Jasmine a special BlackBerry phone that was almost impossible to be hacked into, and it had an FBI-approved app installed on it to track all of her movements via GPS technology. The phone was also going to be the FBI's primary way of contacting her, and she could use it to record incriminating conversations so she wouldn't have to wear a wire.

Jasmine saw that Agent Gosling was calling her phone, but she ignored him as she browsed for a new outfit in the mall, since she and Simone were planning on hanging out later that night.

Finally, at ten minutes past one in the afternoon Jasmine, dressed in a pair of black leggings, open-toe sandals, and a pair of Gucci shades, arrived at Dallas BBQ for her twelve-noon meeting. She tilted her shades slightly so she could see inside the dimly lit restaurant.

"Table for one?" the hostess asked her.

Jasmine gave the hostess a stank look. She scanned the restaurant until she spotted Gosling sitting at the bar. She sauntered up to him carrying two bags from Macy's.

"What did you have?" Jasmine asked after seeing the plate of eaten food in front of him. She could see the fury in Agent Gosling's eyes. His look reminded her of the way her father used to scold her without words by simply giving her a stern look of death.

Agent Gosling got up from the bar and made his way over to a booth table he had been sitting at, about five feet away from the bar area.

Jasmine followed behind him, and the two of them sat down. Agent Gosling still had that stern look in his eyes and hadn't said anything to her at that point, not even hello.

After picking up the menu to look at what she was going to order, Jasmine finally heard words come out of Agent Gosling's mouth.

"Put the menu down."

Jasmine immediately complied.

"Did I not tell you noon?"

Jasmine knew what time the meeting was scheduled for, but she said, "Twelve? I thought we were supposed to meet at one."

Agent Gosling stared at her. "Jasmine, our meeting was for twelve, and you have the audacity to walk in here almost an hour and a half late? Let me be clear on something—I'm not one of your friends in the street that you can just blow off with your disrespectful attitude. You pull some shit like this again, and I'll lock you up on the spot. Are we clear?"

"But—"

"Jasmine, are we clear? There is going to be no do-overs."

"Yes, we're clear."

"And when I call you, I expect for you to call me back within a reasonable amount of time."

Jasmine was about to lie and play it off like she hadn't realized he had called her, but she could sense that Agent Gosling meant business and wasn't going to tolerate any of her bullshit.

"Okay, I will," she replied.

Agent Gosling nodded as he looked at her.

"I apologize," she said humbly.

Jasmine hated to be punked, but she knew she had to toe the line if she wanted to get all of the benefits of being a confidential informant. Even though Bebo was now dead and she could return to Nico's estate and feel reasonably safe, she still wanted to get her free living situation, courtesy of the FBI, squared away.

At that point a waitress came to the booth and asked if they were ready to order. Jasmine looked at Agent Gosling, and he slightly nodded, giving his approval. Jasmine just ordered French fries and a coco-loco. Agent Gosling didn't order anything because he had eaten while he waited for Jasmine to arrive.

"You could have ordered more to eat," he said.

Jasmine shook her head and explained that she didn't like eating food that was messy, like barbecue ribs and things like that.

"What's a coco-loco?"

"I'll let you drink some when it gets here," she replied. "Is Agent Battle coming?"

"No, she isn't coming. Remember, Agent Battle is the case agent, and I'm your handler."

Jasmine nodded as she reached into the basket of warm complimentary cornbread. She took out a piece and began munching on it.

"So how have things gone the past couple of days with Nico since you've been home from the hospital?"

At that point Jasmine's French fries and drink arrived. She immediately sipped on her drink, no longer caring that she had told Gosling that she would let him try some.

"Things went well. Don't worry, I'll get you the info you need. There's a way I have to operate and talk around Nico so he won't get suspicious."

Agent Gosling nodded and, without asking for permission, took hold of Jasmine's drink and sipped some of it. Jasmine felt like a bull that'd seen red. She wanted to reach across that table and slap him for putting his lips on her drink. She had already told him that she would let him have some of her drink, but she was planning on pouring him some in a separate glass. Jasmine was definitely going to order another drink and give him the one he had just put his backwash in.

"But you have hung out with him since you've been home?"

Jasmine knew about the GPS feature on the BlackBerry, so she knew she couldn't lie but so much.

"We didn't hang out, like go out anywhere, but I did see him. He came by my mother's house to check on me."

Gosling nodded his head. "When did you last see Nico?"

"Yesterday I saw him. I've seen him pretty much every day since I came home from the hospital."

"So what is he saying about the Bebo murder that I'm sure you're aware of?"

Jasmine smiled and ate one of her French fries. "See, you have to understand—The streets isn't a game of show and tell, where little Johnny comes to school every day and just starts opening up about what the fuck him and his friends did the day before." Jasmine paused. "What I'm saying is, I can't just start asking, 'So, Nico, did you kill Bebo?' I have to bring things up in the natural course. But, don't worry, I'll get you your info."

"So you've seen him every day since being discharged from the hospital?"

Jasmine nodded.

Agent Gosling cut his eyes at Jasmine the same way he had done when she had first come into the restaurant late for their meeting.

"What?" Jasmine nervously took another bite from her cornbread.

Agent Gosling reached into a dark brown folder and he took out four glossy photos and handed them to her.

"That one right there, that's Mia meeting Nico at the airport in Las Vegas," Agent Gosling said. "And that one right there, that's Mia and Nico having dinner together, also in Las Vegas. And this one, this is Mia and Nico shopping together in Las Vegas. And if you'll notice, each day they have on different outfits, and you'll also notice the date and the time on each photo."

Jasmine could feel sweat forming on her brow. She was beyond embarrassed for being busted in a lie, and at the same time she was also heated with Nico.

"Those dates, Jasmine, they cover the past few days right after Bebo's murder, and you just told me that you saw Nico every day at your mother's house. Kind of hard to do that if your mom lives in Queens and Nico is thousands of miles away."

Jasmine knew there was absolutely nothing she could say.

"Let me explain something, Jasmine. I want to go home alive every night. So therefore I have to be able to trust you, and your lies could get me killed out here. So if I wasn't clear a few minutes earlier, let me be perfectly clear now—If you lie to me one more time—No, as a matter of fact, if I even suspect that you're lying to me, I am locking your ass up, and you'll be doing twenty-five years in a federal pen somewhere out in South Dakota with a bunch of lesbian white butches. Is that understood?"

"Yes, it's understood," Jasmine humbly replied.

"So are you getting the picture about how we need you to operate and cooperate with us? No lies. You do as you're told, and you get us the information that we need. You help us, and we help you."

Jasmine nodded her head, tired of being chastised. She was ready to move on and get the meeting over with so she could figure out how she was going to deal with Mia.

"Now we need to discuss what's going on, and we need to formulate an action plan."

"Okay," Jasmine replied. At that point Jasmine's French fries were cold, the cornbread was cold, and she no longer wanted anything to drink. What she wanted at that moment was some high-grade weed to smoke.

"Before I speak about Nico, we both know that Bebo was murdered two days ago." Gosling paused and waited for Jasmine to speak. "Are we on the same page?"

"Mmm-hmm. Yeah, I obviously heard about Bebo. We mentioned this already," Jasmine replied, not knowing exactly what Gosling wanted to hear.

"So what are your thoughts on it?"

"I don't know," she replied with a nonchalant attitude.

Gosling gave her that stern look again.

"Look, you seem to forget that my hand is going to take another week or so to fully heal, and as you can see, my neck is not fully healed yet either. So it's not like I'm just out and about running the streets. I withdrew from school, and I wanted to take a little time to just heal physically and emotionally, and it's like you don't seem to realize that. All you seem concerned about is just doing your job."

Agent Gosling knew that Jasmine had a point, but he didn't care. He went back into his folder and pulled out more photos—three to be exact.

"Do you know any of these guys?"

Jasmine examined the photos closely. "I know him," she said, pointing to the photo on the right. "I mean, I don't know him like we're super cool or anything like that, but I do know him, and he knows me. His name is Black Justice. He hustles uptown, either in Harlem or the Bronx or Yonkers, somewhere in those areas. And these two, I don't know them, but I think I've seen them before at some of the spots around the city; they look familiar."

Jasmine wasn't that interested or enthused. All she could think about was if Nico was fucking Mia again. With the two of them out in Las Vegas, she knew there was no way Nico wasn't fucking her. Jasmine just couldn't understand what it was that Mia had over her, nor could she understand why Nico hadn't asked her to fly out to Las Vegas with him.

"That's right. That's Black Justice, more commonly known as Black Jus. Now this guy right here is named Homicide. And this guy right here goes by the name of Prince. He's new on the New York drug scene. He was only a 'poo-butt' out in California, but he felt like he could be a shot-caller out here in New York, and that's why he's out here. He's a Crip from California with an army of New York Crips who'll murder on his orders."

"Poo-butt?" She shook her head and chuckled. "Them dudes from California kill me with their slang."

Agent Gosling was glad that Jasmine was showing signs of life, so he kept on. "Well, with the murder of Bebo, and with Nico's strength weakening, we think that—"

"What do you mean, 'with Nico's strength weakening'?"

"From our intel, and from some of our other sources, we gathered that in Ghetto Mafia, Nico is the businessman and Bebo was the killer. With Bebo's death, we feel Nico's strength is going to be tested—other crews throughout the city are going to muscle in on Ghetto Mafia's territory."

Jasmine listened intently. She wanted to let Gosling know that Nico had the heart to murder anyone, but she thought it best to keep her mouth shut and just listen.

"So what we're going to need you to do is get us close to these three guys right here. These three dudes are going to try to fill the vacuum. What we don't want is to get Nico off the street, only to have new menaces to worry about."

Jasmine nodded.

"What we would want you to do initially is act as a cut-out for me."

"What do you mean?" Jasmine asked.

"We would need you to make recorded drug buys on my behalf. You'll let them know that it's on my behalf, and after a few buys we'll ramp up the weight of the buys. At that point, the trust should be there where you'll be able to introduce me, and then from that point on, I'll handle my own transactions directly with them, which will allow us to make arrests."

"Oh, okay. That's cool and all. I can do it. But the thing is, I'll definitely need a place to live, and I need some money."

Agent Gosling went into his folder and handed Jasmine a bankcard. "I'm already ahead of you. There's twenty-five hundred on that card. I'll call you later and give you the pin number."

Seeing the shiny, new bankcard with a Visa logo put her in a brighter mood. She quickly took hold of the card and slipped it into her bag.

"Twenty-five hundred will be your monthly stipend. If you need more than that, you'll have to let me know, and I'll need to put in a request to the suits in Washington D.C."

Gosling was speaking Jasmine's language, and she loved it. Twenty-five hundred a month, and she didn't have to open up her legs and fuck anybody.

"And let me just be completely frank with you about something . . ."

Just then as soon as Gosling said that, the waitress came to the table and asked if she could get them anything else.

Jasmine was feeling much better after getting the bankcard, so she immediately asked for another coco-loco.

"And for you, sir?"

"I'm fine. Thanks," Gosling replied to the waitress just before she walked away.

"Now, like I was saying, I need you to really hear me on this."

"Okay, I'm listening."

"Whether it's Black Just, Homicide, or Prince, or for that matter, anyone else we're targeting, you cannot fuck them under any circumstances. Do you understand me?"

"Not even Nico?"

"No, with Nico that's different because you were involved with him sexually before you started cooperating. But with any of the other targets, if you sleep with them, it will be tough to get a conviction because any lawyer would scream entrapment."

"That won't be a problem because it's not like I just go around opening up my legs to any and every nigga in the hood."

Agent Gosling just gave her a look, and she immediately knew that Gosling was more than likely aware of her prostituting herself on Craigslist in the past.

"Trust me, that won't be a problem."

Agent Gosling's phone rang, and he excused himself to take the call.

While Gosling was talking on his cell phone, Jasmine just couldn't help herself. She took out her phone and sent Mia a one-word text message: *Bitch!* She waited for a reply from Mia but didn't get one.

"Sorry about that," Agent Gosling said. "Okay, so now listen. When you get home, what you need to do is use the bankcard to book the next flight to Las Vegas."

Jasmine looked confused.

"Jasmine, this isn't a free lunch. You need to get out to Vegas and smooth things over with Nico because, at the end of the day, if he doesn't trust you, and if he moves on to Mia and leaves you behind without access to him, then what secrets will he ever spill to you? And if Nico doesn't spill secrets to you, then the government really doesn't need your cooperation, and we would have no choice but to lock you up for murder."

"Ugghhh!" Jasmine was tired of Gosling always throwing the possibility of jail in her face. It was frustrating to her because she knew no one had seen her actually murder her ex-boyfriend Shabazz. She felt in her heart that they didn't have the goods on her for that murder, but yet they were always hanging it over her head.

"Why do you keep saying that? That shit is so annoying. Just do me a favor and please stop hanging shit over my head. It's not like it's helping anything when you say that you'll lock me up."

Jasmine was also pissed off that she was going to have to dip into her twenty-five hundred dollars to purchase the plane ticket.

Gosling was about to reply, but Jasmine cut him off, saying, "And when will I get the apartment or the house that you promised me?"

"By the time you're back, we'll have an apartment for you."

"All right," Jasmine replied. "Where are Nico and Mia staying in Vegas?"

He told her and they ended their meeting. Agent Gosling felt good about the plan he had set in motion. Jasmine would do her best, but she didn't know how she was going to be able to hold back from whipping Mia's ass when she saw her. Her only hope was that it wouldn't derail her new career as a confidential informant.

FIFTEEN

Mia looked at her cell phone and saw Jasmine's text. She and Nico were walking together on the Las Vegas strip, taking everything in. She didn't say anything to Nico about the text, but the very thought of Jasmine made her feel insecure. She wanted her permanently eliminated as a threat.

"You know what? I wish Jasmine hadn't survived that shooting."

Nico was eating the fried corn on the cob he had just bought.

"Did you hear what I said?"

Nico again ignored Mia.

Mia sucked her teeth, and the two of them continued to walk with no specific destination, just enjoying the warm weather and taking in all of the sights.

"Get off that insecure shit, Mia."

Mia didn't want to be walking on thin ice, so she apologized.

"Nah, you don't have to apologize, but I'm just saying, don't wish death on Jasmine like that." Nico threw the corn into a nearby trashcan. "This shit is nasty."

Nico walked over to a huge fountain, where kids were making wishes and throwing coins. He hopped up on the ledge of the fountain and sat down, his legs dangling about two feet off the ground.

He motioned for Mia to come to him, and she walked over and stood between his legs with her back to him. Nico leaned forward so that his chest was touching Mia's back, and he clasped his hands around her waist and held her tight.

Mia felt so good. She was somewhat shocked because Nico had never shown any public displays of affection toward her.

Nico had to make Mia feel secure because, with the feds watching him so closely, he needed her to take on risks that he couldn't take himself. She had already shown that she was willing to do anything for her man, and Nico wanted to keep it that way.

"I'll keep it real with you—I can't say I wish Jasmine was dead, but I do wish she was as thorough as you."

"What do you mean?"

"I mean, with you, I would trust you with my life. I know if them alphabet boys ever put the screws to you, you wouldn't sell me out. With you, I know that, and with BJ, I know that. Loyalty is everything to me."

Mia turned and faced Nico. She gave him a peck on his lips and buried her head into his chest. "Baby, it's about love, and it's about trust. You know me and BJ love you, and we trust you, and you love us and you trust us too."

Nico didn't say anything.

"So what was Jasmine saying when you flew back to New York?" Mia asked. Nico had been back in Vegas for a few days, but Mia had made it a point to not ask him any questions up until that point. She was just hoping that they didn't end up fucking.

"She wasn't really saying much."

Nico made sure not to say anything to Mia about what the streets had been saying in reference to Bebo shooting Jasmine, nor did he say anything about Jasmine confirming that Bebo had shot her. He definitely didn't say anything about having murdered Bebo. He and BJ had made a pact to keep that between themselves.

"You did see her though, right?"

"Yeah, yeah, I saw her. I mean, I went by the hospital and all that, but I just got a feeling she workin' with the police."

Mia lifted her head off Nico's chest and pulled away from him slightly. "Why do you say that?"

"It's a lot of shit that just don't add up."

Mia shook her head before returning to the comfortable position on Nico's chest she had been in before.

"Shit don't be adding up with Jasmine or Bebo," Nico added.

Mia pulled away from Nico again and gave him a serious look. "Baby, I know it's probably not my place to be talking about your business, but it's not hard to tell that Bebo is the biggest hater. He's jealous of you."

Nico nodded his head and told Mia she was right. He kept quiet because he wanted to see if she knew anything about Bebo's death. If she did, then he would have known that she was being too much of a busybody and couldn't be trusted.

"Baby, seriously, I hope I don't offend you or say nothing wrong or disrespectful, but it just seems like with Jasmine, you shouldn't have her around you because of the way she did Shabazz. I mean, if she could murder him, then why wouldn't she murder you or snitch you out to the feds, like you suspect? And then with Bebo, it's like when he was in jail, you had everything poppin' without him, and you built everything without him. That's where all his hate and jealousy comes from—he knows you're the man and that you don't need him. I think he would snitch you out or set you up in a heartbeat, just to satisfy the envy he has toward you."

Nico nodded.

"You need to dead Bebo and Jasmine. And, again, I don't say that with no disrespect or anything like that. I'm just saying that you need to be able to sleep at night and not always be stressed out looking over your shoulder. To do that, you should just go back to the way things were before Bebo came home and before Jasmine came into the picture. That's why I was saying that I wish Jasmine hadn't survived that shooting." Mia paused. "I'm just saying . . . "

Nico was shocked to hear Mia talk with such violent overtones. Being in a constant state of paranoia, he wondered if she was wired and recording him, so he kept quiet.

Mia turned around so that her back was once again leaning against Nico's chest.

"You right," Nico whispered into her ear, knowing a wire wouldn't have picked up his whispered words.

Mia turned around and kissed him. "I love you, baby."

Nico looked at her and nodded. Then he hopped off the ledge, and the two of them continued to walk down Las Vegas Boulevard. For the entire time, he kept his lips sealed about both Bebo and Jasmine.

Nico loved playing blackjack, so Mia accompanied him inside Harrah's Casino. She stood behind him and watched as he played. Within a matter of minutes, Nico was experiencing a hot streak.

"A thousand dollars a bet?" he turned and asked Mia.

Mia was standing in her high heels and looking statuesque and gorgeous, turning multiple heads. "Go for it, baby," she said. "You're doing good." She smiled as she held on to her bamboo-tasseled leather Gucci wallet.

Nico nodded and kept on gambling.

In what seemed like five minutes, Nico had won five thousand dollars, on top of what he had already won. He took two thousand dollars in chips off the table and handed them to Mia.

Mia knew that the chips were for her to cash in and do whatever she wanted with. "Thank you." She smiled and then put the chips into her wallet. Then she told Nico she was going to the bathroom and that she would be right back.

Mia didn't have to use the bathroom; she just wanted to reply to Jasmine's text and didn't want to do it in Nico's presence. Her response to Jasmine was simple and to the point: *Bitches get riches. Snitches get ditches.*

SIXTEEN

After her meeting with Agent Gosling at Dallas BBQ, Jasmine didn't even go back to her parents' home. Instead, she drove to Nico's Long Island estate so she could book her trip to Las Vegas and grab some sexy outfits to take with her.

This was the first time she had been at the house since the shooting. Jasmine remembered being wheeled into the ambulance on the night of the shooting, and wondering if she would ever come back to that house. But now that Bebo was dead, she felt a bit safer.

When she pulled up to the Long Island home, things felt eerie to her. As she pulled into the circular driveway, she noticed yellow-and-black police tape still littered the front yard of the house. The sight of it made her cringe. She exited her BMW truck and made her way to the front door, unlocked it, and went inside. As she closed the door behind her, her heart beat rapidly from nervousness.

Jasmine exhaled as she walked past the spot where Narjara's dead body had been. She couldn't believe that Nico hadn't had a company come in to clean the bloodstains off the floor.

Her heart began to beat even faster after she heard a noise. "Who is that?" she yelled out.

Jasmine paused and listened closely, only to later realize that the noise was just the sound of a fence in the backyard slamming shut in the wind.

"I have to hurry up and get out of here," she said to herself.

She then went on to the computer and turned it on. Then she logged on to Expedia and searched for flights to Las Vegas.

"This is some bullshit," she said to herself after realizing that the cheapest roundtrip flight, which was on JetBlue Airways, was going to cost her a thousand dollars. It was going to eat up almost half of her twenty-five hundred dollars. She reluctantly booked the flight, putting the charges on the bankcard that Gosling had given her.

With the flight booked, Jasmine grabbed a small rolling suitcase that she could carry on to the airplane. Then she went upstairs to her closets and began filling the suitcase. She grabbed three of her sexiest pairs of high-heel shoes, one of which she was going to wear on the plane. Then she grabbed a pair of tight-fitting jeans and two additional sexy outfits that she put into the suitcase. She felt that that would be enough because she didn't plan on staying in Vegas for more than three days. She also went into her panty drawer and grabbed matching lace bras and panties and two rhinestone-studded thongs.

Jasmine didn't want to just leave without first showering, but she was scared to take a shower there. All she could envision playing out was a scene from the movie Psycho, where she would end up getting stabbed to death in the shower.

Jasmine was able to calm herself down, and after taking off the splint on her hand and removing the bandage from her neck, she stripped out of her clothes and took a quick three-minute shower.

As soon as she finished applying baby oil to her body, she once again got spooked. She screamed out loud, and her heart rate picked up. Then she realized it was just her cell phone vibrating.

She picked up the phone and saw a text from Mia.

Bitches get riches. Snitches get ditches.

Jasmine's pressure instantly shot through the roof. She didn't have a ready comeback. If Mia was calling her a snitch, then Nico had to be putting that in her head.

Finally, Jasmine had the confirmation she needed. She had been afraid that Nico was avoiding her out of fear that she was a snitch, and now that she was officially a snitch, she didn't know what to think.

Jasmine shook her head and put her phone away. She continued to get dressed. She was going to put the splint back on her hand, but she realized it was totally screwing up her look, as was the scar on her neck. She quickly retreated to the bathroom and began applying makeup to her neck to conceal the redness and the bruising. Although her hand was a little swollen, she figured that a slightly swollen hand looked a lot better than a hand in a splint. She applied much-needed polish to her fingernails, which were badly in need of a manicure. After they dried, she got dressed and headed out the door, on her way to Kennedy Airport in Queens.

◆◆◆

"This is really some bullshit," Jasmine said to a white man preparing to sit down in the row in front of her. "I paid damn near a thousand dollars for this ticket, and you would think I would be sitting up in the first row of the plane, and here I am all the way in the back of the plane near the fuckin' bathroom."

The white man looked like a straight-laced biology or world history professor. He looked shocked when he heard Jasmine curse.

Jasmine caught on to the fact that she had offended him. "Oh, I'm sorry. Please excuse my language. I'm just frustrated. My hand is hurting, and you know how it goes. Hey, would you mind placing this bag overhead for me?" she asked him. "I just had surgery on my hand, and I really can't lift much with it."

The white guy helped Jasmine out, looking somewhat relieved that she had apologized for cursing. After he helped her with her bag, he told her that she really needed to look into getting some kind of adjustment to her fare because he had only paid two hundred and seventy-five dollars for his ticket.

"Two seventy-five?" she screamed. "See, this is some muthafuckin' bullshit right here!" Jasmine called for one of the flight attendants to come her way.

The white man turned red with embarrassment. He regretted having said anything. He was with his four-year-old granddaughter and wanted desperately to press a rewind button so that she didn't have to hear the filthy language that came out of Jasmine's mouth. At the very least, he was definitely going to ask for a seat change.

Within seconds, an argument ensued between Jasmine and a black flight attendant.

The thirty-year-old dark-skinned stewardess with naturally long, wavy hair and a voluptuous body stated, "Ma'am, I'm going to kindly ask you one more time to please sit down, or otherwise I will have no choice but to have the authorities remove you from this plane,"

"Ma'am, I'm going to kindly ask you one more time to please sit down, or otherwise I will have no choice but to have the authorities remove you from this plane," Jasmine repeated, mocking the stewardess. "You can call whatever fuckin' authorities you want to call, but I can guarantee you one muthafuckin' gotdamn thing—My black ass ain't going nowhere. And I can also guarantee you that JetBlue is going to refund me my money."

Jasmine knew she had the power to press her distress button on the special BlackBerry phone that Gosling had given her, and within minutes she would have cops and federal agents coming to aid her. Although Gosling had stressed to her that she should only use the distress button in literal life-or-death situations, Jasmine was ready to press the button just to check the sassy black stewardess, if she had to.

"Miss, please, can you watch your language? There's children on the plane," one of the passengers yelled out to the relief of the white guy sitting in front of Jasmine.

Another passenger screamed, "Yeah, sit down and shut up, so we can take off!"

"Fuck all of y'all!" Jasmine shouted back before taking her window seat.

Just as other stewardesses were coming to the aid of their coworker, the black stewardess realized that Jasmine was backing down, so she retreated and held them off, telling them that everything was under control.

The six-hour flight was the most miserable flight that Jasmine had ever been on in her life, and when the plane landed at twelve thirty in the morning, she couldn't wait to get off. It seemed like it took forever for the rows of passengers to exit the plane, and to make matters worse, Jasmine was all the way in the back.

Finally she retrieved her bag from overhead, and her hand hurt like all hell as she got it without any assistance. She made her way to the front of the plane. "Tighten up your weave, bitch!" she said to the stewardess who had confronted her before the plane took off.

"Oh, please. This is all natural, baby girl!" The stewardess pulled on her hair to prove it. The stewardess was originally from Newark, New Jersey, so she knew how to handle herself. She would have fought Jasmine in a heartbeat had Jasmine taken it there.

"Whatever. Enjoy your little job," Jasmine said and she kept it moving.

Jasmine was beyond stressed out. She needed a drink in the worst way, just to calm her nerves. As she made her way through the terminal she saw Las Vegas Sports Lounge and decided to go in and have a drink. The Sports Lounge was still inside the terminal, so it was perfect for her because she didn't have to leave the airport or get in a cab or wait until she got to the hotel to get a drink.

Jasmine thought the Lounge was fairly crowded and somewhat poppin' for that time of night. She made her way to the bar, trying to figure out where she was going to sit. She looked around and noticed a bunch of cute guys in the bar. Before she could finish figuring out where she was going to attempt to sit down, a light-skinned black dude, about six foot three and buff, with a thin beard, good hair, and diamond-studded chain that looked like it cost more than the average house, stood up from his seat at the bar and offered it to her.

"Thank you," Jasmine said with a smile. She sat down at the bar and positioned her small suitcase next to her.

"I couldn't have you standing there like that," the gentleman said to her as he held out his right hand and introduced himself. "I'm Derek McGee," he said.

Jasmine extended her hand to his for a gentle handshake. "Hi, Derek. I'm Jasmine,"

Jasmine figured she would cut right to the chase and try and determine if Derek was fronting with fake jewels on, or if he was really 'bout it. From his swagger she could tell that he wasn't a hustler, because he came off way too polite—like he had manners from a two-parent household. And only good dudes with an education would introduce themselves with their full government name.

"Your hands are so soft. Either you don't work too hard, or you have a bunch of women pampering you," Jasmine said, blinded by his diamond-studded Audemars watch.

Derek smiled, and Jasmine noticed that all thirty-two of his Chiclet-looking teeth were perfectly aligned and bright white, another sign that he wasn't a street dude.

"So you stereotyping me based on my hands?" Derek chuckled. "That's a first," he added and then asked Jasmine what did she want to drink.

Jasmine told him, and Derek ordered her a coco-loco, and for himself he ordered a Bacardi and Red Bull.

"So you don't work hard, but you look very successful, you have a ton of women, and you look like a model, and you're at a bar at one in the morning. That could be a dangerous recipe," Jasmine said as soon as their drinks arrived.

Derek drank some of his drink and talked into Jasmine's ear over all the noise and he explained to her that he was a professional football player.

"Okay, so now I have to leave, but thank you for the drink." Jasmine smiled and pretended to be leaving.

Derek stopped her. "What?"

"You're a liar, and if you aren't lying, then that means you're trouble, because all athletes are trouble."

Derek smiled. And then he held out his right hand and showed Jasmine his Super Bowl championship ring from the Green Bay Packers.

"Okay, so you're not a liar; let's cross that off the list." Jasmine closely examined the ring. Then she reached for his left hand to see if he had on a wedding ring. "You married?"

Derek shook his head and told her that he was having way too much fun and wasn't even close to thinking about settling down.

"Yeah, I bet." Jasmine downed her drink because she wanted to get buzzed.

Derek ordered her another drink. "So let me stereotype you now," he said to her as her drink arrived. "You don't work hard, but you look very successful, you have a ton of men, you look like a model, and you're at a bar at one in the morning. That could be a dangerous recipe."

Jasmine smiled. "Why would that be such a dangerous recipe?"

"Because that would make you my weakness."

Jasmine told him she was in nursing school and stressed out because she had to withdraw because of surgery on her hand and neck.

"Wow!"

Jasmine was thankful that he didn't ask her what the surgery was for. Then Derek looked at her hand and asked her if she was married.

"Nope," Jasmine replied, and then she asked Derek if he could watch her bag for her while she went to the bathroom.

Jasmine got up and went to the bathroom, where she pulled out her cell phone and quickly logged on to Google and typed in the words "Derek McGee Green Bay Packers." Jasmine clicked on the second listing, which clearly showed a headshot of the same Derek she was sitting with at the bar. She scrolled down and read about him being a top wide receiver and signing a twenty-million-dollar contract extension with thirteen million dollars guaranteed last summer.

Jasmine was convinced that he was no fraud. She had just used the bathroom on the plane, so she didn't need to relieve herself, but she did wash her hands before exiting the bathroom and making her way back to the bar area.

"Everything good?" Derek asked.

"Yup," Jasmine replied and then joked and told Derek that he better had not put anything in her drink.

"So back to what I was asking you, do you have a man?"

"Something like that."

"What do you mean?"

"I mean, you know how y'all niggas do—Can't keep your dick in your pants. So every time I think I got the man of my dreams and everything is all good, he ends up fuckin' somebody else. Remember what you just said about having way too much fun? Yeah, well, all my men always seem to still be in the having-way-too-much-fun mode."

Derek laughed. He ordered another Red Bull and rum, and Jasmine ordered another coco-loco.

"Derek, you want to open a tab, baby?" the sexy female bartender with over-spilling cleavage asked.

Derek shook his head and reached in his pocket and pulled out a bankroll of hundred-dollar bills. He handed a crisp Benjamin Franklin to her and told her to keep the change. And in the process Jasmine's pussy began to throb. Liquor and a cute guy with money was usually what made her pussy jump, and it was twitching and ready to jump out of her pants. Jasmine hadn't had any good dick in weeks, and she was jonesing for some quality dick, which Derek appeared to have.

"So you got no man, and where'd you say you were from? New York?"

Jasmine nodded. She was buzzing like crazy from the two drinks and couldn't stop smiling at Derek.

Derek had been around every type of chick imaginable, and he knew he could smash Jasmine that night if he wanted to, which was just what he planned on doing. "New York girls are trouble," he remarked.

"No, we're not."

"So you really have no man, you came out here to see nobody?"

"I told you, I was just stressed and I had to withdraw from school, so I decided to just fly out here and chill for a few days and clear my head."

"So where are you staying?"

"At the Wynn Resort."

"Okay."

Derek, originally from Las Vegas, had just flown into town to visit his parents. He had a home in Las Vegas, but he didn't want to take Jasmine there without knowing what she was really about.

"So if we leave here, I can go back with you to the Wynn?" Derek asked, testing her.

Jasmine didn't respond with words. She just looked at Derek and slowly nodded.

"Can I stereotype you some more?" Derek asked.

Jasmine smiled and said yes.

Then Derek whispered in her ear and told her that she looked like she kept her pussy bald and that she probably only wore thongs.

"You funny." Jasmine sipped some more of her drink. The smell of Derek's cologne was making Jasmine so hot, she wanted to grab him by the dick and pull him into the bathroom and fuck his brains out in one of the stalls.

"But am I right?"

"Maybe," Jasmine replied.

Derek took another sip of his drink, and then he placed fifty dollars on the bar and ordered another round for him and Jasmine. He positioned himself so he was right up on her and no one else could see as he unbuttoned and unzipped her jeans and felt around for the crotch of her panties, which he moved to the side, and slowly slipped his middle finger inside her soaking wet pussy.

Jasmine sighed in ecstasy, trying to be discreet, and then she slapped his hand. She zipped her pants and buttoned them back.

"So I was right about one thing," Derek smiled and said.

Jasmine just looked at him and remained quiet.

After their fourth round of drinks, Jasmine and Derek made their way out of the bar and out of the airport. Derek called a number that was provided to all of the players who played for the Green Bay Packers that they could use to call a chauffeured car service to pick them up from anywhere in the country if they were ever out late drinking. Derek wasn't going to put his NFL contract at risk by drinking and driving or getting arrested for public intoxication or something like that, so he always made sure to take advantage of that number whenever he went out partying.

Fifteen minutes later, Derek and Jasmine found themselves inside of an all-black chauffeur-driven Yukon Denali with tinted windows and headed to the Wynn. They both were feeling nice, and although Jasmine wanted some dick, she had let Derek freak her in the bar and now come back to her hotel room to fuck her simply because she was looking at the potential bigger picture, which contained possible NFL riches.

Jasmine loved Las Vegas. She had just stepped off the plane, and without even spending a dime on slot machines, she felt like she had hit the jackpot.

SEVENTEEN

By the time Derek and Jasmine finished fucking, it was a little past four in the morning. Before Jasmine fell asleep, she was still feeling the effects of the liquor she drank, and as she lay in the bed next to Derek, she felt like calling up Agent Gosling and telling him that she was done with her role as a confidential informant.

It was hard for Jasmine to stay focused when she was lying next to Derek's rock-hard body. Jasmine loved his tats, which pretty much covered his entire upper body and both of his arms. She cuddled next to him and continually ran her hand up and down his eight-pack abs until she put herself to sleep.

When morning came, Jasmine woke up as Derek moved about the hotel room.

"Hey," Jasmine said in a groggy tone from underneath a white bed sheet.

"What's up, girl?"

"You were just going to fuck me and slide out real quiet, I see. You see how y'all pro athletes do?" Jasmine joked as she sat up in the bed.

"Nah, actually I had already stepped out real quick and met my man downstairs in the lobby."

Jasmine stretched and let out an exaggerated groan, trying to fully wake herself.

"You left and came back? I must have been knocked out. I ain't hear nothing." Jasmine thought to herself how good dick put her ass to sleep every time.

"Yeah, I had to get my weed," Derek replied to Jasmine's instant delight.

Derek sat down at the table that was diagonally across from the bed and pulled out an ounce of weed and put it on the table. "You smoke?" he asked, emptying the contents of a cigar into the trashcan.

"Do I? Did I tell you that I am loving you right now?"

Derek smiled and continued to roll the weed up. "I figured we would smoke and then go get something to eat for breakfast before I head out."

"Okay, that's cool," Jasmine replied. "What is that? Haze?"

"Nah, this ain't haze," Derek smiled and said as he continued to roll the blunt like a skilled marijuana surgeon. "You from New York, but I know New York ain't up on this shit. This that exotic weed."

"What is it?" Jasmine sat down across from Derek, wearing nothing but her bra and panties, and she was as excited as a kid opening a present on Christmas morning.

"It's strawberry ice. This shit will get you fucked up."

Jasmine was intrigued. Within seconds Derek had put the finishing touches on the blunt, sparked it, and handed it to her.

"Wake and bake! That's what the fuck I'm talking about," Jasmine took a real long pull on the blunt and then handed it back to Derek.

For a good fifteen minutes Derek and Jasmine sat and smoked and got high as kites. Jasmine then went to take a shower, while Derek rolled up another blunt.

The NFL had a strict drug policy, but during the off-season, most of the players violated that drug policy. They'd clean out their system a couple of weeks prior to the start of camp so they wouldn't jeopardize their multimillion-dollar contracts.

After Jasmine had showered and gotten dressed, she and Derek finished off the second blunt and made their way downstairs to a restaurant called Society Café. At that point Jasmine was totally enjoying herself and could have cared less about her mission of finding Nico and getting close to him.

"Table for two?" the hostess asked Derek and Jasmine.

"Yes, please," Derek replied.

"Right this way." The pleasant hostess showed Derek and Jasmine to their table.

As soon as Jasmine and Derek sat down, Jasmine picked up the menu and stared at it.

"Oh, my God! I am so high right now, I can't even see the words on this menu," Jasmine laughed and said.

"I told you, that strawberry ice will do it to you every time."

Forgetting about the menu, Jasmine put it down and reached across the table and took hold of Derek's hand. Derek looked into Jasmine's eyes.

"This is exactly the type of getaway I was hoping for. I'm so glad I met you," Jasmine remarked.

"I feel you. I'm glad we met too. But why you talking like we not going to see each other again?"

Before Jasmine could respond, an Asian waitress approached the table and introduced herself and asked if they were ready to place their order. Derek spoke up and asked Jasmine if she minded if he ordered for her.

"No, not all. You know I can't see that menu anyway."

Since it was getting close to noon, Derek proceeded to order drunken noodles for the both of them, Pad Thai for himself, and a Thai breakfast omelet for Jasmine.

"Okay, and can I get you anything to drink? Coffee, or orange juice maybe?"

"Yeah, you can get us two mimosas," Derek replied.

The waitress jotted everything down. "Be right back."

"You trying to keep me twisted, I see. As high as I am, and you ordering me a mimosa?" Jasmine smiled.

Right after Jasmine said that, she went quiet as she directed her attention toward the entrance to the restaurant, where she saw Mia and Nico enter. Mia immediately pointed in the direction of Jasmine and Derek, like she had a Jasmine radar.

"Shit," Jasmine said under her breath.

"What's wrong?"

"Nothing. I was just thinking about something," Jasmine said, not wanting to alarm Derek.

The last person Jasmine wanted to see at that moment while she was with Derek was Mia.

The hostess seated them on the opposite side of the restaurant, well within Jasmine and Derek's view and vice versa.

Jasmine decided to just ignore Mia and Nico and directed her attention straight ahead to Derek.

At that point the waitress arrived with their mimosas, and she told them that their food would be out shortly.

"Okay, thank you," Jasmine smiled and said.

Derek was about to drink from his glass, but Jasmine stopped him.

"Wait, we have to make a toast first," she said.

"My bad."

Jasmine waited for him to take the lead and make the toast.

Derek finally caught on. "I know what I want to toast. I want to toast to your tight-ass chocha!"

Jasmine started to laugh, and the two of them touched glasses.

Nico looked over in Jasmine's direction, and it was clear by his ice grill that he was heated and getting angrier by the second.

"Nico, what is she doing here? And who the hell is that she's with?" Mia asked. "Please don't tell me you flew her out here."

Nico wanted to tell Mia to shut the fuck up, but he just looked at her and didn't answer.

"Yo, chill right here. I'll be right back," he said to Mia. "Don't fuckin' move." He got up from his seat and headed over toward Jasmine and Derek.

"Well, then I definitely gotta toast you to that quality dick you gave me and to that good-ass weed that still got me fucked up."

They laughed as they tapped their glasses a second time, and then they both drank some of the mimosa.

Jasmine wasn't looking in Nico's direction, so she didn't see him approaching.

"Honestly, Derek, I'm really glad that we met. I feel like I really want to get to know you. I just feel some kind of chemistry between us, and I'm not just saying that. I mean, I can't really explain it," Jasmine said as she looked into Derek's eyes.

"That's real talk."

"Yo, what the fuck you doin' here? And who the fuck is this nigga?"

Jasmine looked up at Nico, a disgusted look on her face. "Really?" she asked him, her voiced raised and her tone sarcastic.

"Jasmine, you know how I get down. I'll smack the shit outta you. Now, what the fuck are you doing out here?"

Derek immediately stood up. Nico took notice of his height and his muscles and his tats but quickly sized him up as soft. The only thing was, he wasn't sure if Derek was strapped.

"My man, is there a problem?" Derek asked.

"Don't do it to yourself, potna!" Nico gave Derek an ice grill and moved closer to him.

"Derek, it's okay," Jasmine stepped in and said.

"Oh, you talkin' for this nigga too?" Nico asked. "Come here!" He then grabbed Jasmine by her arm and attempted to lead her out of the restaurant.

"Nico, get your hands off of me!" Jasmine screamed and tried to break free from his vise grip.

Other people in the restaurant began to take notice of the escalating altercation.

Mia got up from her seat and quickly joined in the melee. She pointed her index and middle fingers at Jasmine. "You a stalker bitch now?"

Jasmine shook her head. Her marijuana high had worn off, and she was seconds from losing her temper.

Nico hollered, "Mia, what the fuck did I tell you?"

At that point Derek grabbed hold of Jasmine and tried to shield her from Nico.

"I don't care! I'm so tired of this stalker bitch! I'm about to fuck her up!" Mia said.

Nico snatched up Mia and bitch-smacked her hard two times across the face. "I told you to just chill. Now go the fuck upstairs before I fuckin' kill you!" Nico screamed and then pushed her hard toward the exit of the restaurant.

The left side of Mia's face was stinging, and she was shocked and embarrassed. Yeah, she was out of line and hadn't listened to Nico, but she didn't understand why he always seemed to side with Jasmine over her. Fed up, she stormed out of the restaurant.

Jasmine was now scared that Nico might beat Derek's ass. She didn't know if Nico had a gun on him, but the last thing she wanted was for Derek to get shot or to catch a beat-down on her account.

"Oh, my God! Derek, I am so sorry about this. I'll be okay. Just leave me for now, and I'll call you later. I am so sorry!"

"Jasmine, I'm not leaving you," Derek replied.

Nico gestured like he was reaching for a gun in his waistband.

"Nico, no!" Jasmine screamed and then rushed Nico and grabbed him.

"Come the fuck on then!" Nico barked. "Fuck around and get both of y'all murdered!" He snatched Jasmine up by the arm and marched her out of the restaurant.

"Derek, I'll be okay. I'll call you in a few!" Jasmine screamed.

Nico was putting so much pressure on Jasmine's arm, it was really hurting her.

"Nico, get off of me. You're hurting me! Stop acting like a fuckin' fool!"

The two of them made it out of the restaurant and to an area in the lobby where they were all alone.

"I can't believe you," Jasmine shouted as she marched toward the elevator, trying to make it up to her room.

Nico knew he had spazzed out, so he was trying to quickly get a grip of himself as he followed behind Jasmine. "A'ight, listen," he said.

Jasmine paid him no mind and kept on walking toward the elevators.

"Jasmine! Jasmine, I'm fuckin' talking to you," Nico hollered as he continued to follow her to the elevator.

Jasmine could see herself in the mirror-lined elevator. "Look what you did to me. Look at my fuckin' arm! Shit!" She examined the bruises on her arm.

Nico had Jasmine in solitude like he wanted her. He really wanted to find out just exactly why Jasmine was out in Las Vegas, and how she knew what hotel he was in.

"I'm asking you one more time—What the fuck are you doing out here?"

As the elevator doors opened on to Jasmine's floor, she ignored Nico and quickly walked out of the elevator and toward her room. She desperately wanted to get to her government-issued BlackBerry so she could have Nico on tape incriminating himself.

"Leave me the fuck alone!"

Jasmine used her card key and unlocked the door to her room, and Nico pushed his way in right behind her.

"Hellloo! Leave me alone, please. I believe your bitch Mia is in another room."

After Jasmine said that, she walked across the room and grabbed her BlackBerry. "Seriously, Nico, leave right now, or I'm calling the cops," she said, discreetly activating the record feature.

"Call 'em."

Jasmine sighed and sucked her teeth. "Okay, you know what? Fuck it!" She walked over to the table that had Derek's weed sitting on top of it and sat down and pulled out a second chair for Nico.

"Since you so hard to find, and now you want to talk all of a sudden, sit down and let's talk, Nico."

Nico noticed the ounce of weed on the table, but he didn't comment on it. He had other pressing questions he wanted her to answer.

Jasmine was ready. She waited for Nico to incriminate himself as the BlackBerry did its job, recording his every word.

EIGHTEEN

Nico's phone began to vibrate. He looked at it and saw that it was Mia, so he hit his ignore button and sent her to voice mail.

"Come on, sit down. Sit, Nico," Jasmine said with sassy bravado, tapping the cushion with her hand.

Nico kicked the arm of the chair and knocked it over in the process.

WHACK!

He smacked Jasmine across the left side of her face. The openhanded bitch-slap was so hard that Jasmine saw stars. She had to catch her balance after almost falling out of the chair.

Although Jasmine was woozy, she was a fighter. She stood and tried to throw a punch, but Nico caught her hand and then took hold of her wrist and twisted it and bent it backwards and took her down to the ground.

"Ahhhh! That's my sore hand!" she screamed, writhing in pain on the ground.

Nico ignored her screams and applied more pressure to her bent wrist.

Jasmine tried to get to her feet, but Nico let her wrist go, grabbed her by the throat, and slammed the back of her head to the carpeted floor. Jasmine couldn't breathe, and she scratched at Nico's strong muscular right arm, trying to free herself from his grip.

"Now we gonna do shit my way! You understand me, bitch?" Nico squeezed harder on Jasmine's neck.

Jasmine felt like she was about to pass out, so she stopped resisting, and tried to nod.

Nico finally loosened his grip from her neck, and Jasmine gasped for air, coughing and grabbing her throat.

"Now tell me what the fuck you doing out here and how the fuck did you know where I was staying at? And don't bullshit me!"

Jasmine was still coughing, trying to get air in her lungs. She knew she had to think quickly, because Nico wasn't playing games.

"Nico, what you think I'm doing out here? I'm out here because I love you and I wanted to be with you."

"How-the-fuck did-you-know I-was-out-here, and-how-the-fuck did-you-know where-I-was-staying-at?" Nico asked with a rhythmic cadence to his words.

Jasmine immediately started to cry, hoping her tears would divert Nico's attention.

"Baby, I'm out here because I was scared, and you make me feel safe. Do you know what it's like for me to almost get killed by Bebo and then not want to go home at night because I'm thinking he might come back and make sure he kills me? And all I want is to know you'll protect me, and it's like all you're doing is running from me! I'm scared, baby! That's all! I'm scared." Jasmine started to weep.

Fortunately for Jasmine, some of her words resonated with Nico's macho character.

"I took care of that situation! I told you I would handle it, and I handled it. Now what the fuck you not gonna do is stand there and make me keep asking you the same shit."

"You handled what? See, this is what I can't take. I'm supposedly your girl, but you don't tell me shit. I don't know where you are at times, and it's just like ugggghhhhh."

Nico was quiet.

"So what did you handle?" Jasmine was trying her best to get Nico to talk.

"You know what the streets is talking about. I did that shit, it's done, it's over with. You can sleep at night now."

Jasmine shook her head.

"Answer me, Jasmine."

Jasmine knew what Nico was referring to, and thankfully she thought quickly.

"You're going to think what you want to think so I don't care. I knew you was out here because I called around to all of the hotels and the resorts and I was asking for Mia's name. And as soon as I found the hotel she was at, I knew you would more than likely be side by side with her. And guess what? Looks like I was right."

Jasmine had no idea if Mia had booked the room, so at that point her heart was pounding. If she were wrong, Nico would probably murder her right there on the spot.

Nico looked at her as she wiped her tears. "You full of shit."

Jasmine exhaled because she knew Nico hadn't caught her in a lie.

"Yeah, I'm full of shit. Ugggghhh! Baby, what is wrong? Like, did I do something or what? One minute everything is all good—We at Mr. Chow eating good and living it up—and then the next thing I know, the cops is at our table, I get arrested, and after that, it's like everything just short-circuited. What is going on?" Jasmine asked, desperation in her voice.

Tears started to fall from Jasmine's face. She picked up the chair that Nico had kicked over and sat back down.

"Nico, be straight up with me and tell me the truth. Were you the one who sent Bebo to kill me?"

"The fuck you talking about?"

"I'm serious, Nico."

Nico plastered a smirk on his face. "What you think?"

"I think you did."

Nico shook his head and chuckled. "You're funny."

"That's why I'm out here. I came out here saying to myself that if you're out here with Mia, then there's no way you didn't send Bebo to kill me. You sent him to kill me, and you're out here fuckin' that bitch that you know I can't stand."

"I ain't fuckin' Mia."

"Oh, my God! This is what I can't stand! Nico, I'm not stupid. I'm home in New York dealing with my injuries after almost dying, and do I see you or hear from you? No. So I'm bugging out and can't understand why. And in my heart I just felt it was something to do with Mia. I know you came out here with her before, so I had a feeling that if you wasn't with me that you was more than likely with her, and guess what? I was right. You out here fuckin' her while I'm in New York scared for my life. That shit is so fucked up." Jasmine stood up and walked over to a mirror and looked at her neck.

Nico could see the bruises he had caused.

"You choke the shit outta me, you left me stranded at the precinct and never explained to me what that was all about, and you really wonder if I think you had Bebo come to kill me? Like, really, you want me to believe you had nothing to do with that?"

"A'ight, so whatever happened with that shit? Why did the cops let you go?"

Jasmine sucked her teeth and looked at Nico and rolled her eyes. "Because they didn't have shit on me. It was all bullshit, and we both know that."

"But what did they say?"

"About what? They took me in and they questioned me, but I didn't admit to shit because there was nothing to admit to. And since they wasn't charging me with a crime, they had to let me go. Nico, you know how this shit goes."

Feeling a small bit of relief, Nico walked up to Jasmine and tried to kiss her on the back of her neck, but she moved away.

"I apologize."

Jasmine shook her head. "You apologize? You out here fuckin' that bitch. You choke me out and you got me home in New York looking like a clueless bird-bitch, and all you can say is 'I apologize'?"

Nico slowly approached Jasmine. "Come here."

"No! Get away from me! Go kiss on Mia. You can't just fuck her and then kiss on me and tell me you apologize. That's supposed to make things right?"

"I'm not fuckin' her."

"So then why is she out here with you? She's transporting kilos for you or something?"

Nico looked hard at Jasmine and tried to figure out where that question came from.

"Is she, or isn't she? It's a simple question."

Nico was quiet.

"Nico, it's simple. If you using Mia as a mule to transport your drugs, just say that and I'll know what's up. But if you fuckin' her then just say that too, so I'll know what's up, and I'll know where I stand."

Nico was no dummy. He knew when to keep his mouth shut, and he also knew the right words to speak. He just smiled.

Jasmine also said nothing.

"So who was homie wit'chu down in the restaurant? This his weed on the table?"

"He wasn't nobody. I met him last night at the bar. He was telling me he plays pro football, and he asked me if I would go to breakfast with him."

"So are you fuckin' him?"

"Nico, please don't try to spin this around."

"I ain't spinning shit, but if you wanna keep shit one hundred, let's keep it one hundred."

"I always keep it real, Nico, and you know that."

"Yeah, I know that. And I also know you murdered Shabazz. And if you murdered him, you think my mind don't wander?"

"Oh, my God!"

"Babe, I saw you murder your ex in cold blood, and I been riding with you and I ain't ever blink about the shit."

"Wait. Hold up, hold up. First of all, you ain't ever see me do shit. And how dare you try to put that shit on me?"

"Nah, hold up, baby girl. You the one slinging those murderous accusations, and you need to cut that shit out. Let's be mature adults about this shit. You feel me?"

Nico's prepaid phone started to vibrate at that moment, and he saw that it was BJ. "My nigga, speak to me," he said and then walked into the bathroom so he could speak in private.

"The coroner finally released the body to homie's family. The funeral is on Friday," BJ explained, referring to Bebo's funeral.

"So whatchu saying?" Nico asked, still being careful not to say much of anything on the phone.

"We need to both be there," BJ replied.

Nico had no plans of ever attending Bebo's funeral, but he trusted BJ's judgment, and if BJ was saying that they both needed to go, then he would go.

"I feel you."

"You know what I mean, right?" BJ asked.

"Yeah, I been outta pocket, so the streets been talking."

"No muthafuckin' doubt," BJ replied. "They on that conspiracy shit, but if we both there, it'll quiet all that."

"Yeah, yeah. So Friday, huh?"

"Yes, sirrr. At Gilmore's in Queens, over there on Linden."

"A'ight, speak to his moms and make sure they straight with cheddar and all that. Let them know that we gon' make sure his kids is straight and that they'll be all right."

"Cool." BJ ended their call.

Nico put his phone back in his pocket and exited the bathroom.

"For the record, I wasn't slinging no murderous accusations. If you heard what I said, I was just saying that I didn't know what to think," Jasmine tried to explain to Nico.

Nico nodded his head at her. "Stop running your mouth," he said to her, knowing his words would have a double meaning.

"What are you talking about?"

"I'm just saying . . . "

Jasmine was getting frustrated because she wasn't getting where she wanted to get with Nico.

Nico walked over to the wet bar and poured himself a Jack Daniel's on the rocks and asked Jasmine if she wanted anything to drink. Jasmine just shook her head.

Nico put his drink on the table and gestured for Jasmine to come to him. She came to him, and then he kissed her on the lips. Jasmine sucked her teeth and told him that she hated him.

He planted a peck on her lips. "You hate me?"

"Yes." Jasmine felt Nico unbutton her pants, and then she heard her zipper get unzipped.

"You ain't give my pussy away, right?"

Jasmine lied and shook her head no. "You can't fuck me, Nico."

"Why not?" Nico asked, unzipping his own pants.

"Because you don't trust me, you don't tell me anything you don't—"

"Stop talking," Nico commanded.

Nico took another swig of his drink, and then he put it back down. He took Jasmine by the hand, led her into the bathroom, and turned on the shower.

"Take a shower with me," he said to Jasmine while he got fully undressed and made his way into the glass-enclosed shower.

Jasmine wanted to resist, but the sight of Nico's naked body turned her on so much, her pussy instantly got wet. She got undressed and joined him in the shower. She started to tongue-kiss him as the water rained down on both of them.

Before long Nico's dick was rock-hard and lathered up with soap. He turned Jasmine around and fucked her from behind in the shower for twenty minutes.

Jasmine didn't know what it was about Nico, but something about the way he fucked her always made her have multiple orgasms and left her literally weak in the knees.

When they had finished fucking and showering, Jasmine was uncharacteristically quiet, dealing with all kinds of emotions and feelings. Overwhelmed and confused, she had no clue what the hell she had gotten herself into.

NINETEEN

Nico ended up staying in Jasmine's room for the rest of the day. Including the session in the shower, he had fucked her four times, to be exact. Her pussy was sore, but she knew one thing: As long as Nico was with her, he couldn't be with Mia.

Jasmine had hoped for an opportunity to catch Nico saying something revealing, but with all of the fucking they were doing, the opportunity never presented itself. By the time ten o'clock rolled around, they were exhausted and decided to order room service instead of venturing out to eat. Neither of them had the energy to deal with Mia and any drama that would have come their way if they bumped into her somewhere.

After they had finished eating their dinner, it was only a quarter to eleven, which was very early for Las Vegas time, but Jasmine found herself dozing off in the bed with Nico.

"You still up?" she asked him.

"Yeah."

Jasmine turned and faced Nico and she kissed him on his chest. She was very groggy and her voice sounded even more tired than she was feeling.

"I just wanted to tell you that I love you."

"Oh, a'ight." Nico had lost trust in Jasmine, so he couldn't reciprocate the feelings that he had felt less than a month ago.

Before long, Jasmine was knocked out and in a deep sleep. Nico knew that the weed she had been smoking combined with the liquor and the sex was going to have her out cold for a while. He was tired, but he wasn't about to let himself fall asleep; it was way too early for that.

After about an hour of just laying there, Nico slid out of the bed and went into the bathroom to take a piss. When he came out of the bathroom, he looked around for Jasmine's cell phone.

Jasmine had her FBI-issued BlackBerry inside of her open Gucci bag, which was not too far from the bed, and she had her regular BlackBerry on the nightstand right next to her head. Seeing the BlackBerry on the nightstand, Nico never thought to look inside her Gucci bag. He walked over and picked up the BlackBerry on the nightstand and walked back into the bathroom with it. Then he locked the door and started searching through the phone.

Nico looked at text messages, incoming calls and outgoing calls, and he figured out how to play back recordings. The only recording he saw was the one that Jasmine had made when Bebo had shot her.

Realizing that she hadn't taped any of the conversations she'd had with him, Nico came out of the bathroom and placed her phone back on the nightstand. He quietly got dressed, got his phone, and made sure that all of his cash was in his pocket. Then he took a long look at Jasmine, and as she slept, he reconfirmed how fine she was. Though he felt some relief that she hadn't recorded him, he still had a gut feeling that she was working with the feds.

Nico slipped out of the room headed to the roulette table, but he decided to go to his room first. When he got there, Mia was nowhere to be found, and her bags weren't there. He called her three times, but she didn't pick up. He decided to just go play roulette for an hour, telling himself if Mia wasn't in the room by the time he got back, he was just going to go to the strip club or back to Jasmine's room and fuck her one more time.

Nico had no idea that Mia had already checked out of the room and had checked into an inexpensive hotel room right near the airport. She was tired of Nico and his bullshit love triangle. And she was even more tired of him just tossing her to the side whenever he felt like it, like she was a piece of trash or something. She had made up her mind to head back to New York the next day, and she was going to go straight to the safe deposit box Nico had her open up for him and take the three hundred and fifty thousand dollars in there and then disappear and spend the money however she felt. That would be the best form of revenge to sting Nico with. Even though it could possibly get her ass killed, she didn't care. She was going strictly off her hurt feelings.

When Jasmine first opened her eyes, she wasn't exactly sure where she was. So much had been going on in her life, she wasn't sure if she was at her mother's house, at Simone's house, or at her and Nico's house. After about a minute she sat up in the bed, and then she remembered that she was in Las Vegas, and that she and Nico had just spent the majority of the previous day fucking their brains out.

Seeing that the light was on in the bathroom and the bathroom door was closed, she assumed that Nico was in there. She walked over to the bathroom door, knocked on it and called Nico's name, and waited for an answer. When she didn't get one, she tapped on the door again and opened it up and went inside.

Jasmine shook her head as she exited the bathroom. When she realized it was five o'clock in the morning and there was no sign of Nico, she knew he had purposely slid out on her.

Jasmine went back into the bathroom and peed and then washed her hands before getting back into the bed. The room was still somewhat dark because the sun hadn't risen yet. Jasmine lay in the bed feeling like a whore, knowing that only hours ago Nico had been fucking the shit out of her, and he was now probably fucking Mia the same way.

She reached over and grabbed her BlackBerry. She called Nico, but she got no answer.

Nico would have answered his phone, but he was in the strip club getting a lap dance and didn't even realize that it was ringing.

"I can't do this shit no more," she said out loud in frustration.

She then sent Nico a text message: *So it's like that, Nico? You just fuck me for hours and leave without telling me???*

Jasmine waited five minutes, and when she realized Nico wasn't responding, she texted him again: *You back on that bullshit AGAIN! It's all good, though. Don't worry I WON'T CHASE YOU!!!*

Jasmine tried to go back to sleep, but she couldn't. It had now been a full hour, and Nico still hadn't responded to her missed call or to her texts. She needed to feel wanted, so while still lying in the bed, she decided to call Derek.

When Derek didn't pick up, she left him a voice mail: "Hey, Derek. This is Jasmine. I know it's early, but I just really need to speak to you. First, I want to really, really, really apologize for yesterday. I am so sorry. But call me back when you get this, so I can explain. It's way too much to explain in a voice mail."

After about five minutes Jasmine decided to send Derek a text message: *Hi Derek, it's Jasmine. I just left you a voice mail. Call me as soon as you can.*

Jasmine grabbed the remote, turned on the TV, and started to flip through the channels. Two minutes later, she heard her BlackBerry vibrating on her nightstand. She quickly reached for it. She thought it was a phone call, but then she realized it was a text message from Derek.

Jasmine, the pussy was good, but I don't need the drama. LOSE MY NUMBER! Thanks!!!

When Jasmine read that text message, she felt like she had just been dropkicked in the gut. She immediately called Derek, but it went to voice mail. She knew he was done with her and was avoiding her. She was so mad with Nico at that point because not only was he playing games with her, but he had now managed to fuck up the NFL jackpot that had fallen in her lap.

Beyond frustrated, Jasmine got up and went to the wet bar and poured herself a drink. She was done with Las Vegas. It made no sense for her to stay out there any longer. After her drink she was going to take a shower, get dressed, eat breakfast, and then head to the airport and see if she could change her ticket or fly standby so she could get her ass back to New York and reassess everything.

TWENTY

When Jasmine made it to the airport to head back to New York, she asked to see a JetBlue supervisor. She complained to the supervisor about how rude the JetBlue stewardess had been to her on her flight to Las Vegas, and asked if she could be upgraded to the front of the plane so she wouldn't have to be subjected to the same ghetto treatment.

The white male supervisor looked like he could be a weatherman on the local TV news, with his blond hair, bright blue eyes, and perfectly tanned skin. He began furiously typing into his computer.

"Would you like a window seat or an aisle seat?"

"It doesn't matter," Jasmine replied.

"Okay, just give me one more minute, and I should be—Oh, okay there we go. Would the third-row window seat be good?"

Jasmine smiled. "Perfect."

"Sorry I couldn't actually get you in the first or second row."

"No, that's fine. You helped me out a great deal."

Jasmine smiled, took hold of her boarding pass, and thanked him again before going to sit down and wait for the plane to start boarding.

A little over an hour later, she found herself boarding the plane and sitting happily in her third-row seat. She had already put her carry-on bag in the overhead compartment and was reading the latest issue of Essence magazine while the other passengers boarded the plane. She began to flip through the magazine aimlessly before deciding to put it away.

She looked up and couldn't believe her eyes. She saw Mia boarding the same plane and taking her aisle seat in row two just across the aisle from her. Jasmine's heart started to beat rapidly because she was certain that Nico would be soon boarding the plane. Mia was wearing designer sunglasses that hid her face somewhat, but Jasmine was sure that it was her. She intently watched for Nico, but he never walked onto the plane.

Mia searched out one of the male flight attendants and asked him if he could put her carry-on bag in the overhead compartment for her. And as soon as the flight attendant took hold of her bag, she turned and saw Jasmine looking at her. Mia slightly slid her shades downward off her face, just to make sure her eyes weren't playing tricks on her.

"Yeah, it's me, bitch!" Jasmine shouted at Mia, to the shock and dismay of the older white lady sitting next to her.

Mia rolled her eyes and shook her head before putting her shades fully back on. "Thank you so much," she said to the flight attendant. She went into her bag and pulled out a twenty-dollar bill and tried to hand it to the flight attendant who had just helped her. "Here, this is for you," she said, purposely ignoring Jasmine.

"Oh, no. Thank you, but I can't take that."

"Just take it, buy coffee or something when we land in New York."

"He said he can't take it. Now sit your ass down, so we can take off! Bitch!"

Everybody seated in the front of the plane was shocked and surprised at Jasmine's language, not to mention confused.

Mia smiled and calmly walked toward Jasmine and stood over the white lady sitting next to her. "You're frustrated. I understand, sweetie. You'll be okay," she said in a soft, nonthreatening tone.

"If you were smart, you would sit your ass down in your seat."

"Ladies, is everything okay?" a gay black male flight attendant walked up and asked both Mia and Jasmine.

"Everything is fine," Mia replied right before taking her aisle seat. "She's just going through a little of life's frustrations."

The flight attendants stood watch for about a minute, and then they realized that Jasmine's emotions had subsided. They continued on with their duties, and the flight eventually took off.

For the remainder of the almost six-hour flight, Jasmine and Mia both ignored each other. Jasmine sat with more of a screw face, but that was because her prospects for the future didn't seem as bright as Mia's.

Mia sat through the entire flight knowing that within a matter of days, if not hours, she would have her hands on three hundred and fifty thousand dollars in cash, which would go a long way to helping her feel good, regardless of what Jasmine and Nico chose to do.

◆◆◆

When the flight was approaching the airport, Jasmine sent Simone a text and asked her if she could pick her up in thirty minutes from LaGuardia Airport, which wasn't too far from Simone, and Simone agreed.

So when the plane finally landed, Jasmine and Mia continued to ignore each other, and they both exited the plane, with Mia walking in front. Mia had luggage that she had checked in, so she had to go to the baggage area. When she went to the left, Jasmine went to the right toward the passenger pick-up area outside. She saw Simone and she walked toward her, pulling her carry-on bag behind her.

"Hey, girl." Simone rolled down the passenger side window. She popped the trunk, so Jasmine could put her bag inside.

"Thank you so much. I flew out of Kennedy Airport, and I got my truck parked there. But there was so much drama, I ended up flying back in to LaGuardia," Jasmine explained.

"Oh, okay. So you need me to shoot you over to Kennedy?"

"Yeah, if you can."

Simone gave Jasmine a look. "If you didn't have your car parked at Kennedy, then I would be driving you home. So what's the difference?"

"No, I'm just saying I don't want to be all rude and assuming, that's all." Jasmine smiled.

"So you went to Vegas and didn't even tell me?"

"Drama, drama, drama—I can't even begin to tell you!"

"In Vegas? What happened?"

"So I go out there with this dude named Derek McGee. He plays football for the Green Bay Packers—twenty-million-dollar contract, fine as hell, muscles, all that. So . . ."

"And when were you going to tell me about him? Hook a sister up with one of his friends!"

"No, just listen. So me and Derek are at the Wynn Resort. We chillin', smoking good weed, good sex, eating good and all that. So we at brunch at this restaurant, and who the fuck walks in? Nico!"

"How did he know you were there?"

"I got no idea. So Nico comes to the table beefing, like, 'who the fuck is this nigga?' Yadda yadda yadda. So Derek stands up from the table, and he ain't a street dude, and inside I'm saying to myself, 'Derek, I know you got muscles and all, but I hope your ass knows how to use your hands.'"

Simone chuckled. "Nico ended up knocking his ass out, right?"

"No. So I stand up and I step in between them. But Derek starts talking shit, so next thing I know, I see Nico reaching for his gun."

"Jasmine, no." Simone held her hand over her mouth.

"So I screamed, 'Nico, no!' and I rushed him and held him so he wouldn't do nothing crazy. So Nico is going crazy like, 'What the fuck are you doing out here?' and he's snatching me up, like, 'Come on, let's go.'"

"And what was Derek doing?"

"He was just standing there, asking me if I was all right, so I ended up telling him that I would be right back and I was sorry and all that. And Nico marches me out of the restaurant, and it was just crazy!"

"So what else happened?"

"It's too much to tell, but I wasn't trying to have Nico murder my ass."

"So you just left Derek out there?"

"Well, his punk ass ended up texting me, talking about my pussy was good and all that but for me to lose his number because he don't need the drama. Look." Jasmine handed Simone her phone to look at the text Derek had sent to her.

"Wow! But, Jasmine, that's twenty million you leaving on the table."

"I know, I know. Don't even remind me. I am so through right now."

Jasmine shook her head and slumped in her seat and kept quiet before turning up the volume on the radio.

"So where's Nico?"

"He's still out there. He had some business to take care of. And you know what? I'm glad you asked me that, because you need to come chill with me in Long Island until he gets back in a few days."

Simone looked at Jasmine but didn't say anything. She was well aware of what happened the last time one of her friends went to her and Nico's house, and she wasn't trying to end up dead.

"Okay, well, at least chill with me for the rest of the day, and then let's hang out later tonight or tomorrow, or something."

Simone agreed.

The two of them ended up driving to Simone's house, where Simone parked her car and got into Jasmine's truck, and they headed out to Bell Boulevard, in Bayside, Queens.

On the plane Jasmine had made up her mind to get a tattoo, and she wanted to do it right at that moment so she wouldn't change her mind.

"You have got to be the wildest chick I know. You just barely healed up good and you getting a tattoo?"

Jasmine smiled and nodded, maneuvering her truck on the Cross Island Parkway toward the Bell Boulevard exit, and before long the two of them were at a tattoo shop called Murder Inc. Jasmine felt her government-

129

issued phone vibrate, and she looked down and realized it was a text from Agent Gosling that said, That was quick.

It instantly filled Jasmine with anxiety. She knew that the clock was ticking, in terms of how much time she had to come up with the information they needed, or else her ass was going back to jail. And, to make matters worse, she had to figure out how to delete some of the conversation that she and Nico had, when he basically put Shabazz's murder squarely on her.

She responded, Yeah, we'll talk. Working on something

She had to quickly make a move and get her ass in the streets, so she could at least give the FBI some of what they wanted.

Jasmine put her phone away, blew out some air from her lungs, and turned off the ignition. "Let's go do this," she said to Simone, even though Simone wasn't getting a tattoo.

"You are crazy. On your neck? Jasmine, you sure you want to do this?"

"Positive!" Jasmine shot back as they walked toward the shop. "On my neck I am going to get a tattoo in cursive letters that says LOVE IS CURSED. And on my hand I'm going to get a cobra tattoo."

"And you thought about this already?"

"Yup."

◆◆◆

Jasmine was excited by how her tattoos turned out. Her excitement didn't last too long, though, because Agent Gosling was texting her again and asking when could they meet.

Jasmine sent back Soon. Just give me a little more time. You'll be happy.

And before should could look at her tattoos for a full five minutes, she began plotting and scheming about how she could quickly get close to Black Justice.

TWENTY-ONE

Bebo's wake was a mad house with people wall to wall. There were relatives, baby mommas, friends, undercover police and federal agents, and celebrities. Almost all of the members of Ghetto Mafia were present, but Nico, BJ, and Lorenzo, BJ's cousin and right-hand man, were all noticeably absent.

As people milled about and huddled in their circles of two, three, and four, rumors about why Nico wasn't there began to surface. Some people had heard that it was Bebo who had shot Nico's girl, Jasmine. Others dismissed that rumor as nothing but bullshit, while still others believed it and fed into it. For those who believed it, they all agreed that Bebo was dead simply because Nico had retaliated, like any real man would have.

Others believed that the two masked men who had gunned down Bebo were BJ and Lorenzo because Nico would send his two lieutenants to carry out his orders for him, instead of doing the dirty work himself.

Two and a half hours had passed, and many people had kissed Bebo's cold, lifeless body as it lay inside a twenty-thousand-dollar casket. The undercover cops and federal agents discreetly milled around and mixed in like regular mourners while subtly taking photos and video both inside and outside the funeral.

With about a half an hour left in the wake, Nico, BJ, and Lorenzo pulled up to the funeral home on Linden Boulevard in Nico's Maybach, driven by Nico's most trusted driver. Nico's driver illegally parked the Maybach in front of the funeral home and got out and opened the rear door so that Nico, BJ, and Lo could exit the vehicle.

It was dark outside, and the curtains inside the Maybach were drawn, so no one knew who was inside, until Nico and his two homies emerged. Immediately the three of them began to get a lot of love from the different mourners.

"Keep ya head up, my niggas," a Queens thug said to Nico, BJ, and Lo after he exhaled smoke from a blunt.

Nico nodded to him, and they kept it moving. Nico led the way, followed by BJ and Lo.

It seemed as if everybody wanted to give Nico a pound and a hug, and in the process it took them about twenty minutes to make it inside the funeral home. The three of them made their way to the front row of the mourners, and they each addressed the family one by one, shaking their hands and telling them that they were sorry for the loss they had suffered.

"Auntie Rose," Nico said to Bebo's aunt. He too called her auntie because she always cooked tons of food for him and all of Bebo's crew, and she was like an aunt to everybody. "You was like a mother to Bebo, and you like a mother to me. That's not going to change. Whatever you need, just let me know, and I'll always be there for you," Nico added directly into her ear while he held on to her hand.

Auntie Rose squeezed Nico's hand and pulled him toward her, so she could now speak directly into his ear. "Just promise me you'll find the people who killed my nephew."

Nico didn't know what exactly to say. He felt so fucked up at that moment, knowing that Auntie Rose was looking right at her nephew's killer. "Most definitely." Then he patted her on the shoulder and kept it moving.

By this time BJ and Lo were both already at the Bebo's casket looking at his body. All BJ could think about was the day he had murdered Bebo, and now there he was standing at the casket, looking at his victim. Deep down inside he knew that he had carried out the proper justice because

Bebo had broken codes of the street and therefore deserved to die.

Nico touched the side of the casket—a casket he had paid for—and stared at Bebo. All Nico could think was that they wouldn't have been there if Bebo hadn't tried to kill Jasmine and hadn't let his ego get the better of him.

The three of them stayed at Bebo's casket for about two minutes, and then one by one they turned and walked away from the casket and out of the funeral home. Lo took out a cigarette and offered one to BJ. Nico didn't want one, but he stood on the steps of the funeral home while Lo and BJ smoked.

"That shit is fucked up," Lo said.

BJ knew how to keep his mouth shut, so he had never even told his cousin Lo that it was him and Nico who had murdered Bebo.

"That's the streets," Nico replied real coldly.

"Word up," BJ added.

It was starting to drizzle lightly, and although the wake was nearing its end, it seemed as if there were now more people standing outside the funeral home than at any other time during the wake.

The funeral was scheduled for the next day, Friday morning at 9 A.M., at Allen A.M.E Cathedral, which wasn't too far from the funeral home.

"So in the morning we riding together or what?" Lo asked BJ and Nico as they continued to stand on the steps.

Before either Nico or BJ could answer, an all-black Hummer SUV sped up to the front of the funeral home. The Hummer, driving eastbound on Linden Boulevard, was driving so fast, people had to scurry out of the way to avoid getting hit.

As the Hummer came to a skidding halt on the slick roads, the front and rear passenger side windows both rolled down, and masked gunmen in the front and back seat both stretched their bodies out of the windows and started firing toward Nico, BJ, and Lo.

"Oh shit!" BJ hollered, ducking for cover behind one of the funeral home's wooden pillars.

The gunman in the front passenger seat had fired off sixteen shots from a 9mm handgun and was quickly out of bullets. He pulled his body back inside the Hummer and began to urge the driver to pull off. "Drive, nigga! Drive!" he yelled.

The driver didn't listen because he didn't want to pull off too quickly and have his other homeboy fall out of the rear passenger window.

TATATATATATATATATATATATATAT

That was the sound of gunfire coming from the second gunman's Calico M960 that had the capability of letting off 750 rounds a minute. Luckily for all of the innocent bystanders, he only had a one-hundred-round magazine in the gun.

After emptying the magazine, the gunman slipped his body back inside the truck, and it peeled off down busy Linden Boulevard before making a quick right turn onto 195th Street.

Within seconds, police and ambulance sirens could be heard blaring from every direction.

Lo had been hit multiple times in the back, legs, and ass, and was laying on the steps of the funeral bleeding and writhing in pain.

BJ had also been shot multiple times. He was hit in the stomach and in his right arm. He was doubled over in pain and hiding in bushes he'd jumped behind after unwisely stepping from behind the wooden pillar.

Everyone outside the funeral home began screaming when the shots rang out, and a good majority of them rushed into the funeral home fleeing from bullets.

Nico had managed to make it inside the funeral home. He was kicking himself for not being strapped. He was trying to figure out which way to go, and then he saw a sign that said "exit" and he headed toward it and ran down some steps that led to the basement. In the basement there were about five dead bodies on silver tables and there were caskets everywhere. Nico saw another exit sign all the way on the other side of the basement, and he bolted toward it. He was breathing hard and moving as fast as he could.

Nico knew that he shouldn't have come to Bebo's wake, but he'd gone against his better judgment. Now he felt like he was going to have to pay for it with his life.

He pushed open the other basement door, and that triggered a loud alarm that scared the shit out of him. When he emerged from that door, he realized he was in the back of the funeral home. He saw people running down the street in a panic.

At that point he didn't hear any more gunshots, but he did hear a ton of police sirens, so he figured he was safe. He leaned against the brick rear wall of the funeral home and tried his best to catch his breath. It was at that moment that he realized that BJ and Lo weren't following behind him.

"Muthafucka!" Nico yelled out loud. He then left safety and ran down the block toward the funeral home. He was running in the opposite direction of all of the people who were trying to get away.

As soon as Nico made it to the front of the funeral home, he saw twelve different people, who had been shot, lying on the ground. Including a four-year-old girl.

He looked for BJ and Lo and saw them both on the ground, and from his vantage point, they both looked as if they weren't moving. "Ahhh fuck!" he hollered.

Cops had quickly roped off the scene with police tape, and where there wasn't police tape, the cops wouldn't let anyone near the funeral home. They were trying their best to clear everybody from the streets.

Nico's driver had been forced to move the Maybach, so Nico couldn't locate his car. But it wasn't his car that he was concerned about; he was worried about his two homeboys. When he was prevented from getting closer to them, he had no choice but to think the worst.

Nico helplessly looked on at the chaos until he was forced by police to leave the scene, which he reluctantly did. He later learned that fifteen people had been shot—four fatally—and more than twenty people who hadn't been shot were also injured. He had gotten no word from BJ or Lo, and his calls and texts to their phones went unanswered.

TWENTY-TWO

The morning after the shooting at the funeral home, Agent Gosling called Jasmine on her government-issued BlackBerry. Jasmine was hesitant to answer, but she didn't want to duck him, only to have him pop up unexpectedly in person somewhere.

"Can you talk?" Gosling asked.

"Yeah, I can talk."

"Talk to me about the shooting last night at Bebo's wake."

Jasmine paused.

"What is Nico saying? The funeral is this morning. Is he going?"

"Listen, things have been so crazy and happening so fast, I haven't even seen Nico since I got back from Vegas. I'm going to—"

"Let me explain something to you, Jasmine. I need you to treat this like it's a full-time job. You need to eat, drink, shit, and sleep what you agreed to, and cut out this half-ass bullshit you've been offering up."

"But I'm trying. You just don't understand."

"Well, try harder. I need information, and you're not giving me anything. Before you left for Vegas, you had nothing. You go out to Vegas and come back with nothing. There is a major shooting, and you have nothing. You do understand what we agreed to, right?"

"Yes," Jasmine meekly replied.

"Well, then what's the problem?"

Jasmine sighed. She was tired of getting chewed out. "I just need more time."

"Time? That's all I keep hearing: you need time."

Getting close to Nico was going to be tough, but she didn't want to tell Gosling that. She also didn't want to tell him that she had found out where Black Justice hung out and that she had formulated a plan to get close to him. What she wanted to do was first get something concrete and then let Gosling know what she had come up with.

"How much time do you need?" Gosling asked in a disgusted tone.

"Two weeks."

"Two weeks . . . "

Jasmine waited for Agent Gosling to tell her how he was going to throw her black ass in jail if she didn't come up with the info they needed.

"I tell you what. Make it a full thirty days. But in thirty days I don't want any excuses. None. Are we clear?"

A slight smile appeared across her face. "No excuses."

After the call ended, Jasmine went back to the mirror and continued to examine the tattoo on her neck. She loved the way the tattoo looked, even though it would take at least another two weeks for it to fully heal.

Jasmine had heard that on Friday nights Black Justice could usually be found at a strip club called Sue's Rendezvous. Sue's was located in his hometown of Yonkers, which wasn't too far from the Bronx and Harlem, areas of New York that Black Justice pretty much controlled.

Jasmine and Simone weren't the biggest fans of strip clubs, but Jasmine had convinced Simone to go with her to Yonkers. She explained to Simone that they had spent too much time fucking with dudes from Brooklyn and Queens, and that it was time for them to start mixing it up with dudes from Harlem and Bronx.

Simone continually stayed on the prowl, hoping to land a baller who would spoil her and take care of her, so it didn't take much convincing. The only thing Simone couldn't understand was why Jasmine wanted to play with fire. Simone couldn't exactly put her finger on it, but she instinctively knew that things were on a downward spiral between Nico and Jasmine.

◆◆◆

It turned out that Jasmine and Simone had picked the right night to go to Sue's Rendezvous. Two of the chicks from Basketball Wives were scheduled to make an appearance at the club, and a popular porn star was also dancing there that night. When Jasmine and Simone pulled up to the club at one o'clock in the morning, the streets were flooded with high-end cars, and there was a long line of people waiting to get in.

Jasmine didn't want to spend fifteen minutes circling around looking for a parking spot, so she let the valet park her truck for her, and she and Simone made their way toward the entrance of the club.

It was summer time, so Jasmine was wearing a pair of tight shorts and a twelve-hundred-dollar pair of black Jimmy Choo peep-toe suede shoes with a five-inch heel and back zip. Simone was also dressed sexy, but she was more conservative with a pair of form-fitting jeans and much less expensive high heels.

As the two of them approached the front of the club, a bouncer spotted them and called out to them. "It's just the two y'all? No dudes?"

"Yeah, just me and her." Jasmine smiled.

"Okay, that's what's up. Y'all don't have to wait on line. Just stand right here, and as soon as he's done with them, he'll frisk y'all, and y'all can go right in."

"Thank you," Simone responded.

"Do me a favor and open up your bags, so he can check those too."

Before long Jasmine and Simone had been frisked, and they both paid their twenty-dollar cover charge to get in. When they walked into the club, they quickly saw how rammed it was.

"This shit is way too packed up in here!" Simone screamed into Jasmine's ear.

Jasmine ignored Simone. She started looking around to see who she knew and tried to figure out where to go. Simone wanted to go to the bar area next to the main stage, but Jasmine wanted to get closer to the tables, where all the ballers were poppin' bottles.

Jasmine felt somebody tug on her arm. She turned around and saw Ish, who was part of Ghetto Mafia and real cool with Nico. That was just what Jasmine didn't want. She hoped she didn't see anybody she knew.

"Hey, baby," Jasmine yelled with a smile. She gave Ish a kiss on his cheek. "What you doing here?"

"What the fuck you doing up in here? That's the question."

"I just needed to get out. I been cooped up in the house ever since I got shot, and this is my first time out," Jasmine yelled into his ear.

"Oh, right, right. The streets is crazy right now. You got shot, Bebo got murked, then Lo. Shit is on fire."

Jasmine had heard about BJ and Lo getting shot, but she didn't know if Ish was trying to say that Lo had died, and she didn't want to ask any questions.

"Exactly. That's why I just wanted to get out and get my mind off everything, and when I heard my girl Tami from Basketball Wives was going to be here, I had to come."

"Oh, so that's what the fuck you doing here. That Basketball Wives shit. I feel you. Nico coming through too?"

Jasmine shrugged her shoulders. "Ish, you ever met my girl Simone?"

Ish squinted his eyes to look at Simone, who was attracted to him from the moment she saw him. Ish had that thugged-out look that she loved. He had a deep caramel complexion and full lips and hazel eyes. Ish was about six two, and two hundred pounds of lean muscle, and his deep-set eyes gave him a very menacing appearance.

"Nah, I don't think I ever met shorty before." Ish smiled as he extended his hand to Simone.

"Well, buy her a drink and a lap dance and then get to know her," Jasmine playfully commanded.

"No doubt, no doubt."

"The drink would be fine, but no lap dances, thank you very much."

Simone was "strictly dickly." In fact, she'd told Jasmine that the strippers had better not come near her, trying to grind and dance on her. Simone followed Ish, and they made their way to the bar.

Jasmine walked through the club, and before long she spotted Black Justice sitting with about five other dudes who were drinking and tossing money at strippers. She got as close as she could to him and his crew, and then she found a seat and started to move her body to the music.

One of the dudes with Black Justice asked her, "Want a drink, ma?"

Jasmine nodded, and within seconds the dude poured her a glass of Ace of Spades. Jasmine thanked him and started sipping the champagne.

"So what's your name?" he asked.

"Ask your boy. He knows who I am."

"Who? Black Jus?"

Jasmine sipped more of her champagne and nodded. Then she put the drink down and stood up and started dancing by herself to one of Drake's hit songs.

The dude told Black Jus what she said, and Black Jus looked in her direction and stared at her, trying to remember her name. Black Justice was a half-black, half-Colombian pretty boy who had fucked many bad chicks in his lifetime. He was trying to remember if he had fucked Jasmine.

The dude who had given Jasmine the drink walked back up to her and told her that Jus wanted to see her. Jasmine nodded and turned around and looked in Black Justice's direction. She kept dancing and waved at him, and then she signaled for him to give her a minute. She didn't want to seem all eager and desperate. When the song ended, Jasmine made her way over to Black Jus, who stood up as she approached.

He looked at the tattoo on her neck. "Love is cursed—I like that. You just got that tat?"

"Thank you," Jasmine replied. "Yeah, I just got it."

"Yo, I know that I know you, but I'm trying to figure out from where."

Jasmine gave Black Jus a disgusted look. "Jasmine."

"Right, right. You from Queens, right?"

Jasmine nodded and smiled.

"You used to fuck with that nigga Shabazz?"

"Yo, I swear me and Shabazz might as well have been married or some shit. Everybody links me to him, and I wasn't even fuckin' with him for that long before he got killed."

"So what's up wit'chu?"

"I'm just doing me right now, trying to make my own moves."

"Whatchu mean?"

Jasmine looked at Black Jus, and then she drank some more of her champagne. "It's too noisy in here. I can't really talk like I want to, but I gotta get wit'chu and discuss something."

"Fuck the music! Let's talk now."

Jasmine didn't want to talk right then and there because she wanted to record the conversation. Turning on the recorder at that point wouldn't have made any sense because the music would have drowned them out.

Jasmine stood on her tippy toes and yelled into Black Justice's right ear. "Here's what it is. I just need a new connect right now. I got this nigga from North Carolina, and I had him going through Ghetto Mafia niggas, but you know how hot shit is right now with them."

Black Justice was as greedy as any drug dealer, and the only thing he cared about more than money was his looks.

"So what's good, ma? Talk to me. He lookin' for weight?"

Jasmine nodded her head.

"I gotchu. You know how I gets down."

Jasmine smiled.

"So you fuckin' with that nigga? It's your man or what?"

"Something like that."

"Whatchu mean?"

"I mean, I ain't trying to tie my pussy down."

Black Justice laughed, and then his man came with a brand-new bottle of Hennessy and handed it to him.

"You want some?" he asked Jasmine.

Jasmine shook her head. "So let me get your number because I see you about to get twisted."

Black Justice took out his cell phone and gave Jasmine his number. "Call me right now, and I'll lock you into my phone, and you can lock me into yours."

Jasmine didn't know which number to give him, but something told her to just give him the FBI-issued number, and that's what she did. She took out her FBI BlackBerry and dialed his number.

"Two-five-two?" Black Justice commented, referring to the area code of Jasmine's number.

Jasmine froze because she didn't have a ready-made excuse as to why the number was out of state. In fact, that was the first time it had dawned on her that she should have known the number.

"Yeah." Jasmine nonchalantly locked in Black Justice's number.

"Oh, that's that North Carolina area code, right?"

Jasmine's heart began to race. She didn't know what to say because she had no idea if it was in fact a North Carolina area code. She just smiled and nodded.

Jasmine and Simone both ended up having a great time at the strip club. Simone had managed to hook up with Ish, and Jasmine had made the initial inroads into Black Justice.

Jasmine was able to exhale later that night. She knew the "confidential informant gods" were on her side because, as luck would have it, the 2-5-2 area code was, in fact, a North Carolina area code.

TWENTY-THREE

The following afternoon, Black Justice found himself waking up next to a stripper named Bella, who had recently relocated from Miami. Although Bella had a small frame, she had a huge ass, which was what had attracted Black Justice to her. In spite of Bella's ass, Black Justice found himself unable to get his mind off Jasmine. He got out of the bed and walked over to the vertical mirror on the back of his bedroom door.

"We would have some cute kids," Bella said as she partially sat up in the bed with her elbow on her pillow and the palm of her hand supporting her head.

Black Justice walked into the bathroom and put water in his hands and then ran it back and forth through his hair, causing it to curl. He then went back into the bedroom and looked at himself again in the mirror.

"Yeah, we would have some fly-ass seeds," he replied.

Bella got out of the bed, walked up to him, and rubbed on his dick.

"I'm good, ma."

"You good?" Bella smiled as she continued to rub on his dick.

Bella was always trying to use her position as a stripper to land a baller like Black Justice, and now that she had one in front of her, she felt like she had to impress him with her sex skills as much as she could. She had already let Black Justice fuck her when they'd come home from the club, but she wanted to exhaust him with her pussy.

"I said I was good." Black Justice pushed Bella away. It wasn't a hard push, but it got her attention. "I'm going to the barbershop, and then I got some moves to make."

"Oh, okay."

There was a moment of awkward silence as Black Jus looked through his phone.

"So can I chill here until you get back?"

Black Jus didn't say anything as he put on his watch and chain and walked into the bathroom to brush his teeth.

Bella wanted to jump in the shower, but she decided against it. She just threw on the same pair of thongs and the same bra that she'd had on the previous night, and she started to get dressed.

"I got another shorty coming through in about a hour or two; otherwise, I would let you chill with me until I get back."

Bella felt like shit after that comment, but she was sort of used to being treated like a whore. She tried to play things off like it didn't affect her. "So you a pretty boy playa? Playa, playa, playa," she chuckled and said.

Black Justice smiled as he looked into his mirror again. Then he put on some cologne before quickly getting dressed.

"I just do my thing. You feel me?"

Bella nodded as she put on her stilettos. Then she grabbed her bag, walked up to Black Jus, and kissed him on the lips. "Call me if you ever need me."

"No doubt." Black Justice reached into the pocket of the jeans he'd worn the night before and pulled out a wad of cash. After peeling off three hundred dollars, he threw the jeans to the ground and handed Bella the cash.

"Thank you, sweetie." Bella gave Black Jus another kiss.

"Yo, how these kicks look with these jeans?"

"It's official." Bella was surprised at how vain Black Jus was. She had been around a lot of thugs in her short lifetime, but Black Jus was definitely more preoccupied with his appearance than any other dude she knew.

Bella made her way out of the house and into her Mitsubishi Galant, and she headed to her Harlem apartment.

Black Jus ignored the missed calls he had on his phone from about five different chicks and called Jasmine.

"Hey," Jasmine replied after answering on the third ring.

"What's good?"

She stretched and yawned at the same time. "Nothing. Just woke up."

"So, yo, I'm heading to the barbershop. What you doing later? Why don't you come through?"

Jasmine didn't respond.

"Hello?"

"Come through where?"

"To the crib."

Jasmine knew that if she went to Black Justice's crib that he would make a move on her and try to fuck her. She remembered Gosling's warnings about no sexual involvement with any of the targets. "Jus, I told you I got a man. I can't disrespect him like that."

Black Jus was quiet.

"You understand what I'm saying?"

"Yeah, yeah, so just come through anyway, so we can chop it up about what we was talking about last night."

Jasmine knew she had to get something incriminating on Black Jus, and therefore she had to play the game on his terms. So she got his address and made plans to meet up with him at his crib at four o'clock.

◆◆◆

At four o'clock Jasmine found herself at Black Justice's huge New Rochelle home just off North Avenue in Westchester County.

Black Jus opened the front door to his house. "You found it okay?"

"GPS." Jasmine smiled while her Blackberry lay in her bag recording everything that was said. "You have a nice house." The house was nice, but it couldn't touch Nico's estate.

"Yeah, it's cool. It's quiet up here, you know, when you want to get away from all the noise and drama."

Jasmine nodded. "Does Irv Gotti live around here?"

"Yeah, that punk-ass nigga live about two blocks away."

Jasmine chuckled. "I thought so." She had been to a party before at his house and thought the area looked familiar.

"So them Ghetto Mafia niggas is dropping like flies," Black Jus commented. He was referring to Lorenzo, who had succumbed to the gunshot wounds.

"Yeah, that's so fucked up." Jasmine had always thought that Lo, like BJ, was so cool.

Jasmine hadn't spoken to Nico, but with Lo's death, she knew she would hear from him soon and, at the very least, would find out about funeral arrangements and would run into him at Lo's funeral.

"So shit is fucked up with them?" Black Jus asked.

Jasmine caught on really quick to what Black Jus was saying. "Yeah, I mean, I don't exactly know what's going on. I mean, they can get product, but the shit is just real weak, you know?"

Black Jus smiled. He loved to hear about the failings of his enemies.

"Muthafuckas don't know what they doin'. See, a nigga like me, I gets that fish scale straight off the boat! You feel me now?" He reached behind a picture frame on the mantle of his granite-finished fireplace and held up a brick of cocaine.

Jasmine smiled.

"Ain't nobody in New York fuckin' with the quality of this shit."

"Jus, you are crazy! You keep them bricks in your crib like that?"

Black Jus nodded once as he put the kilo back behind the picture frame. "It's different up here. You want anything to drink?" He walked into his kitchen and handed her a Corona before she could even respond and took out a Heineken for himself.

Black Jus opened both bottles, and he then got a lime and cut a piece of it and handed it to Jasmine for her Corona.

"What you mean, it's different up here?"

"New York City, you got the biggest gang in the world that you going up against, the NYPD. Them NYPD cats is forty thousand cops strong. That shit is like a small muthafuckin' army. But out here, New Rochelle, they got their own little police department. And that shit is like fuckin' with Boss Hog and that Dukes of Hazzard shit. You understand what I'm saying?" He laughed.

"Nah, you lost me."

Black Jus took a swig of his Heineken and then explained to Jasmine that, with a smaller police force like New Rochelle's, it was real easy to get to the top people in the department and have them on the take.

"Ohhh, okay, I gotchu. So they on the payroll?"

"Exactly." Black Jus smiled before he guzzled down the rest of the Heineken and cracked open another one.

"I got a two-year-old daughter and a four-year-old son, but word is bond, I done already put about five kids through college already. And all they daddies are cops."

Jasmine smiled and sipped on her Corona. Having that admission on tape alone was enough to start an investigation into a corrupt police force.

"You heard of diplomatic immunity? What I got up here in Westchester County, I call that shit 'thugmatic' immunity. You feel me?" Black Jus laughed.

He walked back into the living room and examined his hair in the mirror. "Yo, I hate the way this muthafucka lined my shit up. Every time my barber ain't around and I fuck with one of them young barbers, they fuck my shit up!"

Jasmine had no idea why he was complaining because his hair looked perfect, like he could immediately go do a photo shoot for a Sean John ad campaign or something.

"Aight, so let's talk business. Your man is really moving weight down there in North Carolina or what? What would he need? He ain't just sticking his toe in the water on some bullshit, is he?"

"I mean, I don't want to talk for him, but I would say definitely like nine ki's or better."

"Nine ki's?"

Jasmine figured that using some random uneven number like nine was the best way to avoid suspicion. Nico had once told her that undercover cops and feds always made the mistake of trying to buy shit in perfectly even numbers, and to him that was a red flag that would make him proceed with caution.

"Yeah, but if you don't got nine, then I'm sure he would—"

"Nah, nah, nah, I got it. That ain't no problem."

"What part of North Carolina you said he was from again?"

Jasmine began to panic because she couldn't remember if she had said a particular area, and she didn't want to make a mistake and get caught in a lie. She blew out air from her lungs.

"Okay, look. Please, whatever you do, when you meet the nigga, don't relay none of this shit, because he would kick my muthafuckin' ass."

"Yeah, yeah. I don't run my mouth like that. What's up?"

"See, you know them colleges like Duke and the University of North Carolina?"

"Yeah."

"That whole college scene, and all them white boys with the rich parents, he got that whole shit on lock."

Black Jus smiled and nodded because that explained why her boyfriend was moving so much product in North Carolina.

"So listen. He gave me twenty-five hundred to purchase an ounce from you, you know, just so he could sample it and shit."

"That ain't nothing."

"No, but it is. The thing is, I already spent most of the money, and right now all I got is a grand on me."

"So I'll get you half an ounce."

"Okay, thank you."

"I gotchu." Black Jus moved closer to Jasmine. "I wanted to get wit'chu ever since I used to see you out with that nigga Shabazz."

Jasmine moved back. "Oh, really?" She smiled.

Black Jus nodded. He looked possessed—like he just wanted to bend Jasmine over right there in his living room and fuck her. He came closer, but she held out her hand and stretched out her arm and held Black Jus at bay.

She told him, "Don't even do that."

"Do what?"

"Push up on me like that. With the harem of bitches that I'm sure you got, I ain't trying to be in your stable."

"What women?" Black Jus leaned in and tried to kiss Jasmine.

"Jus, as good as you look, stop it."

"Don't nobody got to know nothing. It's just me and you right now. Your man ain't here, and my girl ain't here."

"I know that." Jasmine managed to escape from his clutches and went into her bag. "Let's just keep it about business, though. Here, let me give you this money." She tried to discreetly stop the recording device, but since she couldn't do it without making it obvious, she gave up on the idea. She pulled out the cash and counted off a thousand dollars.

Black Jus took hold of the money and counted it. He then told Jasmine that he didn't feel like getting out a scale and chopping up a brick just to weigh out a half ounce of coke. It was like he felt like he needed to impress her. He told her that when they left his crib, he would drive her to get the half-ounce of cocaine and then take her to some different spots in Yonkers.

Jasmine told him that she was okay with that plan. She knew that Black Jus was now going to go real hard at her and try to fuck her, but she had made up her mind to be strong and not give in to him and to only promise him that she would let him fuck her later, just not then and there.

Jasmine knew how to play the game. The best bait was the prospect of him fucking her. In fact, the prospect of pussy was even more powerful than the pussy itself. And it was the prospect of getting at Jasmine's pussy that had allowed Black Jus to let his guard down, and with his loose lips and his huge ego, he walked right down the road she wanted him to walk down.

TWENTY-FOUR

Nico had not left Jamaica Hospital since the night of the shooting at the funeral home when both BJ and Lo were rushed to the trauma unit. That would be the equivalent of betraying his two most trusted lieutenants. He was at the hospital when BJ came out of surgery. The doctors told him that the prognosis was good, and it looked like BJ would pull through.

But then a different set of surgeons informed him that they had tried everything they could but weren't able to save Lo. Nico was devastated. He felt all kinds of guilt because he was certain that Lo would be alive and that BJ wouldn't be clinging to life if he'd followed his gut and skipped Bebo's wake.

It was nearly four in the morning when he decided to call Jasmine from the hospital. His cell phone battery had died, but one of the nurses was kind enough to let him use the phone at the nurses' station. When Jasmine didn't pick up, he decided against leaving a message and ended the call. He desperately needed somebody to talk to, share his pain with, and he knew that regardless of any past drama, she would be there for him. It was late, so he figured Jasmine was sleeping. He decided he would just drive home to Long Island when he left the hospital and give her the news about Lo face to face.

"You okay?" the nurse asked Nico after he hung up the phone.

"Yeah, I'm good."

"Listen, I'm not supposed to do this, but the staffing is real light at this time of night, and the anesthesia should be wearing off right about now, so if you want, I can take you in to see your friend but only very briefly," the head nurse explained to Nico.

"That's what's up. I would appreciate that."

The head nurse stood up from her leather chair and looked around and saw that, aside from a janitor, the hallways were empty, and she told Nico to follow her. The two of them made it to BJ's room in the intensive care unit, and she opened the door and let Nico inside.

"No more than five minutes, okay?"

"Okay," Nico responded.

Nico closed the door behind him and walked up to the side of BJ's bed. BJ was almost unrecognizable because of all the bandages and surgical tape, and the wires, IVs, and monitors attached to him, and the breathing tube attached to his mouth. He noticed the Velcro handcuffs on BJ's arms, hooking his wrists to the bed railing to prevent him from trying to remove any of the medical equipment.

"BJ, it's Nico. Can you hear me?"

BJ was silent, his eyes closed.

Nico was as tough as they come, but the sight of his homie in that condition almost made him shed tears. He undid the Velcro handcuff on BJ's right wrist and clutched his hand.

"BJ, it's me, Nico." He could feel BJ starting to squeeze his hand. That was the best feeling. It felt like a surge of electricity shot through his body when BJ squeezed his hand. "You gonna be all right, my nigga. I promise you that."

BJ squeezed Nico's hand. Nico could see that BJ was starting to sweat. He looked around and he saw a box of napkins, took a few, and then blotted the sweat from BJ's brow.

After he did that, Nico could see BJ trying to motion something to him. BJ couldn't talk if he wanted to, because of the breathing tube attached to his mouth.

Nico tried to figure out what was going on, and was wondering if he should call the nurse. But then he realized BJ was motioning for a pen or a pencil so he could write something. Nico told BJ to relax, that he would be right back with a pen and paper. He quickly left the room and approached the nurse, who gave him a pen and a small notepad, and reminded him that he only had a few more minutes in the room. Nico assured her that he wouldn't be long and quickly made it back to BJ's room, where he put the pen in BJ's hand and held the pad for him.

BJ mustered up all the strength he could and struggled to write the letters L and O.

Nico held on to BJ's hand and squeezed. He didn't want to tell him anything about Lo at that point because he knew BJ needed to focus all of his strength and energy on trying to recover from his own wounds.

"Everything is good. Don't worry about nothing. Just relax, so we can get you healed up and outta here."

BJ motioned for the pad, and Nico again positioned it so he could write.

BJ then scribbled the words NO KIDS. BJ didn't want his kids to come to the hospital and see him like that. Nico reassured him that he would get word back to his girl and make sure that she didn't bring the kids with her to the hospital.

The nurse walked into the room and told Nico that he had to go. Nico told BJ that they were making him leave and that he would be back to check on him the next day.

Nico felt drained when he left the hospital and made it down to the parking lot, where his driver was waiting for him. He instructed the driver to take him to his crib out on Long Island. The roads were deserted because it was nearly the break of dawn and no one was out, which allowed Nico to make it to his house rather quickly.

When he realized Jasmine wasn't home, he decided to have his driver drop him by Mia's house. Without calling before showing up, Nico arrived and let himself in with his own key.

"Oh my God!" Mia screamed out when she awoke to feel Nico touching her.

Mia wasn't expecting Nico, or anyone else for that matter, and since she had withdrawn that cash from the safety deposit box earlier that day, she was terrified that someone had broken into her house to rob her.

"Baby, it's me," Nico said.

"Ugggghhh! My God! You scared the shit outta me! Why didn't you call before you came?" Mia sat up in the bed and turned on the lamp on her nightstand. She saw that Nico looked kind of ragged, and she then asked if everything was ok.

"Lo got killed."

"What? Baby, oh no."

"BJ is in ICU. Shit is so fuckin' crazy right now, I don't know." Nico sat down on the bed and ran his hand down his face.

Mia, in her short lace nightie, positioned herself behind Nico on the bed and began to massage his shoulders. "What happened?"

"We was leaving Bebo's funeral, over on Linden, and muthafuckas pulled up in a Hummer or some shit and just sprayed everybody. The shit was a zoo. Niggas was running, and bitches was screaming and shit. BJ and Lo got hit. Ambulances and five-o came, rushed them to the trauma unit and . . . "

Nico stopped talking in the middle of what he was saying, and Mia knew not to push for more information. She just wrapped her arms around him and hugged him real tight and told him that she was so glad he was okay.

"It ain't about me, though."

"I know, baby, but if something had happened to you, I couldn't live."

Mia then thought about the money hidden inside her freezer. She knew she couldn't let Nico know about it. "Do you know who was shooting?"

Nico slowly shook his head, and then he stood up from the bed. "I don't know, but I'm going to find out."

Mia was quiet, and so was Nico.

Mia knew Nico really well and could always read his vibes. "What you thinking about, baby? You can talk to me."

Nico blew out air from his lungs and fell backwards on the bed, his face to the ceiling.

"I need you to go down to Miami to take care of some business for me. I'll be down there with you as soon as I can. I gotta handle this shit in New York first, though," Nico explained.

Mia had heard Nico talking about Miami before and knew he was starting to get a lot of money down there with the Haitians, but she didn't know exactly what he needed her to do.

"I'm here for you, baby." Mia got on top of him and kissed him softly on his lips and neck. She then positioned herself next to Nico and lay with her left arm draped over him. "Everything is going to be okay."

Nico just nodded. He was worried about what his future held. For the first time in a while, he felt like his chances of being killed were much greater than his chances of being locked up, and he seriously wondered to himself if it was all worth it.

TWENTY-FIVE

B lack Justice took Jasmine along with him everywhere he went around town. It allowed her to get a ton of information to take back to Agent Gosling. Black Justice was a dream for Jasmine in terms of the way he constantly bragged and ran his mouth. He had even shown her one of his two stash houses located around the corner from New Rochelle High School.

It was getting tougher and tougher for Jasmine to keep rejecting Black Justice's sexual advances, and she definitely used that to her advantage when it came time for her to meet up with Gosling.

Agent Gosling had actually been forced to go out of town for five days due to a death in his family. So he had to move back his scheduled meeting with Jasmine until the day after he returned from the funeral.

Gosling couldn't wait to meet with Jasmine, and had actually arrived twenty minutes early for their three o'clock meeting at Chipotle in downtown Brooklyn. Unfortunately for him, Jasmine didn't share his enthusiasm, and she showed up late.

"It's three forty," Gosling said to Jasmine.

"Parking is crazy around here. Why did you pick this congested-ass area? And how was your funeral? Who died anyway?"

Gosling shook his head. He knew there was no use in trying to control or discipline Jasmine because she was who she was.

"It was sad. I lost my sixteen-year-old nephew. He died in a car accident."

"Oh, I'm so sorry to hear that," Jasmine said with genuine emotion.

Gosling thanked her, and then the two of them went to the counter and ordered food. They took their food to the seating area upstairs, so they could talk with a little more privacy.

"So I told you to give me some time, and I think you'll be happy."

Gosling knew that Jasmine had been spending a lot of time with Black Justice, because he had two agents follow her everywhere she went when he went out of town for the funeral.

"Talk to me."

Jasmine pulled out her BlackBerry and she had her recorder ready to play at the point that she knew would intrigue Gosling. "Listen to this," she said.

"New York City, you got the biggest gang in the world that you going up against, the NYPD. Them NYPD cats is forty thousand cops strong. That shit is like a small muthafuckin' army. But out here, New Rochelle, they got their own little police department. And that shit is like fuckin' with Boss Hog and that Dukes of Hazzard shit. You understand what I'm saying?"

"Nah, you lost me."

"Ohhh, okay, I gotchu. So they on the payroll?"

"Exactly."

"I got a two-year-old daughter and a four-year-old son, but word is bond, I done already put about five kids through college already. And all they daddies are cops."

Jasmine stopped the playback and took a sip of her margarita.

"That's Black Justice." She reached in her bag, put an ounce of cocaine on the table, and pushed it across the table to Gosling. "I made that purchase from him, which by the way, you need to reimburse me for, and I got him on tape basically admitting that he got the New Rochelle cops in his hip pocket."

Gosling smiled a huge smile because he definitely wasn't expecting the kind of bombshell like the one Jasmine had just dropped on him.

"Wow! Excellent work, Jasmine! This is powerful, very powerful. Much more than I was expecting."

"I know what I'm doing out here. But I just have to say this, and I need you to really hear me. You need to talk to Agent Battle or whoever you got to talk to and get me that apartment ASAP. I mean, on one hand you tell me that under no circumstances am I to fuck anybody, and I'm good with that. But, on the other hand, I need the right tools. I mean, I was going everywhere with Black Justice. He was parading me around town like he was my man and shit. He drove me past one of his stash houses, and he even had me all up inside his own house and all that. So it gets to the point where him or any nigga is gonna want the pussy."

"Please tell me you didn't go there, Jasmine."

"No, I didn't. But what I'm saying is, if I had my own spot, I could control the rules of the game better."

"Give me three days, and you'll have the apartment."

Now that she was giving the FBI what they wanted, it made it much easier for them to give her what she wanted. Gosling was certain that Agent Battle would finally sign off on the apartment paperwork.

"So you said you know about a stash house?"

Jasmine nodded as she ate some more of her food.

"Did you actually go inside the stash house?"

"No, but I'm confident that it really was his stash house. He runs his mouth like a chick, I swear to God." She chuckled.

Gosling nodded in contemplation.

"What are you thinking about?"

Gosling ignored Jasmine's question, shaking his head.

Jasmine then let him have it for not letting her know that the phone he had given her had a North Carolina number, but Gosling insisted that he had informed her of that fact.

"You didn't," she said emphatically.

Gosling didn't fight with her.

"Well, anyway, I did what you told me to do. I made the first purchase and set it up where you are my man from North Carolina and you're looking to buy nine kilos. I also told him you got all the colleges in North Carolina on smash."

"So do you think he would meet with me, or does he want everything to go through you?"

"No, he trusts me. But if we don't meet with him soon that could spook him, and he'll think I'm bullshitting."

"Okay, so nine kilos?"

"Uh-huh."

"You're talking several hundred thousand dollars."

"And?"

"What I'm getting at is, there is a process before I can get that kind of cash allocated to me."

"Oh, my fuckin' god!"

"We can get the money, but we need some time."

Jasmine shook her head. "And meanwhile he's going to keep pushing up on me, trying to fuck me."

"Work something out."

At that moment it was as if Jasmine and Gosling had talked up Black Justice. Her phone began vibrating.

"It's him right here."

"Answer it."

"Hello."

"What's good with your man?" Black Justice asked with his deep, gravelly voice.

"He just got in town today."

"A'ight. That's what's up. So we still doing this or what? Speak to me."

Jasmine paused because she wasn't sure how she should answer. Her heart started pounding, but she thought quickly on her feet.

"Yeah, everything is a go. But what price you talking?"

"For nine, right?"

"You know what? I don't like talking on the phone like this. He's in town. I'll hit you back, and we'll figure out where we can link and talk face to face."

"Jasmine, don't take him to nobody else."

"Jus, we good. Not on the phone, though. I'll hit you back, or you can hit me back in an hour."

"No doubt."

Jasmine looked at her phone to make sure the call had ended.

"I bought you some time, but you gotta get money to make this shit go down. He's going to call me back so we can meet up and talk about price."

Gosling smiled, impressed with Jasmine and the way she was handling herself. For the first time he found himself looking across the table at Jasmine in another light. He had always kept things on the up and up and strictly professional, and he planned on keeping things that way, but he would have been lying to himself if he'd said that he wasn't attracted to her.

"Why you looking at me like that?" Jasmine asked, feeling a bit uncomfortable.

"So love is cursed?"

"Oh, you looking at my tattoo? It's fire, right?"

"No comment."

"No comment? Yeah, okay. All I know is, you better step up your swagger before we meet with Black Justice. Don't come looking as lame as you be looking," Jasmine said with a laugh.

Agent Gosling had conducted many undercover assignments, so he wasn't worried. He knew he would be able to pull off a meeting with Black Justice. He had to end the meeting with Jasmine so he could contact several of the North Carolina field offices to get some names of some of their confidential informants to see if they would be willing to vouch for him, just in case Black Justice started to sniff around and inquire about Gosling.

The meeting ended without Nico's name coming up, nor with any talk of Lo's death or the funeral home shooting. That was fine with Jasmine because she didn't have anything on it. She was starting to think she was smart enough to pull off this confidential informant thing on a long-term basis.

TWENTY-SIX

They met up the next day near the Brooklyn Bridge, where Jasmine parked her car, got in the FBI-issued BMW 760 Agent Gosling was driving, and headed uptown to Manhattan. Jasmine had arranged for the two of them to link up with Black Justice at a Dominican storefront restaurant located off Broadway in the Washington Heights section of Manhattan, of which he was part owner. Black Justice often used a small back office inside the restaurant to conduct business.

When Jasmine and Agent Gosling arrived, they parked their car on the opposite side of the street from the restaurant, crossed the busy street, and made their way inside.

"Hi," a sexy Spanish waitress said to Jasmine and Gosling. "How can I help you?"

The place was small, and there were only six tables where customers could sit down and eat. Mostly it was a take-out restaurant.

Jasmine smiled. "Hi, we're here to see Black Jus."

The waitress nodded and turned around and screamed out something in Spanish to another sexy Spanish lady at the cash register.

"You can have a seat. He should be right out."

Jasmine and Gosling thanked her, and they took a seat inside the tight restaurant.

After about five minutes, a muscular brown-skinned dude standing six foot five and looking like he could play on the defensive line for the New York Giants emerged from the back of the restaurant. Jasmine thought the guy was black, so she was surprised when she heard him speak to the waitress in Spanish. The waitress looked annoyed, and she responded in Spanish with an attitude. She pointed out Jasmine and Gosling, who looked in the direction of the tall dude, and he motioned for them to follow him.

When they made it to the back of the restaurant, he introduced himself as Poppy and shook Jasmine's hand.

"Hi, I'm Jasmine."

Gosling held out his hand for a pound. "Jimmy," Gosling replied. Gosling was a second generation Jamaican who didn't have the slightest bit of a Jamaican accent, yet he'd decided to go with the street name Jamaican Jimmy.

"Watch your step. This floor is slippery," Poppy said as he led them through the kitchen and down a narrow set of metal stairs that led to a basement.

As soon as Jimmy opened the door to the basement, the sound of loud hip-hop could be heard bouncing off the walls, and a strong smell of weed smacked them in the face.

When they made it to the basement, Black Justice was sitting at a metal rectangular desk in front of a huge cage made out of chicken wire with two large pit bulls inside. Both of the dogs had the hugest heads that Jamaican Jimmy had ever seen on a pit bull before. He was certain that somebody had been injecting the dogs with steroids.

Black Justice was eating a plate of Spanish rice and chicken. He nodded to Jasmine and Jamaican Jimmy and motioned for them to have a seat at the two chairs positioned in front of his desk. Poppy stood off to the side.

Jasmine had her recorder on, but with the sound of the music blasting, there was no way it would pick up any conversation. Jimmy didn't tell Jasmine, but he also had a recording device strapped to his ankle inside the brand-new construction-style Timberlands he was wearing.

Black Justice motioned for Poppy to lower the volume on the music, and Poppy turned the music off completely.

"I said turn the shit down, I didn't say turn it off," Black Justice hollered. "That was my shit right there."

Poppy turned the music back up, but not as loud as before. Agent Gosling was glad that Poppy had turned the music down because he was certain his recorder could pick up everything being said.

Black Justice took a pull on the blunt he was smoking and began nodding his head to the music. He then stood up and took another pull before passing it to Poppy.

"Black Justice," he said to Jimmy and extended his hand for a pound.

"Jimmy," Agent Gosling replied as he clasped Black Justice's hand.

"What's good, Jasmine?"

Jasmine smiled. "Nothing. You see we here and we ain't front on you."

Black Justice nodded, and then he sat down and ate some more off his food.

Poppy passed the blunt back to Black Justice, who held it out for Jimmy, but Jimmy held up one of his hands and waved off the weed. Jasmine wanted to cringe, but she held it together. Then she reached over and took the weed from Black Justice and took some pulls on it.

Black Justice asked Jimmy, "You don't smoke?"

Jimmy shook his head.

"He's Jamaican and he don't smoke weed," Jasmine said, trying to ease some of the tension that had suddenly filled the room. "Can you believe that shit?"

"Jamaican Jimmy, I like that," Black Justice said. Then he asked Jimmy if he knew an Italian dude name Joey from North Carolina. "The Italians call him Joey Six-Pack."

"Yeah, I'm cool with him," Jimmy replied.

Joey Six-Pack was an FBI informant the Raleigh, North Carolina field office had briefed Jimmy on.

"Why you ask?"

Black Justice asked, "How you know him?"

"From the fuckin' streets! What the fuck is all these questions for, my dude?"

Black Justice cocked a half smile, and then he asked Jasmine and Jimmy if they wanted anything to eat.

Jimmy said, "Nah, let's just talk business,"

"Jimmy about that bread! My muthafuckin' man." Black Justice stood up, took the remaining scraps of food on his plate over to the dogs, and spilled it into their food bowls. "So what kind of whip Joey pushing now?"

Jasmine was feeling very uncomfortable. She finished the weed and dropped the last of the blunt on the basement floor and stepped on it.

"Joey always switching up cars. The last thing I think he was pushing was a white Range Rover."

Black Justice nodded. "And what about you? I see you got the seven sixty parked outside. What else you got?"

Jimmy and Jasmine both were surprised that Black Justice knew what kind of car they had pulled up in because they hadn't even parked directly in front of the restaurant, and it wasn't like Black Justice or anyone else for that matter had ever seen Jimmy driving around New York.

Jimmy was starting to wonder if Joey Six-Pack and Black Justice had spoken. And with Jimmy not fully knowing Joey Six-Pack's credibility, he wasn't sure what to make of Black Justice's questions.

"I got the NSX. But my main toy is my muthafuckin' sixty-foot Viking Sport Cruiser. Y'all New York niggas ain't up on that shit."

Jasmine had no idea what the hell Jimmy was talking about.

Black Justice looked at Poppy, and he got no response from him.

"The fuck is that?"

"That's my yacht. You need to come down to North Carolina, and we can party on that shit. Bring some New York bitches wit'chu, and trust me when I tell you them bitches will be taking off their panties as soon as they step on that muthafucka."

"Ahhhh shit! Okay. Fuckin' yachts and shit. That's what's up. What that cost you?"

"Seven figures brand-new."

Black Justice sat back down at his desk. He went into the top drawer and pulled out what looked like a pound of weed and sat it down on top of the desk.

"A'ight, so Jasmine said you lookin' for nine kilos."

Jimmy nodded his head. "Nine, maybe more, depends on what price we talking."

"Thirty-five."

"Thirty-five? I got niggas that can beat that."

"The fuck outta here. Ain't nobody beating that price for fish scale."

Jimmy ran his hand across his face. "Do it for thirty."

"You saying you got muthafuckas that'll sell you a kilo for thirty? You full of shit."

Jasmine was getting nervous because she had no idea where Jimmy was going with everything. She couldn't understand why he was haggling like he was at a fucking flea market or something.

"So you got the cash?"

"I wouldn't waste your time."

Black Justice went inside his top drawer once again and this time he pulled out a vanilla Dutch Masters cigar in a plastic clear wrapper and tossed it to Jimmy. He then pushed the bag of weed across the desk toward Jimmy.

"Do me a favor—Twist that up for me," Black Justice said to Jimmy. "I need to think on your price. My mind functions better when I smoke."

Jimmy put the cigar on the table and reminded Black Justice that he didn't smoke.

Jasmine knew that Black Justice was testing Jimmy, who was making one false move after another. Her heart was in her throat.

Black Justice looked over at Poppy, who smiled and motioned his head in Jimmy's direction before gesturing toward his own waistband. Black Justice shook his head to indicate to Poppy that he didn't want him to do anything at that moment.

Jasmine said, "I'll roll the shit up," and she reached for the cigar. She knew in her gut that Jimmy had never rolled up any weed and was hesitating because he didn't want to look stupid.

Black Justice went into the bottom side drawer of his desk and pulled out a chrome .44 Magnum and placed it on top of his desk. "Nah, Jasmine, I want this nigga to twist that shit up for me."

Jimmy didn't know what to say or do.

Black Justice reached forward and grabbed hold of the gun and held it sideways and pointed it directly at Jimmy and Jasmine. "Roll that shit up right now if you and Jasmine wanna walk outta here alive."

Jimmy stood up to his feet and pushed the cigar and the weed off the table and onto the basement floor, and Poppy immediately made a move toward him.

"Nah, Poppy, I got this shit," Black Justice said, his gun aimed at Jimmy.

The pit bulls sensed their master was angry and began barking violently.

"Jus, come on, chill," Jasmine pleaded.

"The fuck this nigga think he is?" Jimmy squinted his eyes, trying to muster up the meanest screw face he could.

Black Justice was watching Jimmy's hands to see if he was going to make a move for a gun and if he did Black Justice was going to blast him.

"You gon' shoot me 'cuz I won't roll your fuckin' weed up? Come on then. Shoot me, nigga!" Jimmy yelled, his open right hand pounding on his chest. "You got big balls! Shoot me, nigga!"

Jasmine's heart was racing more than on the night when Bebo had tried to kill her.

"Jimmy, shut up!" Jasmine pleaded. "Jus, please, come on, this ain't necessary." She stood up.

"Jasmine, who the fuck is this muthafucka?" Black Justice stood up.

"He's my man!"

"Poppy, turn that music all the way up!"

Jasmine was ready to shit and piss on herself.

"What? You think I'm a cop? You think I'm fuckin' five-o?" Jimmy lifted up his shirt to show that he had no gun on him and that he wasn't wearing a wire.

Poppy turned the music up so loud, the sound of the dogs barking could no longer be heard.

Jimmy's heart was racing as his life flashed before his eyes. Not knowing what else to do, he pulled his shirt all the way up and over his head until he was standing there shirtless. Then he reached for his pants and unbuckled the belt and quickly unbuttoned and unzipped his pants and pulled them down to his ankles.

"I ain't no muthafuckin' cop!" Jimmy yelled as he walked around in circles with his pants pulled down to his ankles, exposing his black briefs, and his hands raised above his head.

Jimmy looked as stupid as anyone could look, but he did that to convince Black Justice that he wasn't strapped or wearing a wire. The move was brilliant because, in the process of making himself look like an absolute fool, he still managed to hide the wire strapped to his ankle on the inside of his Timberland boot.

Poppy couldn't help but laugh at Jimmy. Black Justice motioned for Poppy to turn the music down.

Jimmy's heart was coming out of his chest as he stood there with his hands still in the air, the dogs still barking loudly.

"Pull your muthafuckin' pants up!"

Jimmy felt somewhat relieved, but he knew he wasn't out of the woods yet. He quickly scooped his shirt up from off the basement floor and put it on and pulled up his pants.

"The lowest I'm going is three hundred thousand for the nine kilos," Black Justice said. "Have the cash tomorrow. I'll have Poppy hit y'all up to arrange the location."

Jimmy kept quiet, and Jasmine said okay.

Poppy held open the basement door that led upstairs to the kitchen, and Jasmine and Jimmy both headed toward the stairs, Poppy following behind them.

"It's disrespectful not to roll up a man's weed for him when you in his spot," Black Justice said out loud, a sinister grin on his face.

Jasmine, Jimmy, and Poppy made their way up the stairs and out.

"No muthafuckin' games! Word up!" Black Justice shouted out to Jasmine and Jimmy.

Jasmine and Jimmy made it through the restaurant's kitchen and then out the front door. They had never been so happy to see daylight.

"I'll hit y'all and let y'all know what's up," Poppy said to Jasmine and Jimmy just before they walked out of the restaurant.

As soon as they got in the car, Agent Gosling asked Jasmine with a real stern voice. "Where is his fuckin' stash house?"

"I told you to step up your swagger, and you up in there haggling like you at a fuckin' car auction or some shit. He tell you thirty-five, you suppose to roll with that number."

"Where the fuck is the stash house, Jasmine?" Agent Gosling hollered.

Jasmine screamed back at him that it was in Yonkers and that they would have to drive to it and she would be able to point it out.

"Gosling, it's weed we're talking about. Everybody knows how to roll up weed. Oh, my fuckin' God!"

"Look, shut the fuck up!" Gosling was seconds from slapping her. He had just gotten punked by a drug dealer and didn't need Jasmine in his ear.

Gosling drove off, and they headed toward Yonkers. After he had driven about two miles from the restaurant, he pulled the car over, got out, and left it running. He told Jasmine he would be right back.

Gosling called Agent Battle and told her what had just happened at the restaurant. He then told her that he was heading over to Yonkers to drive by Black Justice's stash house and that he would call her back in an hour. He also told he needed her to get a judge to sign off on three emergency warrants—one for the stash house, one for the restaurant, and one for Black Justice's residence. He then cautioned Agent Battle against telling the New Rochelle Police Department about the raids on the stash house and Black Justice's house until all of the FBI teams were in place and were ready to storm the locations.

Gosling was taking a major chance that Jasmine would be right about the location of the stash house; otherwise, it would not only make the FBI look really bad, but it would also put Jasmine's life in jeopardy on the streets of New York. He was going more on emotion than intellect because Black Justice had just played him. He no longer wanted to wait until the next day and show up with the money to do the deal and then make the arrests. He wanted to get Black Justice off the streets that same day for punking him.

TWENTY-SEVEN

Jasmine was shocked when Gosling told her that Black Justice, Poppy, and ten other members of Black Justice's drug organization had been arrested. She didn't feel one ounce of guilt or remorse for the role she played in setting up Black Justice, but she did have doubts about whether major charges would stick. The feds weren't able to catch him red-handed with major drugs, nor were they able to directly link him to the stash house because the house wasn't in his name, but they did catch him with an illegal gun and four pounds of marijuana when they nabbed him at the Dominican restaurant.

Jasmine had expressed some concern that Black Justice would quickly beat his charges, and, within a year or so, be back on the streets looking for her. But Agent Gosling tried to assure her that there was enough rock-solid evidence on Black Justice to get him indicted and convicted on a federal conspiracy charge and send him away for a very long time.

It didn't take long for Jasmine to forget about Black Justice. In fact, three days after he had been arrested, Jasmine was reimbursed by the feds for the money she had spent buying the half-ounce of cocaine, and she received another twenty-five-hundred-dollar installment payment. On top of the money, she also had the keys to a ninth-floor loft apartment in the trendy SoHo section of Manhattan.

Jasmine couldn't believe her eyes when she walked into the pristine, newly furnished apartment in a building with a doorman. It was way more than she ever could have imagined.

"You like it?" Agent Gosling asked.

Jasmine was beaming. "Are you kidding me?" She knew that only high-end doctors and top runway models could afford to live in SoHo, and here she was a drug dealer's girlfriend and an FBI snitch, living just as good as them.

After Jasmine had finished touring the apartment, Gosling had to bring her back to reality.

"The apartment is nice, but remember, you have a job to do, so don't let the apartment become a distraction."

Jasmine nodded.

Gosling reminded her of her next two targets, Prince and Homicide. He gave Jasmine a rundown of the different intelligence reports the FBI had accumulated on them, including the cars they drove, the clubs where they hung out, the restaurants where they ate, and the different women they were fucking.

Jasmine took in everything that Gosling was saying, and she told him to give her a few days and she would come up with a plan to get close to the two targets.

"I got faith in you," Gosling said.

"Oh, now you got faith in me? A few weeks ago you couldn't stop reminding me about how I was going get locked up and all that shit."

Gosling chuckled. "That was before you proved yourself."

Jasmine sucked her teeth and playfully rolled her eyes.

"Seriously though, you're a talent that is hard to find and hard to cultivate, and we really value you."

Those words made Jasmine feel good because she liked being praised for things other than her good looks and her pussy.

"I'm serious," Gosling added.

"Thank you," Jasmine replied.

"But listen. Be smart, and be very careful out here. These guys are wolves, and you can't take anything for granted."

Jasmine gave Gosling a funny look. "You learn how to roll weed yet?"

"Fuck you," Gosling jokingly shot back.

Jasmine walked up to Gosling and innocently began to massage his shoulders. "I'll be smart. I know how to maneuver."

Gosling liked the way Jasmine was massaging his shoulders. He felt his dick starting to rise, so he stood up from the love seat he was sitting on.

"Okay, so I got some work to do. I'm going to head in to the office. I'll check in with you in, say, seventy-two hours."

Jasmine rolled her eyes.

"What?"

"I just told you to give me a few days to formulate a plan, and then you tell me you're going to check in with me in seventy-two hours? You don't have to micromanage me."

"Like I said, I'll check in with you in seventy-two hours."

Jasmine rolled her eyes once more.

"But call me if you need me."

"Good-bye, Gosling."

Gosling made his way toward the door, but he didn't leave before asking Jasmine about Nico.

Jasmine told him that Nico had called her the day before just to check up on her and to ask her to visit BJ in the hospital.

"Did you go?"

"No, not yet. I'll get over there probably today."

Gosling was about to say something else, but Jasmine cut him off.

"Good-bye, Gosling!" And then she playfully pushed him toward the door.

"Okay, I'll talk to you later. And, seriously, you be careful out there."

"I will be."

TWENTY-EIGHT

When Jasmine entered BJ's hospital room, she was surprised to see Simone in the hospital room with BJ's homeboy Ish.

"Hey, BJ." Jasmine's smile was mixed with genuine compassion as she walked up to the head of BJ's hospital bed carrying ten get-well-soon helium balloons and a box of chocolate candy. She bent over and gave him a kiss on the cheek.

"Jasmine, what's good, baby girl?" BJ replied with a smile.

BJ was slowly getting his strength back with each passing day, but he still wasn't able to eat on his own and had to be fed through IV. She noticed he had lost a lot of weight, but she didn't comment on it.

"I know you all hard and stuff," Jasmine said, "but you better take these balloons and candy."

BJ chuckled and told her it was all good. He thanked her for the balloons and candy and told her where to put them.

"What's up, Ish? And, Simone, what the hell you doing here?" Jasmine gave both of them a kiss on the cheek.

"I'm with my baby."

Jasmine laughed and shook her head. "BJ, I introduced these two at the strip club and, I swear, they been attached at the hip ever since. Every time I call this heifer, she talking about, she'll call me back, because she's with Ish."

"That's how us Ghetto Mafia muthafuckas do," BJ replied. "He put it on her the same way Nico put it on you."

Ish laughed as he walked over to BJ to give him a pound.

"Here we go. See, you ain't even hurt. Get your ass up and get dressed. We taking you home right now," Jasmine said.

BJ asked Jasmine, "What's that shit on your neck?"

"It's my new tattoo. You like it? And look at the one I got on my hand."

BJ looked at it and responded in the same manner as everyone else whenever they saw it, repeating what the tattoo said. "Love is cursed."

"Yup. That shit is hot, right?"

BJ nodded, but it was easy to tell he was reluctant. He asked Simone and Ish to give him a few minutes alone with Jasmine.

Ish and Simone told him they were going to step out and go to Wendy's on Jamaica Avenue and then come back.

As soon as Ish and Simone were out of the room and out of earshot, Jasmine looked over at BJ like she wanted to cry.

"Oh, BJ, I didn't want to say nothing, but you sure you okay, boo?"

BJ could see the tears beginning to form in Jasmine's eyes. "Yo, cut that shit out. There ain't gonna be no fuckin' tears up in here."

"I know, but I don't like seeing you up in here like this."

"Jasmine, I'm gonna be all right."

Jasmine bit down on the inner part of her lip to prevent herself from crying. She really cared about BJ on a human level and loved him like a brother, so her feelings of sadness and concern were genuine. Flashbacks of when she'd almost died added to her sadness.

"So what the hell happened? I mean, I been hearing all kind of shit from the street, but you know how that goes."

"I don't wanna talk in here. I'll be home next week, though. When I get out of here, we'll talk."

Jasmine nodded, but at the same time she was hoping that BJ would start talking because she had her recorder going from before she walked into his hospital room.

"Okay, no problem. So you are coming home next week? That's good."

"Yeah, but I been fighting with these doctors. They been telling me that it's a fifty-fifty chance that I'm going to need a colostomy bag for the rest of my life."

"No way." Jasmine covered her mouth with her right hand. "BJ, don't say that." She couldn't stop the tears from streaming down her face.

"They had to remove part of my large intestines."

"But they did say it's a fifty-fifty chance, so that means that maybe you won't have to." Jasmine wiped some tears from her cheek, trying to maintain emotionally for BJ.

"That's what I'm hoping. I told them niggas I would pay whatever, just as long as they fix my shit up right. Word is bond, they might as well kill my ass if I have to walk around with a fuckin' bag attached to me."

Jasmine shook her head and she wiped more tears from her eyes. "They probably was just giving you the worst case scenario to cover themselves. But, believe me, from what I learned in nursing school, as long as you can pay, they'll fix you up right. But let your ass be poor or up in here with a damn Medicaid card, and you would be ass out."

Jasmine wasn't trying to be funny, but her words made BJ laugh.

"It's true," she added with emphasis.

"Yeah, I know. Money talks."

Jasmine walked over to a chair underneath the TV in the corner of the room and sat down.

"I'm gonna be all right, though. Niggas is gonna die behind this shit. You better believe that."

Jasmine looked at him and nodded.

"So what's up with you? Nico, told me to make sure you was straight."

Jasmine sucked her teeth and blew air out of her lungs.

"What's that about?"

"BJ, it's like I don't even know Nico anymore. I don't see him, I don't speak to him. It's like—"

"Jasmine, just hold the nigga down. You know how shit go sometime."

"I mean, I am holding him down. It's just I don't know what we got anymore."

"Whatchu mean by that?"

"I mean, am I still wifey or what?"

BJ chuckled. "Jasmine, that nigga love you. Trust me when I tell you. And you know Nico's like a brother to me, so I know what's up."

Jasmine smiled. "I know he loves me, but he don't trust me like he used to."

"It ain't you, Jasmine."

"Well, then what is it?"

"You see where I'm at right now? Laid up in a fuckin' hospital with half of my intestines missing and shit. And you seen on the news how the feds just nabbed Black Justice and caught forty bricks in the process. That's what it is—he's trying to stay one step ahead of death and jail. You feel me?"

Jasmine thought about just how smart Nico really was to have been avoiding her; otherwise he would have likely been facing the same fate as Black Justice. "I feel you, but I still need to—"

"You still need Nico to make you feel like a woman and all that lovey-dovey shit, right?"

Jasmine smiled. "No, it's not that."

"Yes, it is. You wanna feel like wifey, like you just said a minute ago."

"What I mean is, I don't want to come across all needy and shit like that. I know how to play my position. I know what I signed up for. I just need Nico to trust me and be straight up with me. That's all."

"If Nico caught a charge and had to do time, would you do the time with him?"

"Of course, I would."

"You full of shit."

"No, BJ, really I would, because if he was in jail, then I would know where I stand, and I would know what's up."

"Well, listen. Between me and you, I told Nico to stay outta New York for a while. And if anybody wants that nigga in New York right now, it's me. I want Nico here going to war for me, but I know the game, and I know the streets. This shit is like playing chess. And right now, you got the feds coming at us, you got NYPD coming at us, we got snitches in Ghetto Mafia looking to snake us, we got other crews coming for our throat, and we got confidential informants helping the feds build a case on us. So it's coming at us from all sides right now. I know that, and Nico knows that. So for right now and for the time being, it just makes sense for us to get this bread outta town. And we getting it right now in Miami. And when the time is right, Nico will be around, and you'll be feeling like wifey again and all that. But for right now you just got to hold the nigga down just like if he was doing a bid or something."

"I understand."

"You ain't hurting for nothing, right?"

"No, I'm good." Jasmine made sure not to say anything about her new SoHo apartment.

"You keeping your shit tight for Nico, right?"

Jasmine gave BJ a look that told him not to even go there.

"I gotta ask."

"No, you don't. You already know the answer to that question."

BJ chuckled. "Nico will be around when he's around. But we trying to stay off them phones, and we staying off the radar until the time is right. When all these dumb-ass niggas out here go to prison, we gonna be the only smart ones still getting it. You feel me?"

"You leaving town too?"

"Me and Ish gonna be right here keeping an eye on your slick ass."

179

"What you mean by that?"

Jasmine was already feeling self-conscious about the comment that BJ had made earlier about confidential informants.

BJ chuckled. "I'm just fuckin' wit'chu. I gotta deal with these surgeries that I got coming up, so I'm here."

"I'm sorry about what had happened to Lo."

"This is our life. You know how it goes."

Jasmine didn't immediately reply to his words, but she definitely understood where he was coming from.

"This is our life, baby girl," BJ repeated. "Just hold your tongue."

Jasmine immediately looked BJ square in the eyes but didn't say anything, and neither did he. She moved closer to him and kissed him on the forehead before telling him that she had to go.

The streets were definitely Nico's, BJ's, and Ghetto Mafia's life, and it was also now Jasmine's life. It was a life that came with riches and fame, but it also came with violence, death, prison, and all kinds of worries. Jasmine was super worried. She was wondering if BJ and Nico were on to her role as a confidential informant. She knew that to really survive and make it in the life they lived required a certain level of smarts and skills like a chess player, and a certain level of acting, like an Oscar winner.

Jasmine knew that she was acting and playing the role as a confidential informant. But she just hoped that BJ and Nico weren't better actors than she was. If they were, there was going to be a murder scene in which she would be playing the victim. She wondered if she should heed BJ's advice to hold her tongue.

TWENTY-NINE

"*Sak passé.*"

"*Sak passé,*" Mia replied, smiling as she sat up in her beach chair to take a break from tanning her body on Miami's famous South Beach.

Mia was trying her hardest to remember the Haitian girl's name. She didn't want to be rude and ask, so she just continued to smile and play things off as she sipped on her piña colada.

"Yeah, so like I was saying, if you want me to take you around later on and show you some different areas, I can do that."

The name finally hit Mia. The chick's name was Pascale.

"Well, I think I'm just going to let Nico handle that. I appreciate the offer, though," Mia replied.

"Oh, okay. So you want to go shopping or do something else later?"

"I'll let you know." Mia then put her shades over her eyes and reclined in the beach chair. She was hoping Pascale would leave her alone.

"So when I come up to New York, I want you to take me everywhere. I don't want to rest for one second."

Mia kept quiet.

"And I never been to New York. I can't wait!" Pascale added.

Mia continued to keep quiet.

"You okay?" Pascale asked.

Mia nodded but didn't say anything. She was loving her time in Miami with Nico, but she hated being around Pascale because she would never shut up. She reminded Mia of a nagging and annoying little sister. Pascale was the girlfriend of Nico's right-hand man in Miami, Haitian Jack.

While Haitian Jack and Nico were out running the streets or at the gym lifting weights, Pascale felt it was her duty to show Mia a good time so that she wouldn't be bored. And while Mia appreciated the hospitality, Pascale would never give her more than five minutes to breathe.

Pascal was drop-dead gorgeous with her light skin, Indian hair, and voluptuous body. She had high cheekbones, which defined her face and accentuated her green eyes. There was no denying her beauty, but it definitely seemed like God forgot to dish out a fair share of brains and common sense when it came to Pascale.

"It's just that time of the month for me," Mia lied, hoping that would explain her silence.

"Oh, do you get really bad cramps?"

Mia nodded her head.

"When we leave here, you have to come with me and let me take you by this herbalist. She is the best. I'm telling you, I used to have the worst cramps, and when I went to see her, she told me what to take, and I never had a problem since."

"Really?" Mia asked, trying to sound like she was somewhat interested.

"Oh, she's the best. We'll go when we leave the beach."

Mia nodded and sat back up and sipped some more of her drink. There was no sense in trying to relax and get a tan with Pascale and her annoying motor mouth sitting a couple of feet away from her.

Mia couldn't wait to speak to Nico later that day to let him know that she had to somehow ditch Pascale, or else she was going to go crazy.

When it was all said and done, Mia knew that putting up with Pascale and her annoying self was a small price to pay in exchange for the good life that she and Nico had been experiencing on a daily basis in Miami.

Every night Nico and Mia were going to the best restaurants, and in the morning, they were having breakfast on South Shore Drive. Every day they were seeing different celebrities, and at night when they went out, they were treated like royalty at every night spot they went to, since Haitian Jack had the city on smash.

Mia and Nico were living ghetto-fabulous in Miami, and at the same time they were getting money without all of the headaches and drama going down in New York. The way Nico looked at it, he was getting the best of both worlds. He was New York to the core, but as long as he was getting money, he really didn't care what city the money was coming from.

◆◆◆

While Mia was experiencing the spoils of the Miami good life, Jasmine was in New York trying to decide if she was going to answer Agent Gosling's phone call. Gosling had been blowing up her phone repeatedly for the past hour. All Jasmine could think about was BJ's words about her holding her tongue.

At the same time she knew that now that she had the SoHo apartment, there was no way she would be able to duck Gosling for long, so she decided to answer on the tenth call.

"Hello," she answered nonchalantly.

"I been calling you."

"I'm sorry. I was 'sleep and didn't hear my phone."

"Well, wake your ass up and get to Madison Square Garden by eight o'clock. We got you seats two rows from the floor, Knicks and Lakers, and you'll be in the same row as Homicide."

Jasmine didn't respond.

"Work your magic," Gosling added.

Jasmine sighed. "Just one ticket?"

"No, two tickets. Bring somebody with you. Pick the tickets up from the box office window. Both tickets will be under your name."

"Okay," Jasmine responded.

Jasmine was reluctant to go, but she had no choice. She had signed up for this role and now she had to live it out or risk being thrown in jail and giving up her monthly stipend, her apartment, and all the perks that came with being a snitch.

She sat down on the couch and thought about how she should play things. She thought about calling Simone, but then she remembered her fourteen–year-old cousin who loved basketball to the point where he ate, drank, and dreamt basketball. She figured she would call him and see if he would want to go.

"Jasmine, you lyin'!"

"No, Corey, I'm serious. Good seats too."

"Don't play with me like this, Jasmine."

Jasmine couldn't help but laugh. She loved her cousin's innocence. "You know where Spike Lee sits at, right on the floor?"

"Yeah."

"Well, we're two rows behind Spike and all the celebrities."

"Oh my God! Jasmine, are you serious?"

"Dead-ass."

"Yo, I love you! I definitely want to go."

Jasmine laughed. It made her feel good that she could make his day the way she did.

"Just let your mother know that you won't need no money or anything and that I'll drop you off at your house after the game. I would come pick you up now, but by the time I get dressed and head to Brooklyn and then drive to Manhattan, we'll get there too late and miss the start of the game."

Corey told her that he would let his mother know and that he was going to get dressed and be on the A train in fifteen minutes.

"Just keep your phone on in case we can't find each other," Jasmine warned.

Jasmine jumped in the shower, but seeing that she hadn't had a chance to bring any of her clothes to her new apartment, she put on the same clothes she had been wearing all day long.

She went out for about a half an hour to find a new outfit to wear to the game. She purchased the outfit, and then she ran back to her apartment and got dressed.

By the time Jasmine finished getting dressed, it was close to seven-thirty. So instead of driving her own car, which would have slowed her down and gotten her to the game later than she wanted, she hopped in a yellow cab and got to Madison Square Garden by seven forty-five.

Jasmine linked up with her cousin, and before long the two of them had their tickets and were headed into the world's most famous arena to see the Knicks play the Lakers.

THIRTY

"Jasmine, I can't believe this!" Corey gushed. "There go Kobe right there, and there's Carmelo Anthony."

Jasmine smiled like a supermodel in her black oversized Dior shades, her Gucci signature bag dangling from her wrist as they finally reached their seats. She reached into her bag and pulled out a twenty-dollar bill and handed it to the usher who had helped them.

"Thank you," the usher said to her. "Are you familiar with The Ainsworth Prime?"

"No. What is that?"

"It's a restaurant bar that's located on the third-floor terrace level. It's open to all club-seat holders such as yourself. I think you would like it."

"Oh, okay." Jasmine replied.

The usher walked away, and Jasmine and her cousin both took their seats under the bright lights. Corey looked at the NBA stars with amazement as they warmed up and got ready for the game.

Jasmine looked around trying to locate Homicide, but she didn't see him or anyone that looked like him. She took out her phone and sent a text to Agent Gosling and asked him if he could send her a photo of Homicide.

Fifteen minutes later the photo arrived on Jasmine's phone. She opened it up and studied it for about two minutes and then looked around some more to see if she could locate Homicide, but she still didn't see him. She decided to chill and just relax and enjoy the game with her cousin and not stress out about him.

"You want anything to eat or drink?" Jasmine asked Corey.

He shook his head and told her that he was all right.

Jasmine went into her bag and pulled out a fifty-dollar bill and gave it to Corey. "Here. You don't have to be shy around me. I want you to have a good time."

Corey thanked her and took the money and made his way to the concession stand and to the bathroom. Just as Corey walked out of the row, two guys began to make their way into the same row Jasmine was sitting in. Immediately she recognized Homicide from the photo. Homicide had on a black snap-back Yankees hat, so it was kind of hard to get a great look at him, but Jasmine was sure it was him.

Homicide was a lot shorter in person than Jasmine had imagined him to be. He also had a full beard, even though none of the pictures she'd seen of him depicted him with a beard.

"Pardon me, miss," Homicide said to Jasmine as he carefully made his way past her.

"No problem."

Homicide was wearing a pair of Stash House jeans, a black shirt, a gray biker's leather vest, a pair of Adidas sneakers, and a big-linked platinum bracelet flooded with diamonds. Homicide's homeboy was taller than him and much skinnier. He was wearing a pair of brand-new Levi's, a pair of Nike GTX boots, and a black-and-purple Lakers hoodie.

As Homicide and his homeboy took their seats, Jasmine thought of exactly how she was going to approach them. She wasn't sure about what move to make, but she was definitely happy that Homicide had come to the game with another dude and not a chick.

At the end of the second quarter and during halftime, mostly everyone got out of their seats and headed either to the bathroom or to get something to eat or drink. Jasmine and Corey stayed in their seats, while Homicide and his homie made their way out of the aisle.

"My man, that's your girl?" Homicide asked Corey, referring to Jasmine.

Corey shook his head no.

Homicide gave Corey a pound, and then he looked at Jasmine, who didn't say anything.

"You a CO on Rikers Island, right?"

"Who, me?" Jasmine asked.

Homicide nodded and continued to stare Jasmine down.

"Far from that."

"I know you're a cop or some shit like that. You look too fuckin' familiar."

Jasmine instantly got nervous, but she kept her cool, just slowly shaking her head.

"No?"

"I told you she wasn't no CO," Homicide's homeboy said.

"You look familiar too," Jasmine said to Homicide. "What's your name?"

"Homicide."

Jasmine smiled. "What did your momma name you?"

"Aziz," Homicide replied, and then his cell phone starting ringing. He answered the call, and then he told Jasmine he would be right back, and he and his homeboy walked off.

"So you good?" Jasmine asked her cousin.

"More than good!" He continued to watch the sexy Knicks City Dancers perform their halftime routine.

"OH, MY GOD!" Jasmine said in a slow cadence to herself but loud enough for her cousin to hear.

"What's the matter?" Corey asked.

"Oh, nothing," Jasmine replied, not wanting to tell Corey what she was thinking. She pulled out her BlackBerry and looked at Homicide's picture again. I can't believe this, she thought to herself before the full name Aziz Zahir came to her mind.

Jasmine was certain that Homicide was the same person she'd had a secret childhood crush on since she was in the fourth grade. Her palms started to get sweaty, and she started to get both excited and nervous at the same time. Immediately she deleted his picture from her phone.

Jasmine and Aziz had been in the same class at Public School 22 on St. Mark's Avenue in Brooklyn before she moved to Queens. She wondered if she should say anything to him when he got back to his seat, or if she should just play things cool and see where they led.

The second half of the game started, and a lot of people including Homicide had not yet made it back to their seats from the halftime intermission. As Corey watched the NBA action, Jasmine combed her mind and thought back to her years in elementary school. She remembered how all of the kids laughed at Aziz's name when their teacher introduced him to the class. She also remembered how the kids teased him because he was two years older than all of the kids in his class. Aziz was a smart kid. He was two years older than everybody because he had started school late in Egypt, where he was born, and when he'd moved to the United States at the age of eleven, he was considered a fourth grader by United States standards.

Jasmine could not believe that the former teacher's pet, who was very religious, and a borderline nerd, had grown up to be the feared drug hustler and murderous stickup kid from Brooklyn known as Homicide. After graduating from Public School 22, Jasmine soon moved to Queens, and she had not seen or heard from him since.

By the middle of the third quarter of the game, Homicide and his homeboy came back to their seats, both carrying a box of chicken fingers, French fries, and beer.

"Excuse me, sexy," Homicide said to Jasmine.

Jasmine smiled as she stood up so he could get by her. As weird as it was, she had waited more than a decade to hear him call her sexy—since she was a skinny fourth-grader with pigtails.

Homicide and his friend were six seats from her and Corey. Jasmine didn't know what to say or do, but she figured she had to say something. She thought about taking things back to fourth grade, scribbling something on a piece of paper and then passing the note down to Homicide, but she changed her mind about that and just waited.

Before long the third quarter had ended, and Jasmine took off her shades so her face was fully visible. Some people in her section were milling around, standing and stretching their legs, and others stayed put in their seats. Jasmine looked down her row and saw Homicide on his phone. He looked as if he was texting somebody.

Jasmine's heart started racing. She was about to make a move and was hoping that Aziz would remember her. She was able to get the attention of Homicide's homie, and she signaled for him to tap Homicide for her. When Homicide looked in Jasmine's direction, she smiled and motioned with her index finger for him to come to her, and he got up and made his way toward her.

"What's good, ma?" Homicide asked with a slight smile.

Jasmine looked at him, a huge smile on her face. "I know you."

Homicide looked at her as the two of them stood in the aisle so people could freely walk in and out of their row. "From where?" Homicide loved the scent of Jasmine's Burberry Brit perfume.

"Is your last name Zahir?"

Homicide squinted his eyes as he looked intently at Jasmine. He slowly nodded his head. "How you know my government name?"

"I been sitting here since halftime, and I was bugging, trying my hardest to remember where I know you from. And you are not going to believe this."

"What?" Homicide was a man of few words, so he wanted Jasmine to hurry up and get to the point.

"Remember Mrs. Freeman? P.S. twenty-two?" Jasmine continued to smile.

Homicide thought back for a minute. "Ohhhh, shit! Get the fuck outta here!" he yelled. "Little skinny Jasmine with the pigtails. Ohhhh, shit! What the fuck!"

Homicide laughed, and then he extended his hand to Jasmine's. Jasmine took hold of his hand, and he pulled her toward him and gave her a firm hug.

When the fourth quarter of the game started, people were rushing back to their seats. Jasmine thought quickly and formally introduced her cousin to Homicide, explaining that she knew him from back in the days. She asked Corey if he would switch seats with Homicide, and he agreed.

"This is crazy, right?" Jasmine said, leaning in to Homicide. The crowd was cheering real loud, so it was hard for them to hear each other.

"Word up. So what's good wit'chu?"

Jasmine yelled into his ear, "It's so much to tell you and catch up on."

Homicide took out his phone and asked Jasmine for her number. She gave him her regular cell phone number, and he told her he was going to call her, so she could lock his number in.

"We gotta link up," he told her.

Jasmine couldn't stop smiling. She leaned in to Homicide. "You know you were the first boy I ever had a crush on?"

Homicide looked at Jasmine and didn't say anything in response. All he could do was look at how sexy she looked and imagine what it would be like to fuck her. He wasn't sure if he could fuck her that night, but he was definitely going to try.

"You still a Muslim?"

"No doubt."

"I can see you aren't a nerd anymore."

"Nah, these streets changed a muthafucka."

Jasmine nodded her head.

"As sexy as you is, I know you got a man or something."

"Long story."

Homicide took Jasmine's response to mean that she wasn't putting up any resistance. "So what you doing after you leave here?"

Jasmine shrugged. "Nothing. I just have to make sure my cousin gets home okay, and I'm free."

"That's what's up. So let me take you to get a drink or something. We can hang out and just kick it."

Jasmine nodded.

As the game went on, neither Jasmine nor Homicide paid any attention to the score or the outcome. They were both just so much into each other.

Homicide's main thoughts were about smashing Jasmine that night, and he wasn't really trying to think past that. But Jasmine's emotions were having a field day with her. She didn't know how to describe her feelings. The only word she could come up with was nostalgic.

Jasmine knew she had to stay focused. She hoped that nostalgia wouldn't compromise her mission as a confidential informant.

THIRTY-ONE

Jasmine woke up at three in the morning in her SoHo apartment, and for a moment she forgot where she was. It was the first time that she had actually slept there, so the unfamiliar surroundings had thrown her off. In addition, her head was pounding from all the liquor she'd drunk hanging with Homicide after the Knicks game.

Jasmine realized that Homicide was no longer in the bed with her. She had ended up bringing him back to her apartment and fucking him, and after they had finished fucking, they both fell asleep. What Jasmine didn't realize was that Homicide had never actually fallen asleep. He had just waited for her to fall asleep, so he could case her apartment.

While Jasmine had slept, Homicide went through her bag, her clothes, her closets, and her phone. Going through her phone, he saw Nico's name, BJ's name, Lorenzo's name, Ish, Bebo and a bunch of other drug dealers, so he immediately knew how Jasmine got down and exactly how she got her money.

Homicide was looking through Jasmine's government-issued phone and trying to figure out how to get to her text messages. He was familiar with BlackBerry phones but had never seen that particular model before. As he was trying to figure out the phone, Jasmine walked into the kitchen of the apartment and caught him by surprise.

"Hey," Jasmine said, sounding real groggy, her eyes squinting from the light in the kitchen.

"Yeah, yeah," Homicide replied, and he stood up and placed Jasmine's phone on the counter.

Jasmine saw the phone, and her heart started pounding. "Everything okay?" she asked. She saw that Homicide was fully dressed.

Homicide walked up to her and gave her a hug. "Listen, I'm about to bounce. Some shit came up, and I gotta get back to BK."

Jasmine was wearing a long T-shirt with nothing else underneath. She wondered if Homicide could feel her heart pounding, so she quickly pulled away from his hug and retrieved her phone.

"Your phone was vibrating crazy."

"Please tell me you didn't answer it."

Homicide slowly shook his head but didn't say anything.

Jasmine wondered just what he knew and what he had seen on the phone. "So you was just gonna leave and not say anything?"

"I'll hit you up later today. Go back in the bed and get some sleep."

"What's wrong?"

Homicide knew that Jasmine had caught him looking at her phone and didn't want to come across like the grimy nigga he was. "A'ight, I'll keep it one hundred wit'chu."

"Please do." Jasmine didn't want to feel used, like some stripper slut who got fucked by a random dude, and at the same time she desperately wanted to know if Homicide was on to her.

"We ain't have enough time to chop it up like I wanted to, but yo, the thing is, I got a lot of enemies in this town, and it don't take much to get caught slippin'."

"I'm lost."

"When you fell asleep, your phone was vibrating, and I saw a text message from BJ. So—"

Jasmine sucked her teeth and rolled her eyes. "Ugggh." She was about to flip, but she held her cool.

"So I know that name, and the first thought was, is it the same bitch-ass BJ that I know who almost got killed? So I looked through your phone book, and I see all these Ghetto Mafia niggas' names in your phone."

"Homicide. Okay, first of all, you looking through my phone—that shit is real whack."

"Hold up, Jasmine. On the real, I'm not one of these chump-ass niggas on the street or one of these clown-ass dudes you be fuckin' with."

"I didn't say you was."

"Shut the fuck up when I'm talking!" Homicide shouted. He had a real short fuse, and Jasmine had not been in his life to know that. But immediately he had her respect.

"I'm sorry."

"What I'm saying is, I'm up in here laying up in your shit with no burner or nothing. Anybody could walk up in this muthafuckin' apartment and start blasting. You know what I'm saying? Especially them Ghetto Mafia niggas. Them niggas don't fuck with me, and I don't fuck with them."

The liquor she had been drinking had just about totally worn off, and Homicide was helping her come to her senses. She realized how stupid she had been to let him fuck her that easily.

"Homicide, this is my apartment, and if I bring you here, you're good. I mean, yeah, did I fuck with them Ghetto Mafia niggas? Yes, I did. And I thought I told you that before we left Madison Square Garden that I was fuckin' with Nico. Would I be so stupid to bring you up in here and risk my own ass getting killed? No, I wouldn't be that stupid. You're good here."

Homicide understood Jasmine's reasoning, but his primary occupation was setting up drug dealers to get robbed, so he always saw things from a different lens. To him everything was a conspiracy or had the potential for a setup.

Homicide kissed Jasmine on the lips. "I'm out."

At that point Jasmine was wondering if she had just blown her assignment. "Okay, but I really want to see you again."

Jasmine knew how to make herself cry at the drop of a hat, and at that moment she called up some tears to her eyes. They didn't roll down her cheeks, but her eyes were visibly starting to water up.

"You got my number. Hit me up," Homicide replied.

Jasmine stopped him at the front door and prevented him from leaving. "I don't want to just be a fuckin' booty call."

A smirk came across Homicide's face.

"So you out just like that?" Jasmine asked.

Homicide nodded his head and told Jasmine once again to just hit him up, and after that he opened the door and made his way out of her apartment and out of the building.

Homicide was far from the lovey-dovey, cuddling-in-the-bed type of dude. He had fucked Jasmine and was good from that standpoint. Jasmine didn't know he could sense that she was an emotionally needy chick that he was going to use to his benefit if he could.

THIRTY-TWO

After Homicide left, Jasmine wanted to stay up, but her head was killing her, and her stomach was also bothering her. She still had the lingering effects from her hangover and was feeling stressed out. She wanted to reply to BJ's text message, and at the same time she also wanted to call Homicide, but she decided against both, and instead she got back in the bed and went to sleep for a few hours. Close to four in the morning, and within a few minutes of lying down, Jasmine was in a deep sleep.

At eight o'clock that morning, Jasmine's ringing doorbell and the knocking at her door woke her up. She hadn't told anyone about her SoHo apartment, so she thought it could only be Homicide. She got up as quickly as she could, feeling extremely tired, and walked to her apartment door and looked through the peephole.

"Jasmine, it's me."

Instantly her blood pressure shot through the roof when she realized it was Agent Gosling. Jasmine was still unfamiliar with the locks on her door, but she did her best and ripped open the door as fast as she could.

"Okay, no disrespect, but what the fuck are you doing here?"

Agent Gosling stared at Jasmine and didn't say anything to her. He invited himself in and began looking around.

Jasmine closed the door behind him. "Seriously, what are you doing here? You tryin' to get me killed or what?"

Agent Gosling didn't let Jasmine know that two other FBI agents had followed her after she'd left Madison Square Garden. They had staked out her apartment building, so they knew exactly what time Homicide and

Jasmine arrived at the apartment, and they also knew when Homicide left. They had reported everything back to Agent Gosling, and he made it his business to stop at Jasmine's apartment before going into the office that morning.

"So how'd things go with Homicide? Were you able to make any contact with him?"

Jasmine sucked her teeth.

"Is that a yes or no?" Gosling asked very sternly.

"Yes, I made contact with him."

Jasmine felt really nauseous at that moment, so she rushed off to her kitchen and drank some water to try and settle her stomach. Gosling followed right behind her.

"I had too much to drink last night. I feel sick right now. I was trying to sleep it off, and I was going to call you when I woke up."

Gosling, convinced that he smelled sex in the air, nodded but kept his mouth shut.

"Listen, can we please just get on the same page? I mean, not for nothing, but Homicide was at this apartment and left not too long ago. I don't know how I would have explained your black ass popping up at my door."

"Homicide was here?" Gosling asked, trying to sound like he was learning about that for the first time.

"Yes."

"Jasmine, you apparently had too much to drink, and you know what we discussed, and now you're—"

Jasmine cut him off. "No, I didn't fuck him. I know what you told me, and I'm not trying to jeopardize shit."

"Are you sure you didn't fuck him, Jasmine?" Gosling asked, sounding more like a jealous boyfriend than a concerned FBI case agent.

Jasmine rolled her eyes. "So I'm a slut now?"

"No, no, that's not what I was implying."

Jasmine heard her phone vibrating in the other room, so she walked out of the room to retrieve it. When she got to it, she saw that it was a text from Simone, who had sent her a picture of a dick.

Jasmine shook her head and replied to the text with one word. *Nice*

Simone immediately replied back: *It's Ish's dick. He damn near fucked me into a gotdamn COMA! LOL.*

Jasmine replied right back. *Kind of busy right now. I'll hit you back in an hour or so.*

Gosling had made his way into Jasmine's bedroom. He couldn't help but think about what it would be like to bend Jasmine over her bed and fuck the shit out of her right there on the spot.

Gosling, a recovering alcoholic, had been sober for a little over nine years. But something that night before had caused him to slip up and he'd found himself in a Manhattan bar downing way too many shots of Jack Daniel's.

"You okay?" Jasmine asked him as he stared at her.

Gosling nodded.

"Something isn't right. You popped up over here out the blue. You got this glossy-eyed look about you. Everything is good? You sure?"

Gosling sat down on Jasmine's bed and assured her that he was fine.

"Listen, I wanted to make sure that I told you to stay completely out of Prince's way. We're taking him off your target list."

"Why?" Jasmine asked, not that she was complaining, because as far as she was concerned, that was music to her ears.

"We're ninety percent certain he was behind the funeral home shooting."

"You shitting?"

"I'm serious." Gosling took out a breath mint and popped it into his mouth to help mask the smell of liquor. "We would hate to be walking you into a death trap, so until we get more intel, just do your best to keep your distance from him. He's a dangerous dude. If he shot up a funeral home gunning for Nico and his crew, there's no telling what he would do to you if he found out or knew somehow that you're Nico's woman."

Jasmine felt better at that point because it seemed to her that Gosling had really popped up at her apartment in more of a protective mode than a snooping, micromanaging role.

"Ahhh, you were so concerned about me that you came over this early in the morning?" Jasmine then walked over to her bed and sat next to Gosling and gave him a hug.

Gosling immediately stood to his feet, wanting to get out of Jasmine's apartment. Pretty women were his second biggest vice, and his womanizing ways usually followed his nights of drinking. Jasmine was his new drug of choice, and he was desperately trying to avoid making a move on her.

"I have to get to the office," he told her. "We have an important meeting."

"Okay, I'll call you later in the afternoon and fill you in on Homicide."

"Okay, you do that. And we have to start moving to get Nico back in New York. Agent Battle is starting to grow impatient with me being so lax about Nico being in Miami."

Jasmine nodded.

As Gosling made his way to Jasmine's main door, he turned and looked at her before opening the door. "You look cute when you just wake up," he said to her.

Jasmine was surprised to hear him say that. She didn't know how to take it, so she decided not to read into the comment. "Is that right?"

Gosling slowly nodded. He was seconds from pulling her toward him and sticking his tongue down her throat.

"At eleven o'clock when they start serving lunch at McDonald's, go get a Quarter Pounder with cheese, and get an order of large fries. Eat that, and I promise you all the hangover effects of the alcohol will be gone within a half an hour."

"What are you talking about?"

"The salt from the food, it works wonders on hangovers." Gosling was speaking from years of experience.

Right at that moment, Homicide was calling Jasmine, but she didn't want to answer in front of Gosling.

"Good-bye, silly," Jasmine said to Gosling, and she playfully pushed him out the door as he laughed and told her good-bye.

"Hello," Jasmine said, quickly answering her cell phone before it stopped ringing.

"You up?"

"Yes," Jasmine replied, not knowing what to think.

"I'ma come through and check you this afternoon."

"Oh, okay," Jasmine said with a smile. "I'll be here. I'm not going nowhere."

"That's what's up," Homicide replied before ending the call.

Jasmine exhaled. She was thankful that she hadn't blown her assignment with Homicide. But she was more thankful that her childhood crush wanted to come back and see her. She couldn't stop thinking about him. She made her way back to her bedroom, got in the bed, and smiled her way back to sleep.

THIRTY-THREE

Jasmine woke up at eleven a.m. She decided to jump in the shower and then quickly head to Long Island to get some more of her clothes, since she still didn't have a lot of her things in the apartment. She was trying to rush and be back in SoHo before one o'clock, so she would be there when Ish arrived.

Jasmine made her way to the Williamsburg Bridge and was on the Long Island Expressway when her cell phone started to ring. Using her Bluetooth, she answered the call, and BJ's voice was soon heard coming through the speakers in her truck.

"Jasmine."

"Oh shit! BJ, I'm so sorry. I saw your text, and I meant to hit you back. I was so hung over. I'm just recovering now," she said, laughing lightly.

When BJ didn't laugh or respond, Jasmine could sense that something was wrong. "Everything okay? You doing good?" she asked.

"Yeah, I'm good. I got an operation scheduled in about two hours."

"Oh, okay. I'll make sure I say a quick prayer for you."

"Jasmine, I need you to keep it totally one hundred with me."

Instantly Jasmine's heart started pounding. "Of course. About what? What's up?"

"What the fuck is up wit'chu and Black Justice?"

Jasmine immediately shot back, "Ain't nothin' up with that nigga!" Her mouth started to get dry, and she was trying her hardest to think as quickly as she could.

"You ain't fuck that nigga, did you?"

"Oh, my muthafuckin' God! Hell no, I didn't fuck him! Me and Simone saw him one night up in the strip club, that night Simone met Ish. And he was with his boys and he was drunk and pushing up on me and shit, but I knew he was high, so it was nothing. I wasn't trying to pay his ass no attention."

"Jasmine, you sure?"

"Yes! I'm more than sure."

BJ started to cough. He sounded like he was choking.

"Oh, my God! BJ, I know you checking up on me because Nico is your boy. But honestly you don't even need to be stressing yourself with this bullshit. It's just going to distract from you getting better. Just believe me. I mean, this shit is totally from left field somewhere, and I don't know what's going on. But I do know that I wasn't fuckin' with that nigga."

Through more coughs, BJ continued to talk. "Well, the nigga got locked up, and he's on Rikers Island talking shit. You know how things come back."

Jasmine was beyond stressed and was on the verge of tears, but she had to hold it together. "What kind of shit could he be talking?"

"He telling niggas that he fucked you and that your new name should be Suicide Pussy because every nigga that fucks with you either ends up getting murdered, like Shabazz did, or they end up in jail like he did."

"You know what? I'ma fuck that nigga up! When I hang up the phone, I'm calling Ish, and me and Ish will ride over to Rikers Island right now, and I guarantee you the muthafucka won't talk that bullshit. These lame-ass dudes always act just like bitches whenever I don't fuck with them."

"Fuck that nigga. Don't waste your time going over there. But I'ma tell you this—Just watch where you go. Niggas is saying they saw you coupled up with Homicide at the Knicks game last night, and with this Black Justice shit, it don't look right, you kna'mean?"

Jasmine broke down and started crying.

"BJ, I am so fuckin' heated right now. It's like, damn, can I live? I can't wipe my ass in this city without people being all up in my shit. First of all, I swear on everything, I was at the Knicks game with my fourteen-year-old cousin. I'll give you his number right now, and you can three-way him and ask him. He loves basketball, so I figured I would surprise him and take him to see the Knicks and the Lakers. Now when we got there, did I see Homicide? Yes, I saw him, but I had no idea he was going to be there. And when I saw him I was like, He looks real familiar, so we spoke. Come to find out, I knew him since fourth fuckin' grade when we was in the same class. But I swear to you, before last night, I hadn't seen him in like ten years, if not more than that."

BJ could hear Jasmine's sobs. A small part of him wanted to believe what she was saying, but in his gut he knew she was bullshitting. BJ knew there was no way that rumors like that could start circulating without some kind of truth to them, but he didn't press her on anything.

"A'ight. If that's what you're saying, then that's what it is."

Jasmine sucked her teeth. "You know that's not true because if you're calling me then I know I'm going to have to hear Nico's mouth on this, and I ain't even do shit. Uggghhh! I swear, sometimes I just want to move up out of New York because I can't take this shit. The dudes are worse than these jealous-ass females that be hating on me."

BJ remained quiet.

"And let me guess. Homicide is saying that he fucked me too, right? I'm just opening up my legs and fuckin' everybody."

"Nah, I told you what it is. If I was you, I would just stay in the crib, lay low until things blow over and Nico gets back in town."

Jasmine didn't say anything. She was too frustrated to speak.

"A'ight?"

"A'ight, BJ." Jasmine blew some air into the phone. "Get through your surgery."

"I will."

With that, they ended the call, and Jasmine continued on her way to Nico's house out in Long Island.

When she got there, she rolled some weed and smoked it while sitting on the deck overlooking the sprawling backyard. It didn't help get her mind off what BJ had told her.

With her mind racing, she combed through her closets and picked out a bunch of outfits that she piled in to her truck. At that point, her desire to see Homicide wasn't nearly as intense as it was before she'd spoken to BJ. But she knew she had a job to do despite how uneasy she was feeling.

Jasmine headed back toward SoHo. As soon as she pulled out of the circular driveway, her phone began to ring. It was Simone. The phone was on its third ring, and Jasmine contemplated if she should answer it or not. A big part of her wanted to send Simone to voice mail because she just didn't want to deal with any more stress, drama, or gossip, but at the same time she felt like she had to know everything that was being said about her and exactly who was saying it. So although she didn't want to, she answered Simone's call and braced herself for any new drama that Simone might bring her way.

THIRTY-FOUR

Every word that came out of Simone's mouth seemed to be about Ish. She couldn't stop gushing to Jasmine about how good Ish was treating her. She made it her business to tell Jasmine about the bags and the clothes he had given her, and about the cash he was giving to her to spend any way she pleased.

Simone was a jealous, envious bitch. Although they were friends, Jasmine knew Simone was always in a steady competition with her to look better, dress better, and have more than she had.

As Jasmine drove back to Manhattan, Simone would not shut up even for a moment for Jasmine to respond to anything she was saying.

"Look at me, just talking your head off." Simone chuckled, sounding like a swimmer coming up for air. "So, anyway, what's up with you? And how's Nico? I haven't heard you talking about him. And whenever I'm out with Ish, I don't see him anywhere. Y'all still together, right?"

Jasmine rolled her eyes. If she could have reached through the phone and choked Simone until she passed out, she would have.

"Of course, we're still together, Simone. I already told you he was in Miami doing his thing."

"He's still in Miami? You know he's fuckin' somebody down there."

"Thank you, Simone. I really needed to hear that."

"Oh, I'm sorry," Simone quickly replied.

Jasmine could almost feel Simone's smile coming through the phone.

"I didn't mean for it to sound like that. But I'm just saying . . . you know how these niggas are."

Jasmine kept quiet. Her silence was Simone's cue to continue on rambling about her and Ish.

"Yeah, what I'm saying . . . I knew Nico was still out of town because Ish told me that."

"Do me a favor, Simone—When you're all boo'd up with Ish and y'all are talking pillow talk or whatever, can you please leave me and Nico's names out of your mouths?"

"No, we wasn't talking about you and Nico like that. Ish was just telling me how he's basically been running everything in Brooklyn and Queens since Nico's been out of town, and with BJ in the hospital, and Lo and Bebo dead. That's all."

Jasmine sighed. "Running everything like what?"

"I don't think I need to spell it out for you, Jasmine."

"Actually, you don't. Listen, I have to go. I'll hit you up later." Jasmine had had enough of Simone's boasting. In a way though, she was glad that Simone spoke the way she did because it prevented her from slipping up and saying anything to her about her and Homicide, or about her apartment in SoHo.

"Okay, make sure you do. We have to hang out again real soon."

"We will," Jasmine replied right before hanging up.

Jasmine hated Simone's guts at that point. She didn't see how Simone could be a real friend if she was always in competition with her and always trying to one-up her. She did the best she could to block Simone out of her mind. She didn't want any negative energy flowing through her when Homicide came by to see her.

It was five thirty and Homicide hadn't yet come by to see Jasmine, nor had he called her to tell her if he was still coming by. Jasmine was starting to think that he was standing her up. She thought about texting him, but she didn't want to come across as needy.

Jasmine had some time to just sit by herself, watch TV, and get things off her mind, so in many ways it was a blessing in disguise that Homicide hadn't shown up.

Right at five-forty, the doorman called Jasmine and told her that she had a visitor named Homicide coming to see her. Jasmine almost pissed in her pants laughing at how disturbed the white doorman sounded.

"Okay, you can send him up," Jasmine replied.

Three minutes later Homicide was ringing her doorbell.

Jasmine opened the door with a smile wearing a pair of dark blue biker shorts and a T-shirt that was cut short and exposed her stomach. She had on no shoes or socks, but her recent pedicure made her small feet look perfect.

"You actually told the doorman your name was Homicide?" Jasmine laughed.

"I don't give a fuck about him. That's my name." Homicide handed Jasmine a white shopping bag. "I bought us some fish and brown rice."

"Oh, thank you. And I'm starving too."

Jasmine took the food to the kitchen and got two plates and forks.

"I ain't think you was coming no more."

"Yeah, I know. I was dealing with some shit, trying to get this bread."

Jasmine looked at Homicide and smiled as she fixed the plates. He didn't realize she was looking at him. "Can I get a hug or something?" she said, walking toward him.

Jasmine hugged him real tight and noticed he was wearing a nice-scented Muslim oil. But she could also feel the gun in his waistband. She made sure not to react to the feel of the gun, although she almost pulled away from him quickly.

"What scent is that? Kush?"

Homicide smiled. "Yeah. How you know that?"

"I got some culture." Jasmine laughed. "You want me to warm up your food?"

He shook his head no, so Jasmine handed him his plate and warmed up her plate.

"So what you do today?" Homicide asked, about to put a forkful of food in his mouth.

"Nothing, other than trying not to get stressed the fuck out."

"Stressed about what?"

Jasmine got her food out of the microwave and started to eat it. Then she explained that BJ had called her, and she told him what he had said.

"So you still fuckin' with Nico or what? Break that shit down for me. Be straight up."

Jasmine was silent.

"What the fuck you quiet for? Either yes or no."

"I'm quiet because I honestly don't know the answer. It's like when he wants to see me, he sees me, and when he wants to fuck with other bitches, he does. Right now, he down in Miami, getting money down there, and he's been down there for a minute. Has he called me since he's been there? Not one time. It's like he's running from me."

"You got that suicide pussy, right?" Homicide joked and said.

Jasmine gave him a serious look.

"I'm just fucking wit'chu." Homicide put a forkful of food in his mouth. "I know why you stressed."

"I know too. I just told you why."

Homicide shook his head. "Nah, you think that's why you stressed, but you really stressed because you fuck with weak-ass muthafuckas."

Jasmine just looked at Homicide.

"Your man is supposed to be more than just your man. He's supposed to be your king and treat you like a queen, no matter what it takes. You feel me?"

Jasmine nodded.

"Like, on the real, if Nico was treating you like a queen, he would have had Black Justice touched from inside them prison walls. You know what I'm saying?"

Homicide ate some more food and then he continued on.

"Black Justice talking shit from behind bars, and Nico got his boys calling you basically on some he-said, she-said shit. That's that weak-ass bullshit. And this nigga down in Florida with his feet in the sand while his people is up here in New York laid up in the hospital and having funerals and shit. That's why you're stressed; nothing more, nothing less."

Jasmine had never thought about it from that standpoint, but she had to admit that Homicide was making a whole lot of sense.

"Niggas think the chips they holding is what makes them." Homicide shook his head. "But that's not it. What makes a real nigga is the heart he's born with. That shit comes from Allah. You can't manufacture heart. It don't matter how much bread you holding."

"That's so true, and I didn't even tell you that BJ was asking me if I was at the Knicks game wit'chu."

"You should've told that nigga you was with me, and that you left with me. Fuck that bitch-ass nigga BJ!"

Jasmine laughed. She loved his confidence and his swagger.

"You know how women just on instinct can take care of babies and shit like that?"

Jasmine nodded her head.

"That's because women are earths, and that shit is in y'all nature. But with niggas, we're gods, and gods protect everything. You feel me?"

Jasmine nodded again.

"So if you ever fuckin' with a nigga and you don't feel safe, you fuckin' with the wrong nigga."

"Preach!" Jasmine jokingly said. She didn't want to tell Homicide how his words were ringing so true to her. "See, I knew since fourth grade that you were a good catch."

Homicide chuckled. "I'm too wild for your ass."

Jasmine looked at him and slowly shook her head. She walked up to him and kissed him on the cheek and then whispered that he wasn't too wild for her.

Homicide knew he could have fucked Jasmine right then and there, but he wanted to stay focused on the reason that he had come to see her.

"So this nigga Nico is out of town, BJ is in the hospital, Lo and Bebo are dead, how the fuck them Ghetto Mafia niggas still eating?" Homicide asked.

"They still getting their money."

"I know, but how?"

Jasmine wasn't exactly sure, but she remembered what Simone had said about Ish. "You know Ish?"

Homicide thought for a moment, and then he nodded.

"He's running everything."

"Where that nigga Ish live at?"

"In Rosedale. Why?" Jasmine asked.

Homicide stood up from the chair and started to feel on her ass. Jasmine reached up and she kissed him. Homicide pulled away from her and took out his gun and laid it on the kitchen table. But not wanting to be too far away from it, he made sure not to leave the kitchen. He slid Jasmine's shorts down to her ankles, and she stepped out of them.

Homicide started playing with her exposed pussy. Jasmine gasped as soon as he stuck his middle finger inside of her. With his other hand, Homicide undid his pants and let them drop to just above his knees as he left his sneakers on. He then took his finger out of Jasmine's pussy and lifted her up onto the dishwasher, where she spread her legs as wide as she could for him.

Homicide slid his dick into Jasmine's pussy and started to fuck her real slow, and as her pussy got wetter and wetter, he fucked her harder and harder. Jasmine loved every inch of Homicide, and every second of him fucking her. Unlike the night before when she wasn't totally herself because of the alcohol, this time she was sober and felt totally free. She didn't hold back one bit, and her screams and moans let Homicide know that she was thoroughly enjoying the way he fucked her.

Jasmine wrapped her legs around Homicide's back then clasped both of her hands around the back of his neck. Homicide pulled away from the dishwasher and supported her by gripping her ass and holding her up in the air. Jasmine loved that position, and she bounced up and down on Homicide's dick until she came back to back.

Homicide could feel himself about to nut. He didn't want to nut inside Jasmine, so after a few more real deep strokes, he carried Jasmine back over to the dishwasher, where he had started fucking her, placed her on top of it, and pulled his dick out of her. Within seconds he was shooting come all over her stomach, legs, on her short T-Shirt, and the dishwasher door.

Jasmine hopped off the dishwasher and grabbed him and hugged him. He pulled up his pants and buckled his belt.

Jasmine hugged him, and she wouldn't let him go. She buried her head in his chest and just left it there and listened to his heartbeat.

As Jasmine stood there with her head buried in Homicide's chest, she felt a sense of peace and serenity she couldn't remember feeling before. At that moment she didn't care about Nico and what he was doing, she didn't care about Agent Gosling, and she didn't care about her role as a confidential informant. Homicide made her feel safe and secure, and she just wished that she could stay in that exact same position forever, hugging him with her head placed on his chest, and never have to move or worry about a thing.

THIRTY-FIVE

Two weeks passed, and Jasmine was conscious of what BJ had told her about staying in the house and, for the most part, had listened. But during that two-week period, Agent Gosling was starting to get very suspicious of her relationship with Homicide because she had yet to produce any incriminating evidence on him.

So while Gosling pressured Jasmine to produce results, Homicide was also starting to apply pressure on her to have her set up Ish to get robbed. Initially Jasmine wasn't sure if it was the smartest thing for her to do, but after a long day of seriously thinking about it, she realized it was actually a good idea. For one, she was dead tired of Simone constantly boasting about what Ish was doing for her, and that would be a good way to take a lot of air out of her balloon.

She also figured that if the robbery was successful, she would be able to go to Gosling and have him ease up the pressure on her by convincing him that the FBI needed to really focus on locking up Ish because he was taking over for Nico as the new kingpin. Setting up Ish would also make Homicide trust her and not question her loyalty to him.

So after Jasmine was convinced she was down with Ish getting set up, she started calling Simone more often. Each time, Jasmine reminded her that they needed to go out because they hadn't been out in so long. Simone jumped at the bait because she was itching to show off the new outfits and other gifts Ish had given to her.

"Did you move in with Ish yet?"

"I might as well have. I mean, I'm always at his crib. He loves when I cook for him, so I try to be there as much as possible."

"Mmm-hmm." Jasmine tried her best to stay in character.

"What?"

"You know the only reason you be over there is for some dick! You probably ain't cook that nigga one good meal yet. Remember you are the one who texted me a picture of his dick."

"Oh, my God!" Simone laughed, trying to sound embarrassed. "That shit do look good though, right?"

"I don't know. I deleted that right after you sent it to me. Picture me trying to explain to Nico why Ish's dick is in my phone."

Simone burst out laughing, completely thrilled to talk about Ish any chance she could. After Simone finished laughing she started to talk low and in a real serious tone. "So tell me something—When's the last time you had some dick?"

"Why you asking me like you trying to get the scoop on something? You already know Nico is out of town."

"Jasmine?"

"Yes?"

"You telling me you ain't fuck nobody since Nico been gone all this time?"

"That's exactly what I'm telling you. Unless you know about some dick that I don't know about."

"No, I'm just saying."

"You just saying what?" Jasmine braced herself to hear the latest rumor about her. Jasmine hadn't told her anything about Homicide because she couldn't trust that she wouldn't say anything to Ish.

"I'm just saying I don't know how you go for so long."

Simone was still the dark-skinned, round-faced girl with the pig nose who only recently started looking decent when she had the money to make herself look better. But the way she was speaking, she was trying to make it like, for all her life, dudes were in bidding wars over her pussy and she always had her pick of dicks.

"It ain't that hard, Simone. And you act like Nico is doing time in prison or something. He'll be back."

"I hear you. But just as long as you know, after we finish partying or whatever, my black ass is going home to Ish for some dick. So don't be looking for me to come back to chill with you in Long Island."

"Whatever, Simone."

Jasmine literally couldn't take anymore of Simone, so she ended the call with all of the info she needed to relay back to Homicide.

◆◆◆

With Jasmine's urging, she and Simone made plans to hang out at Sway, a white trendy bar lounge in SoHo. Sway was in walking distance from Jasmine's apartment, but Simone was under the impression that she and Jasmine would both be driving in separately to Manhattan to meet up at the lounge.

"Who told you about this place?" Simone asked Jasmine after she entered Sway and found Jasmine seated at a table by herself. Simone had a stink look on her face.

"I been here before."

"Here?"

"Girl, sit your ass down and let me order you a drink. It'll be poppin' in about a hour."

"I hope so. All these white people . . . I don't party with white people."

Jasmine shook her head, annoyed with Simone already. She managed to get the waitress's attention and ordered two apple martinis.

"None of these white boys better try to talk to me."

"Simone, trust me, these white people in here be on a completely different vibe. They all about having fun and a good time when they go out. Watch how many celebs stroll up in here within the next two hours or so."

"In here?"

"Yes, in here."

Simone rolled her eyes.

The waitress came back with the drinks, and Simone took her drink off of the tray without even waiting for the waitress. She crossed her legs, put the tiny red straw to her mouth, and started to sip on her drink.

"Thank you." Jasmine handed the waitress forty dollars.

"So what's up with school?"

"It's kicking my ass." Jasmine didn't want to tell Simone that she had withdrawn from school for this semester.

"That's cool."

Simone was clearly distracted. She put her drink down and was responding to a text message. After a moment she started to smile, and she texted something.

"Ish said to tell you what's up. And he said he's been to Sway before, and it's a cool spot."

Jasmine looked at Simone and just shook her head. Suddenly Simone had loosened up and was ready to let her hair down after Ish validated the spot.

"So what was you saying about school?" Simone asked.

"Nothing. Never mind."

Simone ordered some Buffalo wings for them. Jasmine knew it was going to be a long night, but she was working, and that's how she looked at it.

She sat for about two hours and listened to Simone talk about how she was so certain that Ish was going to be getting her an engagement ring real soon and how she couldn't wait for him to ask her to marry him.

"No offense, Simone, but do you think Ish is the marrying type?"

"Yup," Simone immediately replied.

Jasmine left it alone and didn't try to argue with her.

Before long, Simone was asking Jasmine what she had planned for Saturday, which was the next day.

"Nothing at all. You don't understand how boring my life is right now. It's like all I do is go to school and come home and study."

"You need to stop acting like you married to Nico and start doing you. That's your problem," Simone had the audacity to say.

Jasmine just nodded. "So what about you? What's up for tomorrow?"

"I'm probably going to go with Ish to the new casino that opened up in Queens." Simone then excused herself to go to the bathroom and told Jasmine that after that she was probably going to get ready to leave.

"Let me guess—You're heading to Ish's house for some dick?"

Simone smiled and pointed at Jasmine, and then she walked off to the bathroom.

As soon as Simone was out of eyesight and earshot, Jasmine pulled out her phone and called Homicide. "We about to leave now, so figure in about thirty or forty minutes."

"That's what's up. I'm good. I'm here," Homicide replied. "Everything sound a'ight?"

"Yeah, everything is good. She talking about she heading there now to get fucked."

"No doubt. Just keep your phone on."

"Okay." Jasmine ended the call.

◆◆◆

Homicide and his homeboy, who went by the name of Cash Out, were parked three houses down from Ish's house, sitting in an all-black Audi with tinted windows. Ish lived on a quiet middle-class block, where all of the neighbors parked their cars on the street, so the Audi didn't look out of place, even though it was two in the morning. Ish's house was completely dark, and the white Mercedes-Benz S550 that he drove wasn't on the block or in his driveway.

At two fifteen in the morning Simone pulled into the driveway of Ish's house and turned off the engine. It took her about two minutes to get out of the car, and when she did she was talking on her cell phone. Simone was fully engrossed in her conversation so she was distracted and didn't see Homicide and Cash Out exit their Audi wearing all-black and black ski masks.

Ish's house didn't have a fence or any bushes. It was just wide-open landscape and layout, so it would have been easy for Homicide and Cash Out to be spotted.

Simone ended her call with Ish just before unlocking the front door. As she opened the door she felt somebody grab her forcefully from behind, rush her into the house, and close the door behind her. Simone's heart dropped to her feet and she desperately tried to free herself from the intruder's grip.

Homicide's left hand was inside of a black leather glove that completely covered Simone's mouth, and with his right hand he gripped a black semi-automatic weapon and pressed it to her temple.

"Shut the fuck up! Stop fighting me, and I won't kill you!"

Simone stopped resisting, but her chest was visibly rising and falling because she was nervous and breathing so hard.

"Who's in the house with you?" Homicide asked.

Cash Out turned on the lights and closed the vertical blinds, so no one could see inside the house.

Simone shrugged her shoulders to indicate that she didn't know who was home. She didn't know who was gripping her from behind, but she could see Cash Out in his ski mask, and the sight of him terrified her.

Cash Out quickly ran through the house and went from room to room just to make sure it was completely empty.

Homicide knew from Jasmine that Simone talked about how Ish would have her get cash and go to the post office to buy money orders for him to pay his bills, so he was sure there was cash in the house.

Homicide slid his hand from Simone's mouth and held her in a headlock, her back leaning against his chest and his forearm applying choke-hold pressure to her neck. "Where the cash?"

Simone, feeling the gun at her temple, was too afraid to lie. "It's downstairs in the basement. Please just don't kill me!"

"Where at downstairs?" Homicide yelled directly into her ear.

"In the stand-alone freezer, under the meat and the food."

Homicide nodded to Cash Out. Cash Out went downstairs, and within two minutes he came back with three large stacks of frozen cash. It looked like about twenty or thirty thousand dollars, but it was hard to determine because it was stuck together.

"I know that ain't it! Where the rest of the money at?" Homicide yelled, and he threw Simone to the ground by her hair and aimed his gun at her.

"I don't know, I swear to you, I don't know," Simone said, trembling.

"You lying to me!"

"I'm not. I swear to you, I'm not." Simone shook her head, and tears began streaming down her face. Simone knew that Ish was on his way home and was hoping he would hurry up and get there before she got raped or killed.

"Where the drugs at?"

Simone was frozen in fear because now she knew she was dealing with dudes who knew Ish.

Homicide nodded to Cash Out.

Cash Out walked up to her and kicked her as hard as he could in her ribs. "Where the fuck is the drugs at?" he hollered.

The kick instantly knocked the wind out of Simone. She doubled over on the living room floor clutching her ribs, gasping for air, and trying to talk all at the same time.

"There's nothing," she faintly replied from the ground, certain she was about to die.

Homicide walked over and picked up Simone's phone and told her to find Ish's number. Simone was barely able to move because of the razor-sharp pain in her side that felt like she was being stabbed with a hunting knife.

Homicide held out the phone, and Simone quickly scrolled through it until she got to Ish's number. Homicide then sent Ish a text message from her phone: *Where are you?*

"Tie that bitch up!" Homicide ordered Cash Out.

Cash Out ripped the lamp from the wall. Then he snapped the electrical cord from the lamp and used it to tie Simone's hands behind her back and to the base of the fireplace mantle.

Simone had just gotten her breath back in her lungs from being kicked, and just as she did, she found Cash Out's gun literally stuffed in her mouth.

"Where the drugs at, bitch?" he asked while he cocked the gun.

Ish was just exiting off the Belt Parkway when he got Simone's text. He was about to text back and tell her where he was, but he decided to just call her instead. Part of him was wondering why she sent him that text if she had just spoken to him five minutes earlier and told her that she was close to home.

The phone rang, and Ish's name popped up on the caller ID. Homicide didn't want to answer it because he didn't want Simone to start screaming or do anything to tip off Ish. Ish called right back when he got no answer, and again it rang out to voice mail.

"Bitch, you got two seconds to tell me where the fuckin' drugs at or your man is gonna come home and find your brains splattered in that fireplace."

Simone knew she had to say something. So she remembered the first night she ever came by Ish's house that he had removed one of the gates to the heating vent and reached inside and took out some weed that he had rolled for them to smoke.

"I swear to God, I don't know, but in the kitchen look inside the heating vent. There might be something there."

Ish called back a third time, and again Homicide sent him to voice mail.

Homicide was now wondering if the text had spooked Ish and if he knew something was up. He was ready to bounce because if Ish sensed something was off, Homicide didn't want to get caught out there outgunned and outmanned if Ish showed up with some of his soldiers.

Cash Out ripped the vent gate from the wall and reached inside and found two pounds of weed. He ran back into the living room and showed it to Homicide. Homicide was pleased with the take, but he was frustrated that the robbery didn't go the way he'd wanted it. He wanted Ish to walk in on the robbery unsuspecting, so he could hold him hostage and find out where Ghetto Mafia's stash house was.

Homicide walked up to Simone, and with his gun, he smacked her across the face. Simone saw stars. Her face spun and hit the wall, and blood from her mouth splattered on to the floor and wall. Three of her front teeth had just been knocked out.

"We out!" Homicide said to Cash Out.

Just as they made their way to the front door, the home phone started to ring. When the home phone went to voice mail, Ish knew something was up. He ran the red light he was at and the next three red lights, trying his hardest to get to his crib as quickly as he could.

When Ish ran the light at 147th Avenue and Brookville Boulevard, a New York City cop saw him and immediately turned on his lights and started to follow Ish.

Ish was only five blocks away from house. Had he not gotten pulled over, he would have literally caught Homicide and Cash Out coming out after the home invasion. But, as it turned out, Homicide and Cash Out made it to their Audi with twenty thousand in cash and two pounds of weed.

Ish tried his best to keep his cool as the cop asked him for his license and registration, so he complied without any kind of confrontation or resistance. He was hoping like crazy that the cop didn't ask him to step out of the car because he was certain the cop would have seen the handgun tucked in his waistband.

THIRTY-SIX

Homicide and Cash Out got about five miles away from the crime scene when they pulled the car to the side of the road and turned the heat on full blast although it was warm outside. They wanted to thaw out the frozen stacks of money. Once the money was thawed out, Homicide counted out five stacks of the twenty grand and gave it to his partner in crime, and he kept the rest for himself. He had also given Cash Out one pound of the weed and kept the other pound for himself before they parted ways, promising to hook up again real soon for another caper.

Homicide would have split the loot fifty-fifty with Cash Out, but it was his masterminding that had got them the loot. Cash Out was really only assisting on the tactical part of things, so the split was fair as far as far as they both were concerned.

By the time Homicide made it to Jasmine's SoHo apartment it was a little past five in the morning.

"Everything okay?" Jasmine asked with a bit of nervous anticipation. Although she would never tell Homicide, in her heart she was hoping that no one had ended up dead at the home invasion.

Homicide handed Jasmine three stacks and told her that everything went off smoothly. He sat down on her couch and ran his hand over his head and down his face.

Jasmine took the money and kissed Homicide and thanked him for it, but in the pit of her stomach, she felt horrible. It was the first time that she could remember money in her hands not feeling good to her and not making her feel genuinely happy.

"I bought some Coronas and some Guinness if you want one," she said to Homicide.

Homicide told Jasmine to bring him a Guinness, which she did, and she sat down next to him on her couch. Jasmine pressed him for details on the robbery, but he had been around the block way too many times and knew to keep his mouth shut. The stone-cold look he gave to Jasmine was all it took to stop her from asking a million questions.

Homicide reached for Jasmine's remote control and turned on the flat-screen TV.

Jasmine desperately wanted to know what was going through his head. "Babe, just tell me one thing—did anybody get hurt?"

"What the fuck you asking me that for?" Homicide stared at Jasmine.

Jasmine knew that he was seriously waiting for her to give him an answer. "I'm just asking, baby, that's all."

"Don't worry about that shit." Homicide stood up from the couch and guzzled down the rest of the Guinness.

"I'm sorry." Jasmine tried to push up on Homicide and give him a kiss, but he wasn't interested in that. Instead he rubbed on his beard and thought about how he had fucked up by not being patient. He should have just waited for Ish to come home on his own instead of sending that text to him.

"Just be yourself. You don't know nothing, you don't say nothing, and you'll be good."

"Okay," Jasmine replied, and she asked him if he wanted another Guinness.

"Nah, I'm about to bounce."

Jasmine made sure she gave him a kiss. "I need you," she said.

Homicide looked into Jasmine's eyes and could feel her sincerity. "I gotchu. Don't worry about nothing."

Jasmine nodded her head, and then she walked Homicide to the apartment door to see him off.

After about five minutes Jasmine called Agent Gosling, who picked up on the fourth ring.

"Hello," Gosling said in a groggy voice. It was clear that he had just woken up.

"You up?"

"No. But what's up? Are you all right?"

"Yeah, I'm okay. Listen, I just got word straight from Homicide that Ish might be using his crib as a stash house."

"Okay," Gosling replied. "How sure was he?"

"Gosling, he robs drug dealers, so whatever he knows, he knows."

Gosling sounded like he was sitting up. "So what are you saying?"

"I'm just saying like I said already—Ish needs to be a priority."

Jasmine was talking in circles and wasn't really saying anything concrete that Gosling could work with. But she had called him to sort of pacify him and make out like she was telling him something about Homicide. She knew he couldn't do anything with the information she was giving him.

"We need something more concrete before we can get a search warrant. Just keep your ear to the ground."

"All right. I'll start calling you more. I think Homicide is comfortable enough with me now where he'll start opening his mouth, so I should have something soon that we can work with and that can get us an angle on him."

Gosling went quiet for a moment.

"You still there?" Jasmine asked.

"Yes, I'm here. Jasmine, listen. What do you think about possibly setting me up and having Homicide rob me?"

"I think I could pull that off with Homicide, but not right now. Apparently my name is hot as hell on the streets, and if I walk Homicide into an arrest, I won't be living for much longer."

Gosling wasn't sure what Jasmine was getting at, until she explained to him how Black Justice had branded her with the nickname Suicide Pussy.

"That's the only reason I been moving real slow on Homicide. That nigga would kill me in a heartbeat if he even remotely sensed that I was snitching."

Agent Gosling knew how dangerous a world Jasmine was operating in, so he completely understood where she was coming from.

Gosling yawned into the phone. "You have to stay alive. I get it," he added with an even bigger yawn. He was dead tired because he had been putting in a lot of overtime hours lately. "Jasmine, I'm going back to sleep. It is Saturday."

"Okay, no problem."

Gosling thanked Jasmine for touching base with him, and like he always did whenever he finished speaking to her, he cautioned her to be safe and to be smart.

THIRTY-SEVEN

Jasmine never went to sleep after she got off the phone with Gosling. She wanted to know for herself if Simone and Ish or anyone else had gotten hurt during the home invasion, but she obviously couldn't just come out and ask Simone. So although it was too early to call her, she decided to send Simone a text message: Girl you won't believe this. I heard after we left Sway that IDRIS ELBA showed up!

Jasmine knew how much Simone loved Idris Elba, so she was certain that she would hit her right back. She had no idea that Simone was in the Jamaica Hospital emergency room getting checked out and seeing if the doctors could do anything about her teeth.

Simone's head was pounding, and her ribs and her jaw were killing her, so Ish had suggested that she get X-rays just to make sure nothing was broken. It was a good thing Simone was dark-skinned; otherwise, she would have had visible black-and-blue marks on her side and on her face.

Simone stood up and walked over to the single mirror in the emergency room. She looked at her face, and tears rolled down her eyes. "Baby, look at me," she said, her lips swollen and three teeth missing.

Ish tried to calm her down by telling her that the swelling would soon go down and that she could get her teeth replaced. Ish felt horrible that he hadn't been there to help her, but at that point there was really nothing he could do but be there for her, help her out with her medical bills, and reassure her that he wouldn't let anything like that happen to her again.

Simone was in the same hospital that BJ was in. BJ was obviously in another section of the hospital, but Ish had gone up to his room to visit him. He had tried to explain to BJ what had happened, but BJ was too drugged up from another surgery he had just undergone. Things weren't looking good for BJ. The doctors were now certain that he was going to have to wear a colostomy bag for the rest of his life. They had done all they could do to prevent it, but the bullets had just done too much damage.

Ish knew he couldn't rely on BJ or Nico, or anyone else for that matter, to help him protect his own home or to seek vengeance for the way he had been violated. He was determined to find out who had run up in his crib, and he was going to make them pay with their lives.

"Simone, you sure nobody knew what was up?"

"I'm sure, baby. I know not to open my mouth."

Ish looked at her and nodded his head as he slowly paced back and forth in the emergency room, while Simone sat on one of the hospital beds waiting for the doctor to come back.

Ish liked Simone, but not nearly as much as she liked him. He had been mainly using her to sign for FedEx packages that contained drugs. See, Ghetto Mafia had a group of corrupt FedEx employees in Miami and in New York's JFK Airport who were able to get drugs on board FedEx airplanes for them and also get them on to specific FedEx delivery trucks.

Ghetto Mafia had been able to get drugs delivered to almost any location in Queens they wanted. They would always switch the drop-off locations to lower the risk of getting busted. They would also always have the package come in the name of a chick that they trusted, and they would have the girl sign for the packages. Just in case they ever got caught, they could always plead that the package wasn't in their name, and therefore they weren't responsible for it.

With BJ in the hospital, Bebo and Lo dead, and Nico laying low in Miami, Nico had been forced to have the FedEx packages go to Ish. Nico never wanted to tell anyone other than BJ exactly where his stash houses were. And even with BJ laid up, and although Nico was running out of options, he still didn't take the chance on telling Ish the location of the stash houses. Instead, Nico had the FedEx re-up packages come directly to Ish's house, so if anything went wrong, Ish would be without excuses.

Nico started having the FedEx packages delivered to Ish's house right after Ish and Simone had met at the strip club. Right from the jump, Ish knew that Simone was real needy and that she was on his dick, so he was easily able to convince her to have her name on the packages. He also convinced her with no problem at all to be at his house on a regular basis to accept the packages and sign for them.

Ish was thankful that the robbery hadn't happened forty-eight hours later, because had it happened on Monday instead of early Saturday morning, the robbers would have made off with a couple of bricks of heroin and coke that would have been in the house. The fact that the masked intruders had only taken the two pounds of weed and a relatively small amount of cash made Ish believe that Simone sincerely didn't have anything to do with the robbery. It would've been very tempting for her to set up the home invasion for the same day that he expected a re-up shipment.

Ish disregarded the hospital rules against talking on cell phones and spoke to Nico on his brand-new prepaid phone. He knew to never use his regular cell phone when talking with Nico, and he also knew to never give out Nico's number.

"Ish, I don't give a fuck what you gotta do, but you gotta find out who those muthafuckas were and handle that shit!" Nico ordered.

Ish tried to explain, as he had done before, that the two dudes had masks on and that Simone hadn't seen their faces.

"Ish, that's your fuckin' problem! We got ten ki's coming on Monday, and you already know that I can't have the shipment stopped. Yo, word on

WIFEY: I AM WIFEY

everything, Ish, don't fuck up this re-up!" Nico ended the call by hanging up on Ish.

"You believe this nigga Nico is upset with me over this shit?" Ish said to Simone.

Right at that point the emergency room doctor walked in.

"Okay, so we have good news. The X-rays were negative, no fractures or broken bones of any kind."

Ish's mind was somewhere else, so he paid the doctor no attention.

Simone had questions about her teeth and getting cosmetic surgery done, but since the doctor wasn't a dentist, he explained to her that he wouldn't be able to give her any real answers. He then told Jasmine that she could get dressed and that he would write up a prescription for her for painkillers.

"The nurse will be right out with the prescription and to sign you out."

Simone thanked him, and she started to get dressed so she would be ready to go as soon as the nurse got there.

◆◆◆

"Don't let Nico stress you, baby," Simone said to Ish while they pulled into the parking lot of Walgreens so she could get her prescription filled.

"Fuck that nigga! He on the phone talking that gangsta shit while his pussy ass is hiding out in Miami."

Simone was feeling a little bad. She was down on herself because she felt like, had she been a little more observant of her surroundings, maybe they wouldn't have got robbed and then Ish wouldn't have been feeling any stress. But there was nothing she could really do.

After they left Walgreens, Simone was too afraid to go back to Ish's house alone. So she asked him to drop her at her own apartment and told him that she would only stay at his house while he was there. Ish dropped her off and headed straight to the barbershop that Bebo had owned while he was still alive.

Ish was determined to find out who had robbed him. He figured, if the streets were talking, then he knew he could count on finding out what was being said by just listening to what the people in the barbershop had to say.

As soon as Simone locked the door to her apartment, she went right to her bathroom mirror and stared at her face. She couldn't believe how horrible she looked, but she knew she was lucky to be alive.

After she finished looking at her face in the mirror, she popped one of her painkillers into her mouth. As soon as she did that, her cell phone started vibrating.

"You don't how to text me back or call me?" Jasmine asked.

Simone sucked her teeth. "So you didn't hear what happened?"

"What happened with what?"

"Last night I got robbed."

"When? After you left Sway? And you just telling me now?"

"No. Well, yeah it was after I left Sway, but it happened at Ish's house."

"You're lying."

"I wish I was." Simone sighed. "Yeah, two dudes pushed their way in and beat me and tied me up and robbed the crib."

"Oh, my God! Simone, are you serious? Where are you right now?"

"Jasmine, I'm dead serious. Ish just dropped me off from the emergency room."

"Emergency room? Where are you at?" Jasmine asked with what sounded like genuine worry.

"I'm home now."

"Okay, I'll be there in forty-five minutes."

"No! I can't let anybody see me like this. My face is swollen, and I got three teeth missing. I look crazy."

Jasmine covered her mouth even though Simone couldn't see her through the phone. Jasmine really felt bad when she heard Simone say she was missing three teeth because she was sure it was Homicide who caused those teeth to go missing.

"You know I don't care how you look! I'm coming over regardless."

"Jasmine, really, I'll be okay. I'm probably going to shoot back over to Ish's house anyway. I have to be there tomorrow when FedEx shows up."

"Fuck FedEx! You don't know what's going on right now, so you don't need to be over by Ish's crib until you find out what's what."

"But, Jasmine, I have to sign for FedEx. You know how that goes."

"What are you talking about?"

"The re-up through FedEx."

Jasmine went silent for a quick moment.

"Hey, let me call you right back," Jasmine said, and then she hung up the phone quickly.

Jasmine had no idea what Simone was referring to about the re-up through FedEx, and she just sensed that she needed to have her recorder going while she spoke to Simone.

Jasmine retrieved her FBI-issued phone and started to record. She then called Simone back and put the call on speakerphone.

"Sorry about that," Jasmine said when Simone answered the phone. "I thought I heard my doorbell, but it was nothing. So, yeah, you were saying something about the re-up."

"Yeah, I was saying I just have to be there to sign for it."

Jasmine wanted to press, but didn't want to raise suspicion.

"Simone, trust me. Let things cool off first before you go back to Ish's house. Don't be hardheaded."

"I can't do that to Ish. Nico was already beefing with him over the robbery, so if this re-up don't go right, then I don't think Ish would let me forget it. I'm just so glad that the delivery didn't come yesterday. Everybody would be sick right now!"

Jasmine kept quiet because she wasn't sure how to respond.

Simone sucked her teeth and sighed. She told Jasmine that she couldn't believe what she was going through.

"Let me go. I'm trying to find a dentist I can go to today."

Jasmine reminded Simone to call her if she needed anything at all.

Jasmine sat down on the couch and thought for about five minutes about what Simone had just told her. "FedEx?" she said to herself in disbelief.

After thinking it through, she called Gosling.

"Got something for you."

"Speak to me," Gosling replied.

"This is the real deal."

"What?" Gosling asked with real anticipation.

"FedEx is making deliveries to Ish that you might want to look into."

"What kind of deliveries?"

"What do you think drug dealers are getting delivered to their house? It ain't no e-commerce merchandise being delivered, I can tell you that."

It instantly clicked with Gosling after Jasmine said that.

"Wow!" Gosling replied. "I'll get right on this right now."

Gosling was hoping that Jasmine was right about what she was telling him. It would make him look good. He was really starting to like the way Jasmine worked.

After he ended the call with her, he wondered why Jasmine, as talented as she was, never tried to get into the law enforcement industry as a career. He always thought that really good confidential informants would make the best cops and federal agents, and Jasmine was no exception.

THIRTY-EIGHT

The FBI contacted FedEx, and they made arrangements to have drug-sniffing dogs check the two packages scheduled to arrive at Ish's house for Monday morning before ten a.m. Based on Jasmine's tip, and like Gosling had suspected, both packages came up positive for drugs, so the FBI, Drug Enforcement Agency, and the New York City Police Department all moved quickly to formulate a plan to raid Ish's home.

FedEx allowed one of the FBI agents to pose as a worker and provided him with a FedEx box truck, a uniform, and a hand-held computer. In the back of the box truck were FBI and DEA agents ready to storm Ish's house as soon as the package was delivered. Sitting five blocks away and ready to provide immediate backup were New York City Police Department units.

Just before ten a.m., the FedEx truck arrived at Ish's house. The middle-aged black FBI agent dressed as a FedEx worker got out of the truck carrying two ten-pound boxes and a hand-held computer. He walked up to Ish's front door and rang the doorbell.

Ish answered the door and immediately suspected something was wrong because his normal FedEx guy wasn't making the delivery.

"I have two packages for a Simone Simmons," the FedEx driver said.

Ish's heart was pounding as he looked around. Nothing looked out of place, but he could sense something wasn't right. "Oh, okay. Let me go get her for you." Ish went back inside his house and closed the door.

The FBI agent wasn't expecting Ish to do that. The last thing they wanted was for Ish to be retrieving a gun. All of the agents inside the FBI truck looked on and waited anxiously.

◆◆◆

Simone was at a dentist in Westbury, Long Island, preparing to get her teeth worked on. She had called around to a bunch of different dentists, and ended up choosing the one who could give her the quickest appointment at the most reasonable fee. One of his scheduled patients had called and canceled their appointment, so he was able to squeeze her in without her having to wait a week to see him.

Her cell phone rang, and she picked up on the first ring. "Hey, babe. Everything go okay?"

"Yo, there's a dark-skinned, black FedEx dude. You ever seen him before?"

"Never." Simone replied. Their normal FedEx guy was a Puerto Rican guy named Juan.

"Fuck!" Ish heard his doorbell ring. He told Simone he had to go and would call her back.

◆◆◆

Ish went to his bedroom and got his gun. He tucked it into his waistband and pulled it over his shirt then ran back downstairs to the front door.

"Sorry about that," he said after re-opening the front door.

"No problem. I don't mean to rush you, but I have one other stop to make before ten a.m., or else I'm going to hear it from my boss," the FBI agent said convincingly.

"Yeah, well, I thought Simone was in the house, but she's not home right now."

The FBI agent had already gone over the different scenarios, so he was prepared. He looked at his computer and pressed a button, then another.

"Oh okay. I was just double-checking. Well, this will require a signature. I don't know if you want to sign for it. If not, I can take it back, and someone can pick it up tonight after six o'clock at our JFK facility."

Ish nodded his head. Everything seemed all right to him. The FedEx worker seemed legit and didn't seem antsy or overly eager for Ish to take the package. Ish had never had any packages go back to the FedEx facility for later pickup, so he wasn't feeling good about that option. He had no idea what the screening process was like if the packages went back to the facility. He could hear Nico in the back of his mind.

"It's a package for my tenant. I had some issues with her, so I'm not really sure if I should take it or not. You know what I'm saying?"

"No problem." The undercover FBI agent reached for a door tag. "Take this door tag, leave it for your tenant, and just have her pick it up later tonight. And if she can't make it, we'll automatically redeliver it tomorrow."

"A'ight, you know what? Fuck it. I'll sign for the shit."

The FBI agent placed the packages on the steps and handed Ish the handheld device and the small pen that went with it and showed him where to sign. Ish thought about asking for the normal FedEx guy, but that would have seemed somewhat weird so he said nothing.

"What's the last name?" the FBI agent asked.

"Jameson."

"Okay." The FBI agent touched something on the computer screen right before picking up the packages and handing them to Ish.

Ish's phone started to vibrate just as he took hold of the packages. It was Simone calling him back. His hands were full, so he couldn't pick up, and it went to voice mail.

He went back inside his house and closed the door, feeling somewhat relieved. It seemed like seconds later he heard a noise at his front door, but he was distracted by looking at the missed call on his cell phone.

The noise he'd heard was the sound of the FBI agents' hydraulic rabbit prying open his metal security screen door. Twelve FBI and DEA agents were lined up on his front steps. The lead agent had pried open the screen door and held it open so the second agent could have free access to Ish's main front door.

The second agent hit the front door with a battering ram. *BOOM!*

The front door burst open, and the federal agents stormed the house.

"Shit!" Ish dropped his phone on the ground and went for his gun.

"Gun!" one of the agents yelled.

BANG!

The agent leading the attack had fired his gun before Ish had a chance to fire his own. The shot hit Ish in the right shoulder and caused his gun to fall out of his hand and on to the living room floor. The force of the gunshot caused him to lose his balance and fall backwards, but he didn't fall to the ground.

Two of the agents grabbed hold of Ish and slammed him face first to the living room floor before handcuffing him.

"Errrgghh!" Ish grimaced in pain on the floor.

Agents flooded the rest of the house looking for others to also arrest.

Outside Ish's house, the block was now crawling with New York City police, FBI, and DEA, and the sound of an ambulance could be heard approaching the block.

Ish was bleeding from his shoulder and still face down on the living room floor grimacing in pain. His pain wasn't only coming from the gunshot wound, but also his jaw that broken when the agents slammed him to the living room floor. With his face on the floor and turned sideways, he could see his cell phone lighting up and vibrating. He could also see it was Simone calling him back.

As the phone rang, one of the agents planted his boot onto Ish's neck to make sure he didn't try to move. It was the ultimate sign of humiliation, but it was a small thing compared to how fucked up Ish was feeling as he laid there on the ground wondering if Simone had set him up.

THIRTY-NINE

The raid on Ish's house and his arrest made the television news and the local newspapers. It was becoming clear to everybody that Ghetto Mafia was falling apart and was at risk of becoming extinct.

Homicide read some of the newspaper stories about the raid and couldn't believe how fucked up his luck was. But the story had energized him to continue to target Ghetto Mafia. He knew they were vulnerable, and he was just waiting to see who was going to step in with Ish now locked up.

During the two weeks that followed the raid on Ish's house, Homicide spent a lot more time with Jasmine. He was genuinely starting to like her, so he wanted to be around her more. And the feelings of love were definitely mutual and growing on Jasmine's part.

Homicide also wanted to stay close to Jasmine because he wanted to know everything about Ghetto Mafia as soon as she knew. His trust in Jasmine was growing with each passing day, but part of him still wondered just how much loyalty for Nico remained in her.

To test Jasmine, one day out the blue, he had her take him to Nico's house in Long Island. Homicide wanted to see if she would put up any resistance to him, and also what vibes he could get from the house. He wanted to know if Nico really had been out of town in Miami. Homicide figured he would be able to tell if the house looked like it had been lived in recently.

Jasmine was caught off guard but didn't resist. "You want to go there now? As in right now?" she asked, as they sat inside the Shark Bar eating.

"As soon as we leave here," Homicide replied.

Jasmine put a forkful of food in her mouth and nodded. Jasmine was starting to come to grips with the fact that Nico had probably written her off for Mia, and therefore she didn't care where she was seen with Homicide or who was reporting what back to Nico. As far as Nico was concerned, Jasmine had nothing to lose. Agent Gosling really trusted her now because she was making him look so good, so he had lowered the pressure on her to hurry and get information on Nico.

It was about ten o'clock on a Thursday night when Jasmine and Homicide left the Shark Bar in Manhattan and headed out to Long Island. Homicide had a gold Yukon Denali with dark-tinted windows that he always drove, but whenever he was going out with Jasmine, he always preferred for her to chauffeur him around in her BMW truck. So Jasmine drove while Homicide reclined in the front passenger seat, his snub-nose revolver in his waistband.

At that time of night, the roads were not congested, so it didn't take any time at all to get to Nico's Long Island estate. She pulled up into the circular driveway and turned off the engine. The house was pitch-dark.

Homicide was used to being in the city where there was always some kind of lights on. But at Nico's remote estate there was no streetlights to help illuminate the property. It was so dark, Homicide could barely see his own hands when he held them up in front of his face.

"It's black as shit out here," he said to Jasmine.

It was also eerily quiet. Jasmine was used to the darkness and the quiet because she had experienced it so many times. She could have walked to the front door of the house with her eyes closed if she had to.

She made it to the front door, let herself in with her key, disengaged the alarm system, and turned on the light. Homicide was thankful for the light that came from inside the house because it allowed him to see where he was walking.

"This shit is like living out in the country or some shit." Homicide walked inside the house and looked around.

"You ain't lying," Jasmine replied, wondering why Homicide wanted to come there. She scooped up the pile of mail that had accumulated and placed it all on the kitchen counter.

Homicide took notice of that. He also took notice of how good Nico appeared to be living. Having finished a five-year prison sentence just over a year ago, he knew he couldn't come close to balling on Nico's level. Homicide felt the envy starting to build up inside of him, but he didn't say anything derogatory about the house.

While Jasmine looked through the mail, Homicide opened up the refrigerator and looked around. He saw that the refrigerator wasn't that full and the expiration date on the gallon of milk had long since passed, giving him further confirmation that the house had not been lived in as of late.

"You want a drink or something?" Jasmine asked.

"I'm good." Homicide walked out of the kitchen and walked into the den and looked around in there.

While Homicide was in the den, Simone called Jasmine. Jasmine wondered about Simone's timing, but she dismissed it as just a coincidence.

"No sob stories," Jasmine said to Simone. She was getting tired of Simone calling her and telling her how much she missed Ish, how Ish wasn't calling her from jail, how he had flipped out on her when she went to visit him in jail three days after he had been arrested.

"No, I promise. No more 'Depressed Debbie talk' from me," Simone replied.

"Thank you. You understand what I was saying, right?"

"Yeah, I get where you're coming from."

Jasmine had been telling Simone that death and jail was part of the game; if she was going to mess with drug dealers, she had to get used to that. She reminded Simone how her ex-boo Shabazz had been killed, and she quickly got over it and moved on to Nico.

"So we hanging out tomorrow?" Simone asked.

"Yeah, if you want to." Jasmine smiled, glad that Simone finally seemed like she was ready to move on.

"And we ain't going back to Sway. I don't care what celebrities be up in there. I just don't really click with that environment."

Jasmine rolled her eyes. "Now let you be the first one who found out about Sway and you had took me there, then Sway would be the bomb and you would be loving it and wouldn't want to go anywhere else."

"That is not even true, and you know it."

"Whatever. I ain't even gonna argue with you. So how are your teeth? They look good?"

"They look amazing! Oh, my God! I went back the other day and got the veneers bonded. Wait until you see me. I look like a Hollywood actress."

"Okay, so you pick the spot, and we'll go wherever you want to go. And, no, we're not going back to Sue's Rendezvous, so get it out your mind."

"I ain't even thinking about Sue's."

"Okay, so just call me tomorrow."

◆◆◆

Simone was mad at herself for not having the courage to mention to Jasmine what she really wanted to tell her. Regardless of the front that Simone was putting on, it was really bothering her that Ish didn't trust her and that he really thought that she'd staged the home invasion as a setup to him getting busted by the feds.

As much as she had pleaded with Ish and sworn to him that she had nothing to do with either the robbery or the raid, Ish wasn't buying it, and he promised Simone that he was going to handle her. He also reminded her that it was her name on the FedEx package.

Simone was desperate to prove her innocence and would stay up at night trying to figure things out. She would brainstorm things on paper. She would replay events in her head, but she kept coming up blank. But three nights ago, she had finally come up with something she thought was concrete.

Simone figured that the masked gunman who'd had his hand around her mouth had to have a full, bushy beard because she remembered seeing what looked like black hair sticking out from the base of the ski mask he was wearing. She also remembered that Ish had told her that BJ was saying that Jasmine was playing Nico by going to a Knicks game with Homicide.

Simone had never said anything to Jasmine about what Ish had told her. She wanted to see if Jasmine would voluntarily bring it up. Since Jasmine never said anything, she kept her mouth shut about it because she didn't want it getting back to Ish that she couldn't hold water.

Simone was now convinced that it was Homicide who had robbed her. She had asked around about how Homicide looked, and people who knew of him all knew that he rocked a full beard. Simone couldn't wait to tell Ish exactly what she was thinking, but she was debating if she should first try and get more confirmation somehow.

Ish was all Simone thought about day and night. She had to have him back in her life. She was even willing to do his bid with him if he was to get convicted. That's just how strongly she felt about him.

Simone felt equally confident about the other concrete thing that her brainstorming had revealed to her, and that was that her friend Jasmine's hands were dirty. Simone couldn't exactly put her finger on it, but she knew that Jasmine wasn't a psychic. Yet to her it was like Jasmine had warned her that Ish's crib was going to get raided.

She replayed Jasmine's words in her mind. "Simone, trust me. Let things cool off first before you go back to Ish's house. Don't be hardheaded." She knew the only reason Jasmine had said to trust her was because she knew what was about to go down the next day. Simone had played detective by agonizing over all of the details. She was certain that she had come to the right conclusions. She knew she had to relay that information to Ish and then hope that he would relent and forgive her, and start to trust her again. She couldn't wait to vindicate herself.

◆◆◆

While Jasmine was on the phone with Simone, Homicide had taken himself on a tour of Nico's crib. Homicide had a photographic memory and was memorizing the entire layout. He didn't know when, but he was definitely going to pay another visit, and he wanted to make sure that he first knew the lay of the land.

FORTY

The day after Homicide and Jasmine were at Nico's house, Jasmine was kicking herself for forgetting to bring some more clothes to her SoHo loft. She and Simone were going to be hanging out later that night, and there was a brand-new outfit and a pair of brand-new shoes she had over at Nico's house that she wanted to wear. Although Jasmine would have wanted to spend her Friday afternoon sleeping and relaxing, she decided to drive back out to Long Island during the early part of the afternoon to avoid the crazy Friday rush-hour and late-night traffic.

She hopped in her truck and made her way out to Long Island by herself. The ride alone did her a lot of good because it allowed her some time to just think about things and to clear her head. It was rare for Jasmine to get quality time by herself because her life was in constant turmoil.

Jasmine made it there relatively quickly. After she parked her truck and went inside, she instantly had a flashback to the time she almost got killed in the house by Bebo. Though a good amount of time had passed, she was still afraid to be in the house alone, even during the daytime.

After closing the door behind her and making sure it was locked, Jasmine quickly went upstairs and grabbed the outfit and the shoes she had come for. She also grabbed a couple more outfits to take back with her to Manhattan and threw them on the bed.

Jasmine entered her walk-in closet and searched for more shoes to take with her. While looking around, she heard the front door close. Her heart dropped, and then it quickly started beating again. She froze dead in her tracks and kept still, not wanting to make a sound.

Jasmine was certain that her snitching had caught up to her and that either Ish, Black Justice, or even Nico had someone following her, and they had followed her to the house to kill her as payback for all of her snitching.

"Fuck! Shit!" she said softly. She cursed herself for being so stupid to come alone and without a weapon. She could hear the person downstairs moving around. She felt that she had no choice but to hide in the closet.

As quietly as possible Jasmine started taking clothes off the racks they were on and created one huge pile about three feet high. She sat down in it and pulled clothes over her so that her face and body were completely covered. The whole time, her heart was racing a thousand beats per second. Now that her head was covered and her heart was beating so fast, it made it very hard for her to breathe, and she started to feel claustrophobic. Even though the claustrophobic feelings were making her panic even more, she knew she had to keep her head under the clothes if she wanted to stay alive.

Jasmine heard someone coming up the stairs, and it was like right at that moment she saw her life flashing before her eyes. She knew she was going to certainly die.

"JASMINE!"

Jasmine heard a booming voice yell out her name, but she stayed perfectly still.

"JASMINE! Yo, you up here?"

With all of the clothes surrounding her, Jasmine could barely make out the voice. After a few seconds, she didn't hear anything. Then she heard a cell phone ringing. She wanted to die. She was so stupid; she had left herself phone in the kitchen when she had first entered the house.

"Yo, this me. I just touched down about an hour ago. I'm at the crib."

Jasmine heard every word being spoken, and then it all hit her. That was Nico's voice. She quickly popped her head through the mountain of clothes, so she could get some air in her lungs. She then stood up and left the clothes on the floor. "Nico?" she said, pushing open the closet door.

Nico had only stuck his head into the bedroom to see if Jasmine was in there when he had called her name, so when he heard her, he came back into the bedroom from the hallway.

"You scared the shit out of me!" she said to Nico.

Nico didn't say anything and just stared at Jasmine. He hadn't seen her in so long, he was captivated by her.

She looked at Nico and noticed that his skin was real even-toned and that he had gotten two shades darker. He looked as sexy as she ever remembered him looking.

Jasmine forgot about everything she had been thinking and was no longer scared. She went right toward Nico and gave him a really big hug. "I missed you so much!" she said to him, and tears instantly started running down her face. She cried while holding him.

"I'm home now. Stop crying."

"I thought you were through with me, baby." Jasmine leaned back and looked Nico in his eyes while still crying.

"I was handling business. You know that."

Jasmine shook her head, and through her tears she smiled and looked at Nico, slowly shaking her head. "I want to be so angry with you right now. And I can't. I hate that about you. Uggghhh!"

Nico looked around the room but didn't say anything.

"You wasn't calling me, you wasn't getting word to through your boys or nothing! It's like ever since I had got arrested that night, you just went funny style on me, and you never explained why."

"I wasn't calling because them boys was listening, and I had to stay off the grid. I was protecting you by not calling you and possibly getting you jammed up in my shot."

"I hate your ass! Uggghhh! God!" Jasmine punched Nico in the chest.

She wanted to go so hard on Nico and let him have it. She felt like all that she was going through, being a confidential informant, was all because of him. She felt like had he not left her to take the weight when she got jammed up and arrested that night, she never would have had to agree to be a confidential informant. But he left her stranded and didn't even have the respect for her to call an attorney. He had left her no choice but to agree to snitch.

While Jasmine was thinking those thoughts, Nico was wondering about her. In his gut he knew she was snitching, and that was one of the main reasons that he had come back to New York. He wanted to get concrete proof for himself that she was a snitch, and he was planning on testing her.

Nico was no dummy. He knew women were caring and attached to their feelings by nature. Therefore, if he wanted to win back Jasmine's trust to the point where she wouldn't fear telling him the one hundred percent absolute truth, he had to fuck her and get back control of her mind through her pussy strings.

He reached out and grabbed hold of Jasmine's arm and pulled her toward him. Then he slid his hand inside her sweat pants and started rubbing on her pussy.

Jasmine pulled his hand away. "You don't speak to me, you disappear on me and just go about doing your thing with absolutely no cares about me at all, and now you want to just play with my pussy?"

"Stop fighting me." Nico slipped his hand back inside Jasmine's pants. He reached inside her thong and felt her pussy lips. He started gently rubbing on her clit. "I did have cares for you. Trust me on that."

"Can we just talk? Seriously, let's just talk and get all issues on the table, so I can really know that you hear me and whether or not you actually give a damn about me. And I can clear up anything that's going through your mind."

Nico guided Jasmine to the bed, laid her down, and took off her flip-flops. Then he pulled off her sweat pants and her thong.

Jasmine couldn't believe that it was so hard for her to resist Nico. While she stared at him, Nico took off his shirt, and Jasmine could tell that he had been working out while he was in Florida because he looked more buff than usual.

Jasmine's pussy was soon visibly leaking. That's how wet she was. No man turned her on the way Nico did. She enjoyed other dicks, but no other dude gave it to her like Nico did, and no other dude made her as wet as he was able to make her.

Jasmine spread open her legs for Nico, who let his jeans fall to the floor of their bedroom, and he slipped his dick into her pussy and started to fuck her harder than he had ever fucked her. Nico was also the only guy who hit Jasmine's G-spot in such an intense way that it made her squirt. Over the next hour and a half Jasmine would squirt a total of three times, and each time she did, she became more and more like Silly Putty in Nico's hands.

FORTY-ONE

While Jasmine was in the shower, she started to get a little paranoid and wondered had Nico really come home to kill her or to make sure someone carried out a hit on her. She started to think he probably just wanted to fuck her real good one last time before deading her.

Jasmine quickly dried off and applied lotion to her body and she got dressed and started to gather the shoes and the outfits she wanted to take back with her to SoHo.

"Where the fuck you going with all that?" Nico asked after coming back into the bedroom with just his boxers on and drinking a small glass of Hennessy with no ice.

Jasmine looked at him and finished stuffing brand-new outfits into a laundry bag. "I'm going out with Simone," she said and started to make her way toward the door so she could leave, but Nico held out his hand and stopped her.

Jasmine moved his arm. "Excuse me, babe. I have to hurry up."

"Nah, chill for a minute." Nico sipped on his Hennessy. "What the hell is that tattoo about? And what's this shit I'm hearing about you and Homicide at a Knicks game?"

Jasmine tried to push past Nico. "The tattoo is what I was feeling, and the Homicide rumors is just that—rumors."

Nico grabbed Jasmine's arm, but she pulled away from his grip and walked down the steps to the living room.

"You want all these answers after fuckin' me like I'm your whore. I don't think so, Nico."

"I wasn't fuckin' you like a whore."

"Well, how about what the fuck was you doing in Las Vegas with Mia?"

Jasmine was starting to get angry. She wondered why she didn't feel this way when he was fucking her half an hour ago.

Nico heard what the streets had been saying about Jasmine being Suicide Pussy, and it was on the tip of his tongue to bring it up. But he didn't want to play bitch games with Jasmine because, to him, it wasn't a game. Shit was serious for him, and he needed to get to the root of why his empire was falling apart. He was back in New York to put his trademark back on the drug game that he had mastered.

"Back to that quiet shit again, huh?" Jasmine made her way to the front door of the house.

Nico finished the glass of Hennessy he was drinking. "Jasmine, I ain't fighting you."

"And I ain't fighting you either. I came for some clothes and I got that. You got some pussy from me, so everything is good. I'm going out with Simone, and I'll see you real late tonight or in the morning."

Nico didn't say anything in response, and Jasmine made her way out to her truck, jumped in, and drove off. Jasmine's confidence and her brashness, mixed with her bipolar ways, was making Nico think she was more of a liability than an asset to him.

FORTY-TWO

When Jasmine walked into her SoHo loft, she saw Homicide doing push-ups bareback in the living room.

"Hey," Jasmine said.

Never did Jasmine think she would get so close to Homicide so quickly that she would feel like she had cheated on him, but that's exactly how she was feeling.

"Just knocking out some sets." Homicide stood up from the floor. He could sense something was up with Jasmine's mood, but he didn't say anything.

Jasmine walked over to a coffee table and placed her clothes and shoes on top of it. "Nico's back," she blurted out.

Homicide scratched his forehead, and then he went back down to the floor and continued doing push-ups.

"I'm just glad he wasn't there last night when we were there."

"Why's that?" Homicide asked, while doing push-ups.

Jasmine didn't answer him because she wasn't sure what to say.

Homicide finished another set of twenty-five push-ups, and then he stood up still waiting for an answer, breathing a little heavy from the push-ups.

"It would have been drama."

"I live for drama!" Homicide replied with emphasis. "That bitch-ass nigga wouldn't want to go to war with me. Trust me on that. I don't want you sexing that nigga. You understand?"

Jasmine slowly nodded her head.

Homicide walked over to a bottle of water he had placed on the floor near where he was doing push-ups, and he opened it up and started drinking.

Jasmine sighed, and tears started to form in her eyes. "Look, baby, can I tell you something? And please don't get upset."

Homicide stopped drinking and listened to what Jasmine had to say.

"I know things are still new with us, but I really love you, and I want you to know that you can trust me."

"I trust you, and I'm just saying I don't want you fuckin' that nigga."

"That's what I'm trying to get at—I just fucked him." Jasmine cringed.

Homicide gave her a real intense look.

"I know it was stupid, baby. I know it. And I was kicking myself the whole way home. And please believe that I really only went out there to get these outfits and I had no idea he was even going to be there." She looked at Homicide to see what his response was going to be.

Homicide said nothing, and Jasmine could tell he was tight.

"I just want you to trust me and know that I'll always be honest with you, and I want you to always be honest with me, no matter what."

Homicide nodded his head and drank some more water. "I respect that."

Jasmine felt relieved to hear Homicide say those words.

Homicide knew no woman had ever been that honest with him. He also knew Jasmine could have kept that to herself and he never would have known. "I respect that because you didn't have to say shit to me."

"I just want us to be able to be completely honest with each other. I'm so tired of these relationships that I been in where no one is totally free to just be who they really are. I don't want no superficial shit between us."

Homicide then asked Jasmine to sit down. "Ever heard of Preme?"

"Supreme?"

Homicide nodded.

"Of course. I never met him, but I know him. Who doesn't know Supreme?"

"Preme damn near raised me. He was like a father to me. He taught me the mathematics and all that. If it wasn't for him, I would have never had knowledge of self."

"I didn't know you were close to him like that."

"Well, the thing is, I woulda took a bullet for Preme without hesitating, and I put that on everything. I would have did a life bid in jail for him. But when we all caught charges and got indicted Preme started snitching. He was ready to cut a deal for himself and send me and a bunch of other cats to prison for a long time. I'm talking a minimum of seventy-five years. You understand what I'm saying?"

"Yeah."

"So I ain't never tell nobody this. You the first person I'm ever mentioning this to. And this is something that has to stay between me and you."

"Okay, it will. Don't worry," Jasmine said, even though she wasn't really sure where Homicide was going with what he was saying.

"So when I was sitting in jail, I find out Preme is snitching and I got in touch with my lawyer and asked him to see if he could cut a deal for me with the district attorney if I was willing to testify against Supreme. And my lawyer pulled it off for me. And I ended up ratting that nigga out."

"Yeah, but if he was going to snitch on you, you was smart to do that."

A bare-chested Homicide walked up to Jasmine. Smiling, he gently placed both of his hands on her cheeks, guided her head toward him, and kissed her on the lips.

"You get it! That's the only reason I snitched him out. The thing is, I would have done no time in jail had I agreed to have my name on the affidavit, but I wasn't down for that. The affidavit I signed was a John Doe affidavit. The district attorney told me that if I didn't reveal my identity,

I would have to do some time. So that's the real reason why I ended up doing five years."

"Wow! I totally wasn't expecting to hear that from you."

"Honesty you said, right?"

"Yes," Jasmine replied.

"See, real recognize real, and that righteousness that you was hitting me with is something I ain't never seen before. You know what I'm saying?"

Jasmine nodded her head. "I got something else to tell you, baby."

"What?"

"Well, you know how you said Preme was going to snitch you out?"

Homicide nodded.

"Well, without making this long drawn-out explanation, let's just say that being around street dudes like Shabazz and Nico forced me to do what I had to do too."

"Whatchu mean?"

Jasmine sighed and looked at Homicide. "Well, there really ain't no easy way to say this, so I'll just spit it out. I'm a CI."

"Stop fuckin' bullshitting." Homicide chuckled.

"I'm not lying. And you were one of those that the FBI had me target."

Homicide was stunned. He bit the inside of his lip. He immediately thought to himself that he was going to have to murder her if she was telling the truth.

"I really love you, baby, and you know I would never have told you that if I didn't truly love you."

Homicide shook his head in disbelief.

"Don't worry." Jasmine walked up to Homicide and kissed him. "All those times you gave me that good-ass dick? That was my way of making sure I could never hurt you, even though they wanted me to target you. From the first day I fucked you, it gave you an entrapment defense against the government."

Homicide smiled and rubbed on his beard. He nodded his head to show that he approved of her. He pulled her close to him, and then he marched her into the bathroom so she could take a shower with him.

Jasmine always thought it would be impossible for someone to make her come harder than Nico did, but that theory was shattered when Homicide fucked her in the shower and gave the most powerful orgasm she'd ever had in her life.

Homicide and Jasmine were truly in love, and Jasmine knew that from that day she was his wifey.

FORTY-THREE

Homicide and Jasmine spoke at length about things and he told her that he could easily make one of her problems go away. Jasmine knew Homicide was referring to killing Nico for her so she wouldn't have to ever worry again about the feds putting pressure on her to get incriminating evidence on Nico.

It was a very enticing proposition for Jasmine because, although the apartment and the money was good, she would much rather have her life back and didn't want to be accountable to anybody.

But while Jasmine and Homicide spoke, she reasoned with him and convinced him that killing Nico at that point in time didn't make any sense. She told Homicide to give her some time to work on Nico so that she could find out where he was stashing his drugs. Once she did, it would then make sense for Homicide to murder him because she was certain that Nico had enough drugs and money stashed that her and Homicide would be able to retire on.

Homicide loved the plan. He was even willing to allow Jasmine to see Nico on a regular basis if he stayed in New York because he knew that would be the only way for her to get close enough to figure out where his stash was.

After Homicide and Jasmine finished talking, Homicide sent her on her way with his blessings to go hang out with Simone. He left the apartment at the same time with her. He was planning on linking up with his homie Cash Out so the two of them could go to Sin City Strip Club in the Bronx.

So while Homicide was chilling at Sin City, Jasmine was bored out of her mind on City Island with Simone. Simone and Jasmine went to a couple of different spots on City Island, and none of them were poppin'.

Jasmine was regretting that she had let Simone ride with her, instead of driving separate cars. Now she was going to have to drive all the way back to Queens to drop Simone off at her apartment.

Simone begged Jasmine to come with her to one other spot on City Island so they could try Henny Coladas. Jasmine had never had that before, so she decided to just try it before putting their night of boredom and misery to an end.

"It's good, right?" Simone screamed into Jasmine's ear over the music.

Jasmine couldn't front. The drink was one of the best she had ever tasted, and before she knew it, she'd ordered a second, third, and fourth Henny Colada.

With liquor her system, Jasmine had lost track of time. It was close to three in the morning and time for last call.

Simone had purposely only had one drink because she was planning on bringing up Homicide's name once she got Jasmine drunk.

"The last round is on me." Simone ordered another Henny Colada and gave it to Jasmine. She pulled out twenty dollars and paid the bartender.

"I'm so drunk right now." Jasmine laughed. "And did I tell you Nico is back home? I put it on that nigga as soon as he walked in the door." Jasmine couldn't stop laughing, even though nothing was funny.

"You should go home when you leave here and give him some more. Wear his ass out!" Simone gave Jasmine a pound. "Fuck marriage and a ring and all that shit. If you want to lock a nigga down, you have to wear his ass out in the bedroom."

Jasmine burst out laughing again. She wasn't able to finish the last drink, and she and Simone went to the bathroom before they made their way out to her car.

"You want me to drive?" Simone asked.

Jasmine gave Simone a look as if to say hell no. She got behind the wheel and made her way off City Island, and soon they were on I-95 South, heading toward the Throgs Neck Bridge. When they got to the E-ZPass lane of the Throgs Neck Bridge, Jasmine's E-ZPass wasn't being read for some reason, and the yellow-armed gate in her lane would not rise up for her to drive through.

"This fuckin' thing!" Jasmine started blowing her horn to get the workers' attention.

A Bridge and Tunnel officer came walking over to Jasmine's side and asked her for her E-ZPass, so he could examine it and make sure it wasn't faulty. As soon as she rolled down her window, the smell of liquor hit him smack in the face.

"Miss, were you drinking tonight?" the officer asked her.

"Yes."

"How many drinks did you have?"

"Oh shit, here we go, Simone. I don't know. I think three drinks."

"Okay, miss, I'm going to need you to turn off the engine, and I need you and your friend to step out of the vehicle."

"Step out of the car for what?"

"Turn off the engine and step out of the car right now!" the cop screamed.

"Right now!" Jasmine screamed back, mocking the officer.

"Jasmine, just do what he says," Simone said, and she followed the officer's directions and got out of the truck.

The officer got on his radio and called for assistance. Within two minutes, three other officers arrived, and Jasmine started to get belligerent.

"I'm not getting out of shit! I'm working for the federal government. Y'all can call Agent Gosling!"

The officers looked at each other; they didn't know what Jasmine was talking about. She hadn't shown them a badge or any kind of credentials, so they dismissed what she had said. But Simone peeped everything.

The uniformed officers were trying to rip open Jasmine's truck door, but they couldn't.

Jasmine took out her BlackBerry and pressed her panic button for the first time, and within five minutes New York City police cars started coming to the scene with their sirens blaring. The FBI had dispatched them to the scene to assess everything until their agents could arrive.

Once all the police showed up, Jasmine got out of the car. And as soon as she did, she was handcuffed and taken down to the ground.

"Call Agent Gosling," she kept screaming, but her screams went on deaf ears.

The police lifted Jasmine off the ground and took her to the Bridge and Tunnel office, which contained a holding cell, a mere fifty yards away from the toll lanes.

The police threw Jasmine into a cell, while they treated Simone with kid gloves.

"She works for the government?" one of the officers asked Simone.

Simone shook her head to indicate no, and then she confirmed for the officers that Jasmine was indeed drunk.

After about twenty minutes, Agent Gosling and three other unmarked FBI cars arrived on the scene. The officers filled Agent Gosling in on what had happened and why Jasmine was being detained. But the FBI had jurisdiction over Jasmine, so she was released into Gosling's custody.

Gosling had one of the uniformed officers drive Simone home and informed them that he would drive Jasmine home. He placed Jasmine in the front seat of his squad car and made sure her truck was driven out of the toll bridge lane and parked in a spot right next to the holding cell.

Traffic had almost come to a standstill because of all of the cop cars near the tollgates. Even though it was real early in the morning, people looked on and rubbernecked, further backing up traffic.

Once Jasmine's truck was safe, Gosling sped off and whisked her away.

"Jasmine, you can't fuck up like this!" Gosling screamed. "You were doing phenomenal. Please don't blow it now by reverting back to your rebellious ways. And, please, for heaven's sake, lay off the liquor!"

Gosling looked over at Jasmine, and her cleavage and her thighs were turning him on. Jasmine also had on a pair of stilettos and Gosling loved to see women in them.

"I'm sorry. You're right. I don't know what happened."

It was hard for Gosling to be angry and give Jasmine real stern looks now that he had feelings for her. He reached over and placed his right hand on her left thigh. "I'm sorry. I shouldn't have snapped at you," he said, caressing her knee.

Jasmine was drunk, but she was fully aware of what was going on. She looked over at Gosling, and Gosling locked eyes with her and didn't remove his hand. He slid his hand up her thigh. She placed her hand on top of his to stop it from going any farther.

Gosling pulled over to the shoulder of the Cross Island Parkway. When the car came to a complete stop, he turned toward Jasmine and, without asking, started to tongue-kiss her, sliding his hand all the way up her thigh until he got to her pussy. Gosling's dick was so hard, it was almost coming out of his pants.

"Wait, wait, wait! What are you doing, Gosling?"

"I want you! I always wanted you," Gosling said, sliding his finger into Jasmine's pussy.

Jasmine exhaled, her mind racing. She didn't want to fuck Gosling, but she felt like if she didn't, he might end up later framing her for something she didn't do to get back at her.

Gosling got out of the car and got in the backseat and told her to come to the backseat with him. Jasmine felt creepy—like she was getting

ERICA HILTON

ready to fuck her father or her uncle or something, but she did as Gosling had told her.

Gosling was like a lion in heat, and as soon as Jasmine got in the car he pulled her toward him and pulled her titties out so that both were fully exposed. Gosling turned Jasmine around so that her ass was facing him, and he positioned her knees on the seat and bent her down so her head wasn't hitting the ceiling. Gosling then lifted up Jasmine's skirt and pulled her thong to the side. He took his gun out of the holster and put it on safety and tossed it on the front seat. Then he feverishly got out of his pants and stuck his dick in Jasmine's pussy from behind and started to fuck her raw.

"Don't come in me," she said sternly to him while he pumped his dick in and out of her.

Speeding cars were whizzing by on the parkway, none of which had any idea that two people were fucking inside the car on the side of the road.

Gosling wanted to last long inside of Jasmine, but all the pent-up excitement caused him to fuck her like a jackrabbit.

Within three minutes Gosling had pulled his dick out and was shooting his load all over the backseat of his FBI-issued car. "Ahhh shit! Ohhhh yeah! Wooooo!"

Gosling was thoroughly enjoying the nut that he had just bust. Jasmine's pussy was tighter and better than he'd imagined during all the times he'd jerked off in his house, fantasizing about his prized confidential informant.

FORTY-FOUR

Agent Gosling cleaned up his come with some tissue he had in the car. Jasmine was dead tired and stayed in the backseat, where she was able to stretch out and close her eyes. She was feeling like she was going to throw up, but she knew that if she just relaxed she would be fine. It was now approaching five in the morning, and she ended up falling asleep.

While she slept, Agent Gosling reached into his glove compartment and pulled out the bottle of vodka he had stashed there. He took a swig and then put the cap back on the bottle and stuffed it back inside the glove compartment. The swig of vodka gave the agent an instant rush. He loved the way the liquor felt as it traveled down his throat and into his stomach.

Gosling had two houses, but the house he liked most was the one in Floral Park, Long Island, relatively close to Queens. With the influence of the vodka he kept taking swigs of, he decided to take Jasmine to his house.

Gosling knew it was a dumb idea, but he didn't care. He wanted some more of Jasmine's pussy. He had come too quickly when he'd fucked her in the car. He wanted to fuck her one more time so she would remember his dick. Gosling woke Jasmine up and told her where she was, and then he walked her into his tidy two-story brick colonial house.

"Let me make you some breakfast," he said to her when they entered the front door. "Here. Have a seat on the couch."

Gosling sat Jasmine down on the couch and then went and made her a nice breakfast that included grits, eggs, sausages, and toast.

Jasmine's stomach was feeling queasy from the liquor, so she wasn't able to really eat the food, but the nibble made her feel better.

"Gosling, what am I doing here? What are we doing? What did we do?" Jasmine shook her head, hoping she could just snap her fingers and then be on an island somewhere far away from all the constant stress and drama in her life.

"Just relax. You done with your food?"

"Yeah. I can't eat any more of it, but thank you."

Jasmine took it on her own to walk over to the couch, where she lay down.

"You want to take a shower? Or you can go upstairs and lay down in my bed."

"No, I'm okay. I just want to lay here for about a half hour, and then I need you to take me back to my car."

Gosling told her he would do that. He then left Jasmine on the couch and went to his cabinet in the kitchen. He pulled out a brand-new bottle of vodka. Then he went into the medicine cabinet in his bathroom and got his bottle of Viagra, took out a pill, popped it into his mouth, and swallowed it.

With the liquor and the Viagra in his system, Gosling was more than ready to fuck, and he wasn't waiting for Jasmine to wake back up. He went to her on the couch and quietly and carefully lifted up her skirt, pulled her panties down, and started to lick on her clit.

Jasmine woke up startled. "What are you doing?" She tried to push him away, smelling the liquor on his breath.

"Let me fuck you one more time?"

Jasmine rolled her eyes, took of her panties and her skirt, and she just lay there, determined not to put any effort into fucking Gosling because she didn't want him getting hooked and then calling her every day for some pussy.

Gosling didn't need Jasmine's assistance. He took off his pants, and the Viagra had his dick standing at attention. He spread Jasmine's legs open and entered her missionary-style, pumping his dick in and out of her for five minutes straight.

Jasmine could feel Gosling about to come. "Remember what I said— Don't come inside me."

She was hoping he would hurry up and get his nut because she could see sweat forming on his brow. The last thing she wanted was for some of his sweat to drip down on her.

Thankfully Gosling pulled his dick out and came before he really started sweating.

After fucking Jasmine for the second time, Gosling was on cloud nine and felt like he was on top of the world. It made her feel dirty, like she was the scum of the earth.

Jasmine was no longer feeling like she had to throw up. Although she was physically feeling better, emotionally she was feeling like shit because she felt like, by letting Gosling fuck her, it was only going to make her feel guilty whenever she saw Homicide. She didn't want to cheat on Homicide, and yet she was feeling like that was exactly what she had just done. Though she had confessed some of her past sins to Homicide, she was certain that confession time was over. There was no way she was going to tell him about what she did with Gosling.

Jasmine's feeling of guilt was a small thing compared to the sheer panic she was feeling while she was walking out of Gosling's house. She suddenly remembered exactly what had happened when she'd confronted the officers.

Her drunkenness had caused her to scream out in front of Simone that she was working with the federal government. Jasmine knew she'd fucked up. Now she was trying to figure out just how to fix her fuck-up. There was no way Simone was going to keep that information under wraps.

FORTY-FIVE

Nico didn't know about Jasmine's SoHo apartment. He also didn't know exactly how much time she had been spending away from the house they shared together. So it was easy to see how he found it strange that she had supposedly gone out with Simone, and at close to seven-thirty in the morning, she still hadn't come back.

What's up with the snitch?—That was Mia's text to Nico, which actually woke him up and made him realize that Jasmine still wasn't home.

Nico didn't respond to it. He didn't need another lengthy lecture or a bunch of texts from her re-explaining why she was so sure that Jasmine was snitching.

Nico had his own brain, and he had a plan for how he was going to set up Jasmine and test her to see if she was snitching. If she failed, he was going to make her life a hell she had never imagined she could experience. He was going to first murder both of her parents before killing her.

Nico couldn't wait around for Jasmine to come home because he had moves to make. He was going to go see BJ in the hospital, and after that, if he hadn't heard from or seen her, then he would call her and find out where she had been all night long.

◆◆◆

While Nico was on his way to Jamaica Hospital to see BJ, Jasmine was on the elevator heading to her apartment. When she unlocked her door and walked in, the loft was very quiet, and although it was still early in the morning, she initially thought that Homicide wasn't there. But when she walked into her bedroom, she found him sleeping in her bed. Jasmine was surprised to see him there, because he always fell asleep in the living room watching sports.

"Babe, wake up. Baby, I have to tell you something," Jasmine said while she shook Homicide.

Homicide opened his eyes and saw Jasmine looking at him, but it took him a few seconds to figure out where he was and to get his bearings.

"Wake up, baby. I need you. I fucked up big time," Jasmine said.

"What's up? What happened?" Homicide asked, his voice hoarse.

"I got stopped by the Bridge and Tunnel police when I was coming back from City Island with Simone. Something was wrong with my E-ZPass, so the officer comes to my window and he smelled liquor on my breath. So he's like, 'Get out the car,' and was asking me, had I been drinking and all that shit. Simone gets out of the car, and I stay in the car with the doors locked and the windows up, and I'm like, 'Nah, fuck that! I ain't getting out.' And I was talking mad shit because I was drunk, so it was the liquor talking for me. So, anyway, the next thing you know is, he calls other officers, and other cops come and they force me out. I was trying to tell them that I'm a C.I. and was asking them to call and check me out, so they can let me go. And I was just talking real loud and—"

"And where was Simone when all this was going on?"

"She was standing right there."

Homicide thought for a moment, and then he sat up in the bed. "Where Simone live at?"

"In Queens."

"Queens?" Homicide said under his breath. "We have to go see her right now before she starts talking." He scooted himself out of the bed and put on the same jeans and shirt he was wearing the day before.

Jasmine was happy that Homicide got it without having to explain anything.

"She got the biggest mouth, and I just hope she went straight home and went to sleep and didn't start calling and texting nobody." Jasmine knew it was do-or-die for her if Simone told anyone what had happened.

Homicide got his gun off the dresser and put it in his waistband and told Jasmine he was ready to roll. The two of them left the apartment and made their way down to the parking lot and got into his Denali, headed to Queens. Jasmine drove, since she knew the way there.

When they reached Simone's block, Homicide told Jasmine to walk to the apartment and call Simone to come open the door, and when she opened the door, stall her for a moment and he would approach and take it from there.

Jasmine took in all of the instructions and exited Homicide's truck. She walked four houses down to Simone's house and called her while standing on her steps. Simone picked up on the second ring.

"Oh, my God! Simone, you are not going to believe what they put me through," she said into the phone.

"You okay?" Simone asked.

"Yeah, I'm good. I'm gonna kill you for getting me that drunk off them Henny Coladas."

Simone laughed. "You was talking so much shit, and I was trying to get your attention so I could tell you to shut the hell up."

"Simone, I'm outside your door. They just released me. I have to shit, and my stomach is killing me, so you was closer and I figured I would just stop by you real quick, instead of driving all the way to Long Island."

"Oh! I didn't hear the bell."

"I didn't ring it."

"Okay, I'm coming right now."

Within thirty seconds Simone was at the door in her short silk pajamas. "So you gonna come and blow up my bathroom?" She laughed.

"Who you dressed all sexy for?" Jasmine asked, trying to stall.

"This ain't sexy. What are you talking about?"

Jasmine just looked at her with a suspicious look. "Let me find out."

"You ain't gonna find out nothing. But hurry up. Come in, so I can close this door."

Jasmine couldn't stall anymore without looking suspicious, so she walked in, not wanting to turn to see where Homicide was.

As soon as Simone tried to close the door, Homicide sprang to the door like an alley cat and stuck his foot in the base to prevent it from closing.

"Who is this?" Simone said with an attitude. She wasn't sure what was going on, and initially she thought it was her landlord who had stuck his foot in the door.

Homicide then grabbed the doorknob and pushed open the door.

As soon as Simone saw Homicide's beard she started to scream.

Homicide grabbed her and repeatedly slapped her in the face until she fell to the ground. "Shut the fuck up!" he said through clenched teeth. "Don't open your fuckin' mouth!"

He pulled out his gun and pointed it at Simone, who remembered it from Ish's house. She was sure it was the same gun. Simone immediately remembered the voice as being the same voice from the home invasion at Ish's house. She also peeped how calm Jasmine was. She knew Jasmine was in on whatever was going down.

"Please just don't hurt me. Please. Jasmine, you don't have to do this. I swear, you don't. You know how long we go back, Jasmine, and you know I wouldn't say nothing to nobody. Jasmine, I won't hurt you. You know that, Jasmine."

Jasmine kept quiet.

"I told you to shut the fuck up!" Homicide punched Simone squarely in the face, and she dropped to the ground like a rag doll. He then dragged her by her hair into the living room.

Jasmine knew what was about to happen and couldn't watch.

Simone tried to put up a fight, but Homicide kicked her in the ribs the same way he had at Ish's house. Simone immediately clutched her stomach in pain and doubled over on the ground.

Homicide grabbed one of the cushions from the couch and placed it over Simone's head and mashed her head to the floor, suffocating her. Simone was trying to free herself, and she put up the best struggle she could, but her screams were muffled by the cushion.

Homicide knew the cushion would also muffle the gun blast.

BLAOW!

One gun blast from Homicide's gun sent a bullet right through Simone's head and blood splattering on the floor. Simone's body went limp. When Homicide removed the pillow from Simone's face, it was clear that she was dead. Her eyes were wide open, but there was no life in her body.

Jasmine walked into the living room, and it was so eerie to her. Simone's eyes were still open, and it looked like she was staring at her. She couldn't help but tremble at the sight of her dead friend.

"Go find some bleach, and see if you can find some gloves," Homicide instructed.

Jasmine went to her kitchen and found plastic gloves that Simone used to wash dishes, and then she looked in the cabinets and found Clorox, and she brought it for Homicide.

"Get me some water too," he told her.

Jasmine ran and got a large glass of water, and then she ran into the bathroom and grabbed the first two towels she saw. She knew what Homicide wanted to do.

With the bleach, water, and towels, Jasmine and Homicide took about fifteen minutes and wiped down Simone's apartment. They made sure to wipe all of the doorknobs and surface areas clean of any fingerprints.

Once the apartment was wiped clean, Homicide poured bleach all over the couch cushion. Then he looked around to make sure there were no security cameras anywhere.

Jasmine saw Simone's phone on the floor and picked it up. She started to go through her text messages and noticed no recent BBM messages or text messages. Then she looked at her call log and saw that Simone had called her on-again, off-again lover Carlos at five o'clock in the morning and spoke to him for half an hour, and also spoke to him again at seven in the morning.

Homicide asked, "We good?"

"We have to make one more stop." Jasmine showed him the phone.

Homicide nodded and then he and Jasmine left the apartment. They made sure all of the lights were off, all of the shades and blinds were drawn closed, and the door was locked. As they walked back to Homicide's truck, he looked at all the houses in close proximity to Simone's, checking for security cameras. He didn't see any cameras that could have captured him and Jasmine going to or exiting Simone's apartment.

Jasmine and Homicide then headed to Carlos' apartment, and a similar murder scene played itself out, with Carlos also losing his life.

"Dead witnesses are the best witnesses," Homicide joked.

Jasmine was way too distraught to make light of the deaths of her two friends.

When it was all said and done, it took weeks before Simone's and Carlos' bodies were found inside their apartments. Jasmine cried her eyes out daily over the loss of her best female friend.

When the story hit the news, police investigators theorized that there must have been some kind of love triangle gone bad. Although they couldn't link Ish to the deaths of Carlos and Simone since he had the best alibi in the world being in jail, Ish's name still emerged as the main person of interest.

FORTY-SIX

After the murders of Simone and Carlos, Jasmine was drained physically, mentally, and emotionally. She explained to Homicide that she needed to go to Long Island for a few days to get the info on Nico they would need in order to retire. The truth was that Jasmine really needed to go to Long Island so she could get a few days to herself and not feel like she was going to go crazy and have a nervous breakdown. Homicide was cool with her going to Long Island, but he was certain to remind her not to let Nico fuck her.

As far as Jasmine was concerned, sex was the last thing on her mind. She loved sex, but she wasn't a sex machine. And over the past couple of days, she had experienced something she had never experienced before when she fucked three different guys within a twenty-four-hour period. Jasmine wanted to give her pussy a much-needed rest, and was hoping that her period came so she would have a good built-in excuse not to fuck.

When she got to her and Nico's house, Nico wasn't there because he was visiting with BJ, who was scheduled to be released from the hospital within two days. But Nico still wanted to go check him.

Jasmine was glad Nico wasn't there. The first thing she did was run a warm bubble bath in the Jacuzzi bathtub in the master bathroom. It was the most relaxing bath she remembered taking. She stayed in the bathtub for more than an hour and a half, periodically adding new hot water to keep the bathwater at a nice, warm, relaxing temperature.

After the bath was over, Jasmine got out and dried herself off and put baby oil all over her body, and she put on a bra and a pair of panties.

Although it was mid-afternoon, she got in the bed and went to sleep.

Like the relaxing bath she had just taken, Jasmine was now experiencing some of the best sleep she'd had in years. She slept and slept, and it felt like she had been hibernating like a bear in the woods. But when Nico came home and woke her up, she realized she had actually only been sleeping for a little over four hours.

"You sleeping?" Nico asked her after he walked into the room.

"I was sleeping until you just woke me up."

"My bad."

Jasmine removed the bed sheet from over her head and explained to Nico how she had got home real late because she almost caught a DWI charge with Simone.

"Get the fuck outta here." Nico then asked her to tell him what happened.

Jasmine lied and told Nico that the Bridge and Tunnel officer had allowed her to pull in front of the barrack offices near the bridge and sleep off the liquor, and he didn't charge her.

"He tried to holler at you?"

"No, not at all."

"You lucky then."

Jasmine sat up in the bed. "How is BJ doing?"

"He's coming home in two days, but the nigga is fucked up. He has to wear that smelly-ass bag and shit for the rest of his life. A nurse or a health aide-type chick is going to have to come to his house every day and help him clean the bag, so he won't get no infections or nothing like that."

"Poor baby."

Jasmine got up out of the bed and checked her phone. Then she put it in her bag and discreetly started recording with her other phone, which was also in her bag.

"BJ talking about getting back in the mix and shit when he comes home. And I didn't wanna crush the nigga's heart or nothing, but I'm saying to myself, BJ, dog, you gotta get out the game. With them kind of injuries, he can't be scrambling on the streets like he needs to. You know what I'm saying?"

Jasmine nodded.

"We got a shipment coming from the Haitians in two days. They gonna do the drop near that vacant warehouse in Brooklyn Bridge Park, and this nigga BJ is saying he wanna be there."

"With a colostomy bag? That's like somebody trying to rob a bank in a wheelchair," Jasmine joked.

"Exactly."

Jasmine got out of the bed and looked for something to put on.

"I just told him that we'll send two of them young gun muthafuckas from Ish's crew. And since Ish is locked up, we can just move them under BJ and have them report to him."

"What did he say when you said that?" Jasmine asked, putting on her jeans.

"I mean, he's with it. You know he reminds me of one of those boxers that don't know when to hang it up, always want one more prize fight."

Jasmine reached for a shirt to put on. "And then they end up punch-drunk and talking with slurred speech for the rest of their life."

"That's what I'm saying."

Jasmine walked out of the room as if she could have cared less about what Nico was saying. "I need aspirin. I still got a slight queasy feeling from these Henny Coladas that me and Simone was drinking."

Nico followed Jasmine down to the kitchen. He changed the subject to something completely different. He had already planted the seed of information into her brain and was ready to sit back and see what that seed would grow into.

FORTY-SEVEN

The day before Nico's shipment of drugs was scheduled to arrive in Brooklyn Bridge Park, Jasmine met with Agent Gosling at Argentina Steak House, located on Queens Boulevard, not too far from the mall. It was the first time Gosling and Jasmine had met or spoken since the day he had fucked her twice.

Gosling had on a brand-new golf shirt, new slacks, and new shoes, and he had a fresh new haircut. He also had on a small gold chain that was visible, since he didn't button the three buttons to his shirt. Gosling's exposed arms looked shiny, and so did his chest and neck area. Jasmine couldn't help but think of how fatherly he looked. He wasn't ugly or anything like that, but she just viewed him in a completely platonic way. But it was obvious to her that Gosling had purposely come to the meeting looking his version of freshly dipped.

When Jasmine first walked into the restaurant, Gosling was waiting in the lobby for her. And when he saw her, he walked up to her and gave her a hug, something he had never done before. His 1990s era-smelling cologne was so strong, it almost made Jasmine's eyes water. She could also smell liquor on his breath.

If Gosling tried to push up on her for sex, she was going to tell him that she had her period and a yeast infection. She was not trying to form a habit where every time they were to meet up he would be expecting to fuck.

"How are you?" Gosling asked.

"I'm good."

"Before we start talking, I just wanted to say, about the other day, it shouldn't have happened. But I also wanted to make sure I thanked you."

His comments seemed weird to Jasmine, but she just nodded and told him that she understood.

The hostess seated Gosling and Jasmine.

"I want you to hear this." Jasmine took out her BlackBerry and played Nico's words from the other night.

Gosling started to smile; it was clear he was excited. "When is two days?"

"Tomorrow."

"Why didn't you call me?" Gosling was concerned that he would have to scramble to get agents in place to help with the raid and the takedown.

"I didn't call you because my gut tells me it's bullshit."

"What if it's not bullshit? We could never get a shot like this again. I want to at least have agents in place."

Jasmine shook her head.

"That's the thing. If it's a setup and Nico spots any agents near that area scoping the place out, he'll never trust me again. Never!"

Gosling thought to himself for a minute. "We have to send somebody."

"Gosling, please just trust me on this."

"I do trust you. Okay, how about this? I know that park, and it's real kid-friendly, right on the water, newly renovated, and everything is visible. So I'll call Agent Battle and have her get four female agents who have small kids. I'll send the agents into the park on different shifts for blocks of like three hours. They'll be in the park with their kids and baby strollers and stuff like that, looking very normal and blending in. This way, if something does go down, we would be able to get some kind of visual observation.

Jasmine felt comfortable with that plan, but she warned Gosling not to send in any unmarked cars and no men, and she also reminded him not to make any arrests or else her credibility with Nico would be shot. Gosling gave her his word.

After they were done speaking, Jasmine ordered an appetizer and a Sprite. She wasn't trying to hang around Gosling longer than she had to. So within twenty minutes after she had arrived at the Steak House, she was leaving, headed back to her and Nico's house.

As it turned out, the next day a drug deal went down in Brooklyn Bridge Park without a hitch at nine thirty in the morning. A young black FBI agent was there near the empty warehouse with her baby, and Nico's young up-and-coming soldiers never suspected a thing. They did see a young black mom taking pictures of her baby, but that didn't seem odd to them at all. What they didn't know was that mother was snapping high-resolution pictures of them as well.

God must have been on Jasmine's side because she was clueless to the fact that she had spared the life of both of her parents. As far as Nico was concerned, she had passed a huge test and would live to see another day.

FORTY-EIGHT

Nico had been spending a lot of time in his house, which was unusual for him, because he was always on the go and out and about. Nico would have never admitted it to anyone, but the truth was, he feared his rival Prince, who was slowly taking over the drug trade in all five boroughs of New York. Prince was ruthless and would gun somebody down in broad daylight whether there were eyewitnesses or not.

Nico had to come back to New York when he had because everything was falling apart around him, including his reputation. All the people he trusted were either dead, in jail, or injured, and he didn't really know how to move. It was like there were two sets to Ghetto Mafia. Nico's set and Bebo's set. When Bebo had first gotten killed, Ghetto Mafia was on the verge of a civil war. People from Bebo's set were convinced that Nico had something to do with his murder, and they planned on getting revenge.

But once Prince had shot up Bebo's funeral, the people loyal to Bebo had a slight change of heart and had to come to grips with the fact that it just might have been Prince who had gunned down Bebo. Everyone knew Prince had killed Lo and maimed BJ, so common sense said that he very well could have been the one that needed to be targeted, not Nico.

So Nico chose to stay in the safe haven of his house until Prince either got killed or locked up. He wasn't bold enough to go hunt him down and kill him. Nico knew Prince was smart, and he didn't want to slip up somehow and have Prince turn the tables on him if he went after him.

With Nico home and Jasmine home, Nico almost by default started to talk about things on the phone while in her presence. One morning, about a week after the drug transaction in Brooklyn Bridge Park, Jasmine woke up but stayed in the bed and acted like she was still sleeping. Nico was talking on his cell phone loud enough for her to hear what he was saying. But the thing was, he was talking in codes, and she couldn't make heads or tails of what he was saying.

Nico eventually walked out of the room, and Jasmine stayed in the bed for twenty more minutes before she made her way down to the kitchen and started to make breakfast. While she prepared waffle batter, Nico walked up to her and kissed her on the cheek.

"What was that for?"

"I just wanted to kiss you."

"What else you want?"

"Whatever you feel like making is cool with me."

Jasmine told him that she was going to make an omelet and hash browns to go with the waffles.

"Let me ask you something," Nico said.

Jasmine looked at him, so he would know that he had her attention.

"We got this major deal going down in Miami and—"

Jasmine stopped mixing the waffle batter and held up her hand. "Wait, I want to be crystal clear on something. I don't want you telling me anything about what you do, about any drug deals, anything happening in the street, or none of that. Because if you noticed, the past couple of weeks have been so cool, I been waking up and making breakfast. I been cooking dinner. We haven't been arguing or anything. And I realized that it seemed like we went off the track when you lost trust in me and you was thinking I was talking to the police. So the best way to solve that is to just not tell me anything, and then we'll have peace and harmony. Okay? And I'm not saying that in a smart-ass way. I'm just being honest."

Nico shook his head. "You wrong about that. I never stopped trusting you. You always read too much into my moods. I be stressed about all kinds of shit. Muthafuckas trying to gun me down and take over blocks and corners that I built up. Shit like that be weighin' on a nigga. And while I'm dealing with bug shit, I don't have time for no pillow-talk bullshit."

"I'm not talking about pillow talk."

"Whatever, Jasmine. I'm not fighting you. I need your advice on some shit! Gotdamn!"

"Okay, so what's up?" Jasmine stopped what she was doing and gave Nico her full attention. Her BlackBerry was on the kitchen counter recording every word.

"I'm supposed to meet with this Haitian nigga named Patrick down in Miami. All these Haitian dudes named Patrick or Pierre, but this Patrick ain't the same Patrick who runs shit. The Patrick who runs shit got murdered two weeks back. And this new Patrick is the other Patrick's lieutenant. He's like BJ to me. But the thing is, I don't know if he had something to do with his boss getting killed, and I'm going back and forth in my head about trusting this nigga. I don't know if I should find a new connect or just trust this dude."

"Don't do it. He sounds grimy, and you'll go down there and get robbed or killed. It ain't worth it."

"Ain't nobody scared of the nigga; it's just about trusting him."

"It's all the same thing. I wouldn't go."

Nico blew air out his lungs and explained how shit was drying up ever since they lost their FedEx hook up. "We gotta get the best product on the street. That bitch-ass Prince got the best product right now. And I can't be second best to nobody."

Jasmine kept quiet.

"I can't send BJ, and Lo is gone. And I don't trust the young guns on something this big."

"How big is the deal?"

"Low seven figures."

"Damn. How you gonna get that up to New York?"

Nico explained that he had a private trucking company owner who would move it for him.

"See, that's different now. You have to do that deal yourself and be riding in that little sleep-away area that they got on them tractor trailers." She laughed.

"Nah. Once it's on the truck, we good money."

"Well, I say find a new connect. But if you go through with it, don't send nobody else but yourself. It's like if Kobe is on the team and they need a last-minute shot to win the championship, only Kobe is taking that shot. They won't have one of the bench players taking the shot."

Nico smiled; he liked that analogy. Nico had been around the block for years and knew the drug game the same way Kobe knew the basketball game, so before he had even asked Jasmine that question, he already knew what he was going to do about the major Miami drug deal.

FORTY-NINE

When Nico left for Miami, the FBI and the DEA had a team of agents following his every move. Jasmine had supplied Agent Gosling with the information on the seven-figure drug deal going down in Miami, and all of the federal and local authorities were all on standby waiting to move in as soon as they got the notice from Agent Gosling, who was leading the task force to take down Nico.

The day Nico left for Miami, Jasmine shot over to her Manhattan loft and called Homicide and told him to come meet her there. When Homicide showed up, he wanted to know if she had fucked Nico.

"There was no way I couldn't fuck him, baby. But it means nothing." Jasmine assured Homicide that it would all be worth it in a just a few short weeks, and reminded him of how they were going to be able to make their come-up and retire and then go off into the sunset.

Jasmine hadn't told Homicide about the seven-figure drug deal getting ready to go down in Miami because she realized that, for a big deal like that, Homicide would be outnumbered and outgunned. He would have been on a suicide mission. Plus, she sincerely wanted the feds to bag Nico and then get out of the world of being a confidential informant. She wanted her life back and felt like she had other options that didn't come with all the drama.

So she kept things from Homicide, but she did let him fuck her as he pleased and when he wanted. Homicide had never fucked Jasmine in the ass before, but all of a sudden, he was telling her that he wanted to fuck her in the ass.

Jasmine wasn't a fan of anal. She didn't want to do it, but she didn't want any drama with Homicide, so she gave in to him.

Homicide wasn't gentle at all. Jasmine howled in pain during the ten-minute episode that felt like torture. She knew Homicide was purposely fucking her in the ass hard to send her a message that things could easily go from sweet to sour between them if she ever tried to play him.

After Homicide came inside Jasmine's asshole, he got up and put on his clothes. He told her he had to leave but would be back later that night or the next day. Jasmine laid on the bed in serious pain. Feeling a little bit delirious, she didn't even acknowledge him.

Homicide stopped at the entrance to the bedroom door just before leaving. "Hurry up and find out where that stash is at. And you don't fuck that nigga again until you do! A'ight?"

"Okay," Jasmine replied meekly.

"I'm not one of these pussy niggas that's out here. Believe that!" Homicide walked out of her bedroom. He slammed the front door so hard the entire apartment shook.

Jasmine gingerly rolled over from her stomach and lay on her back. She closed her eyes and swallowed real hard, a big lump in her throat. She was confident that the feds were going to nab Nico, but now she wasn't optimistic at all that she would get her life back after Nico's arrest.

She knew that, even if Nico went to jail, Homicide would still be around. She wondered if she had made the biggest mistake in her life by letting herself act on her childhood crush instead of staying focused on helping the feds lock him up.

Everywhere Jasmine turned, it seemed like there was always some form of new stress or drama coming her way. She stood up from the bed and saw blood on her bed sheets. She was horrified at the sight, but she knew she had no one to blame but herself for getting so caught up with Homicide the way she had.

FIFTY

N ico sat on a street corner in the Liberty City section of Miami, blocks away from a public storage facility. The drugs were sitting inside a storage unit, ready to be fork-lifted on to a tractor-trailer in the parking lot.

There were agents staking out the public storage facility and agents stalking out Nico, and they were going to take turns trailing him as soon as he decided to drive to the storage facility.

Local undercover cops took turns trailing Patrick as he left his strip club and made his way to the public storage. They all figured Nico would start his engine and make his way to the facility at any moment, but everybody was shocked when they saw Mia pull into the facility in a car she had rented in New Jersey and driven all the way to Miami. Mia had a guy in the car with her—a face no one had seen before.

Federal agents were all in position, but they were told to stand down until the transaction took place. Mia walked up to Patrick's car. He got out, and she gave him a hug. She was wearing high-heel shoes, tight jeans, and a thin short sleeve blouse that was perfect for the Miami weather.

Mia and Patrick walked over to the car Mia had driven. Mia popped the trunk, showed Patrick the money, and then closed it and gave him the keys to the car. The guy in the car with Mia got out and called Nico on his cell phone and was giving him a play-by-play of everything happening.

Patrick got on his cell phone, and within two minutes a young black kid who looked no older than seventeen came wheeling a forklift from inside the public storage facility and placed it on the dock right next to the tractor-trailer.

Out of nowhere unmarked FBI and DEA cars swarmed on the scene, as did marked and unmarked local police cars. Within two minutes a helicopter was also hovering over the facility.

Within seconds, Mia, her male accomplice, Patrick, the young forklift driver, and the tractor-trailer driver were all on the ground and in handcuffs.

DEA agents locked down the public storage facility and searched every inch of it with drug-sniffing dogs.

As soon as Nico heard the sirens, he knew they had been busted. But in the federal agents' haste to get to the crime scene when Gosling gave the order, the agents who had been assigned to watch Nico forgot about him and raced to the crime scene.

Nico had no idea that he had been followed, but he'd started up his car and got out of Dodge as quick as he could. He knew not to venture past the public storage facility.

Once he made it to the interstate, he rolled down his window and tossed all the cell phones he had on him as he tried to figure out exactly where he was heading next.

FIFTY-ONE

The raid in Liberty City was so big, it managed to make national news broadcasts. All of the lead FBI and DEA agents, local police, and federal and local prosecutors held a major press conference, where they had all of the drugs, guns, and cash they had confiscated on display on long tables. The officials took turns coming to the microphone and explaining how grateful they were to have put such a dent into a drug distribution network that spanned the East Coast from Miami to New York City.

Agent Gosling basked in his glory as he stood behind the microphone and spoke about the case. It was rare for agents who worked undercover in the field to show their face the way Gosling was doing, but as he explained to the cameras, he was going to be retiring from the bureau in a few short weeks, and this major drug bust was the perfect way for him to cap off his career.

Homicide was in a Bally Total Fitness gym working out. He stopped and walked over to the flat-screen, tuned to CNN. He listened closely, and as he listened, he seethed with anger. He knew Agent Gosling was Jasmine's case agent, from what Jasmine had told him.

He stormed out of the gym and sped over to the Brooklyn Bridge and into Manhattan, where he weaved in and out of traffic until he got to Jasmine's apartment. The doorman knew Homicide and waved to him as he walked to the elevators.

Homicide banged on Jasmine's apartment door, and after a few minutes she answered the door with her robe on.

WHACK!

Homicide punched Jasmine square in the face, and she saw stars and fell backwards and tripped on to the floor.

Homicide stepped into the apartment and slammed the door shut behind him. "You fuckin' lied to me, bitch!"

Jasmine didn't know what was going on.

"Were you fuckin' Gosling?"

Jasmine's eyes got wide. She didn't know where all of this was coming from because she hadn't seen the news. "No!" she shot back.

All Homicide could think about was how all the drugs and the cash that the feds got could have been his, had Jasmine tipped him off.

Homicide picked Jasmine up from the ground and started to smack her around. "Tell me where Gosling lives! I know you were fuckin' him!"

"Baby, what is going on?" Jasmine screamed at the top of her lungs.

"The feds got the stash, and the only way they knew was because you put them on to it. I know it, and don't fuckin' lie to me!" Homicide pulled out his gun and aimed it at Jasmine's head. "Were you fuckin' Gosling?"

"No, he raped me!" she said, hoping Homicide would go for her lie.

"Get the fuck on your knees right now and put your hands behind your back and face the wall!"

"Why, baby? Why?" Jasmine pleaded, her trembling hands in the air.

"Where does Gosling live?"

"Floral Park!" Jasmine shouted. She had no choice but to tell him because she knew she was a dead woman otherwise.

Homicide knew about the panic button on Jasmine's phone and wouldn't let her get near it. She had told him what he wanted to know, but because she had caused them to lose out on millions, she had to endure a beating that lasted all night.

To prove her loyalty to Homicide, Jasmine drove him to Agent Gosling's house once she was certain he was back from Miami. They went to the house when it was late at night and pitch-dark.

Jasmine was dressed in a sexy silk robe with nothing underneath. She rang Gosling's doorbell, and when he asked who was it, he was pleasantly surprised to hear Jasmine.

As soon as Gosling opened the front door, Jasmine held open her robe. She had on a lot of makeup on her face and her body to cover up the bruises from the beating she had suffered at the hands of Homicide.

"The case is over. You can fuck me the way you want to now."

Gosling didn't even need a Viagra pill for his dick to get hard at the sight of Jasmine's naked body standing on his front steps. "Come in."

Jasmine shook her head and told him she wasn't coming in until he got naked right there in front of her. "Let me see that dick," she cooed.

Gosling almost came on himself. He quickly took off his shoes, unbuttoned his shirt, and took off his pants. He had no idea that Homicide was crouched down on the side of the house in the dark and right next to the front steps.

"That's what I'm talking about. Stroke that dick for me, baby."

Gosling did just as Jasmine said. He didn't care if his neighbors could see him standing naked at his front door jacking his dick.

Jasmine gave Homicide the cue that Gosling didn't have a gun on him or in his hands when she'd told Gosling to stroke his dick. Homicide, in one swoop, jumped onto the stairs with his gun drawn and forced Gosling to go into his living.

Gosling held his hands up in surrender. He knew he should never have trusted a slut-ass confidential informant.

Jasmine closed the front door, and Homicide handed her the duct tape and told her to duct-tape Gosling's mouth and ankles, and his hands behind his back, and Jasmine did just as he said.

"So you raped my girl? Once in your car and once on this couch right here?"

Gosling's eyes got wide, as he shook his head no.

"Yes, you did, bitch!" Homicide kicked Gosling in the jaw as hard as he could. "You know I have to kill for that, right?"

Gosling was in pain from the kick to the face. He violently shook his head to try and get Homicide not to take his life.

"You knew they called her Suicide Pussy, and you still took the pussy. You gotta die. You knew her pussy was suicide," Homicide said.

Gosling was breathing very hard as his life passed in front of his eyes.

"How much money you put in your own pocket from that raid? Enough to retire off, right?"

The room was quiet.

"Jasmine, this nigga don't wanna talk now, but when he was taking your pussy, he had a lot to say then, right?"

Jasmine nodded.

Homicide turned back toward Gosling and then asked him again, "You did know that she has suicide pussy, right? So that means you gotta die." He cocked his gun.

Then suddenly a shot rang out. BANG! And Homicide's body collapsed to the floor.

Jasmine had a small .22-caliber handgun hidden in the pocket of her robe that she always kept with her since the night Bebo almost killed her. When Homicide came up with the plan to go kill Gosling, she hid her gun in the robe.

"That's right, muthafucka! This is Suicide Pussy!" Jasmine said, and then she pumped another bullet into Homicide's head to make sure he was dead.

FIFTY-TWO

Two weeks after Jasmine had killed Homicide, Gosling officially retired from the FBI. On the day he retired, Agent Battle officially thanked Jasmine for all of her efforts as a confidential informant.

And as she handed Jasmine her last check, she told her that her services as a confidential informant were no longer needed. "That's assuming, of course, that you don't want to stay on and help us." Agent Battle laughed.

"Ehhh, no!" Jasmine laughed and replied.

"Open up the envelope and make sure everything is right."

Jasmine opened up the envelope saw the amount of the check. It was two hundred and fifty thousand dollars. "This is my money?" she asked in disbelief.

"Your money," Agent Battle smiled and said.

Agent Battle reminded her that, as a C.I., she was entitled to a percentage of what the FBI confiscated with a cap of two hundred and fifty thousand dollars.

Jasmine, smiling her ass off, couldn't believe it.

"Now," Agent Battle said, pointing her index finger at Jasmine, "you have a clean slate, but stay your ass out of trouble, because if you fuck up, I will come down on you like a pit bull in a skirt."

"Oh, I like that—pit bull in a skirt." Jasmine smiled. "But, trust me, you won't hear a peep from me. I'm done with that life."

"Okay, that's what I want to hear."

Jasmine shook Agent Battle's hand, and then she and Agent Gosling walked out of the office together. Agent Gosling told Jasmine that he would walk her down to the lobby.

As they made their way to the lobby, Jasmine was certain that Gosling was going to start putting the screws to her since they both now had no FBI hold on them. And, strange enough, she started to think that Gosling might not be such a bad catch. Yeah, he was older than her, but at the same time, he was still young enough to do something different with his life. And he wasn't that bad-looking.

When they made their way to the lobby, Agent Gosling held out his hand for a handshake. Jasmine shook his hand and held on to it.

"You know what, Jasmine? I would have loved to wife you. And I never would have guessed in a million years that I would even be saying this. But when we depart from each other now, we'll never speak again and I think that will be for the best."

"Why is that?" Jasmine's ego made her ask.

"We come from two different worlds. And my circle wouldn't approve of you, and I doubt your circle would approve of me."

It pained Gosling to say that, but he was being honest.

"Oh, but I was good enough for you to fuck, right? You didn't check with your circle of friends on that, right? I was also good enough to save your life. On the real, you ain't no better than Nico or Homicide, or any of these get-money dudes on the street. But at least they know who they are. You sound like a confused, weak man. Yeah, you fucked me, but that was because I was vulnerable. Otherwise, you wouldn't have had a chance at this pussy. I know who I am. You need to find out who you are. All you had to do was wish me well and then go off on to your retirement. But it's all good. Hopefully retirement will teach you how to appreciate people and how to say thank you, because you know nothing about that." Jasmine turned and walked out of the building.

Gosling called Jasmine's name, but she was determined to keep walking and never once looked back at him.

FIFTY-THREE

N ico was officially on the run. The FBI and the DEA had warrants
out for his arrest for a drug conspiracy charge, so Jasmine knew
he wouldn't be coming home anytime soon, nor would she probably be
speaking to him anytime soon. She was planning on moving her stuff out
of his house as soon as possible, and was going to have access to her SoHo
apartment only until the end of the month.

The day after she'd left the federal building, she went to Long Island
to get a suitcase and some clothes for a trip she was making to Los Angeles
that same day. When she got to the house, she was surprised to see a letter
from Mia from a correctional facility.

"What the fuck this bitch want now?" She felt like she just couldn't
get drama out of her life, no matter how hard she tried.

She stuffed the unopened letter into the back pocket of her jeans and
told herself she would read it once she got on the plane.

Jasmine drove out to Teterboro Airport, where she met up with Shane
Wright. Shane was a hustler from New Jersey with caramel skin, wavy
hair, perfect teeth, and broad shoulders, and he went by the street name of
Cocaine Shane. Jasmine had met him when she went into Sway one night
by herself, and they hit it off right from the jump. But with all the drama
going on with the case, she didn't have the time to link up with him, but
she'd told him she would get with him as soon as she had the time. She
had used school as her excuse, even though she had dropped out.

Jasmine's timing was perfect because, when she reached out to Shane,
he told her that he was going to be flying to Los Angeles to go to the NBA

Finals. Jasmine was never one to turn down a baller offering her a free trip on a private jet.

She hugged Shane and thanked him for not deleting her number from his phone.

"Nah, I wouldn't do that. I liked the fact that you was about something. That nursing shit is the future."

Jasmine felt like she was in heaven as they sat in the plush leather seats with no one else on the plane except for the two of them and their stewardess.

"Excuse me," the stewardess said. "Jasmine?"

"Yes, that's me."

"I think you dropped this when you were coming on board the plane." The stewardess handed Jasmine the letter from Mia, which had fallen out her pocket.

"Oh, thank you."

She told Shane to give her a minute, so she could read Mia's letter.

Dear Jasmine

I hope this letter finds you in a better place and in better spirits than I am currently in. As you can see from the envelope, I am writing you from jail. I am writing you for a couple of reasons, but I just wanted to tell you from my heart to just be smart. While you have your freedom, you should treasure it and value it.

I could have been anything I wanted to be, but now that is no longer the case, and my life will never be the same. Even after I get out of prison, my life will never be the same.

You remind me so much of myself. Jasmine, you are beautiful, and are smart, and you are determined, and therefore you can be whatever you want to be. I urge you to take to heart what I am saying and just be smarter than I was.

I competed with you because I was jealous of you. I had a lot of hatred in my heart, and I was afraid my star couldn't shine unless I snuffed out your light and prevented it from shining.

But tonight, Jasmine, before you go to bed, do something that I no longer have the freedom to do. Stand outside or open up a window and look at all the stars shining and see if you can count them all. What you will find is that the stars are too numerous to count. I was too ignorant to realize that stars can shine together with no problem. I didn't have to stop your shine in order for my star to shine. I pray that you can learn from what I am saying and learn to be secure in who you are, and you are a star.

I know you have put up with the same things with Nico that I had to put up with. But right now as I sit here in jail I am trying to decide if I will testify against him. I pray that you will never have to be in a similar position. What I know is that if you focus on forgiving and not competing, then you won't end up where I am.

I am not asking you to be my friend, but I needed to write this letter to you so I can move on. If you have ever done anything to hurt me, know that I truly forgive you from the heart. I ask you to find it in your heart to forgive me for all the wrong I have ever committed against you. But if you can't, I will understand, but just remember that a lack of forgiveness is like drinking poison and expecting someone else to die. Ultimately, being unforgiving will have a worse effect on you than on the one you choose not to forgive.

Anyway, I am starting to ramble on, so I will end the letter now. I hope you can understand where I am coming from by writing this letter, and I also hope that you receive this letter in the good and sincere spirit in which it was written.

Jasmine, YOU ARE WIFEY!!!

Sincerely and with Love,
Mia

"What you reading? A book?" Shane jokingly asked Jasmine.

Jasmine didn't know what to make of Mia's letter, but reading it made her feel good. It was definitely not something that she ever expected to receive in this lifetime from Mia. She put the letter away and planned to go back to it later. She didn't want to be rude to her potential new boo.

As the plane took off and lifted into the sky, Jasmine looked out the window and marveled at the beauty of the universe. She couldn't help but keep thinking back to Mia's letter.

Wow! she thought. *Mia actually told me what I always wanted to hear her admit. She actually told me in writing, and she actually openly admitted that I AM WIFEY!*